THE MOZART SCORE

Edwin Leather

M

ISBN 0 333 26547 5

First published 1979 by
MACMILLAN LONDON LIMITED
4 Little Essex Street London WC2R 3LF
and Basingstoke
Associated companies in Delhi Dublin Hong Kong
Johannesburg Lagos Melbourne New York Singapore
and Tokyo

Printed in Great Britain by
THE ANCHOR PRESS LTD
Tiptree, Essex

Bound in Great Britain by
WM BRENDON & SON LTD
Tiptree, Essex

scarborough
public library

For
SHEILA
Sine quo non

CHAPTER ONE

At 10.57 on the night of Tuesday, 4th October 1977, the great golden, richly encrusted curtains of the Vienna Staatsoperhaus wooshed down for the seventeenth – or was it the eighteenth? – and last time as the enthusiastic cheers and clapping of the crowd packing that superb auditorium finally subsided into exhausted contentment. Heinz Wallburg's new production of Mozart's classic comic opera, *Il Seraglio*, which funnily enough he had written in German not Italian, was acclaimed a great success. Hilda de Groote and Horst Laubenthal had belted out their arias and their competitive singing with just that exact mixture of artistry and theatricalism Mozart had unquestionably intended. The audience had done their duty and was ready to retire happily.

A few seconds later the classical marble staircases and the great gilded foyer echoed their customary state of good humoured turmoil as the mass of shuffling, wriggling bodies all struggled at once for the hopelessly overloaded cloakrooms. The work load of the harassed attendants, and hence the delay to the customers, had been multiplied by the quite unseasonable wind and rain which swept down the Danube Valley during the late afternoon from the mountains westward beyond Salzburg. The worst scrum, inevitably, was in the front entrance hall where the normal bottlenecks caused by the doors were increased by the reluctance of those in front to brave the awful weather which suddenly faced them, those in the middle degenerated into one conglomerate writhing mass of humanity struggling to get their own and other people's coats on and their umbrellas

7

up, while the pressure of those behind newly liberated from the cloakrooms surged relentlessly forward.

The temporary adversity of the circumstances did little if anything to dampen the spirits of the satisfied crowd. A burble of approval rose in a gentle haze from more than a thousand throats. In the thick of it a swarthy looking young man wearing a heavy brown overcoat suddenly slumped against the man beside him. 'Look out! This chap's fainted.' A woman behind him let out a little gasp of surprise. 'Stand back. Give him air.' Someone turned and shouted to a uniformed doorman, 'Call an ambulance.' 'Is there a doctor here?' The front of house manager and two uniformed attendants materialised out of the marble columns. 'Please stand back. Let them close that door, please. No, no, it's quite all right. A gentleman has fainted. Please use the other door. No, lady, the door on your right.' It was the sort of unfortunate little event they were well accustomed to handle. Within minutes, the wailing siren of an ambulance could be heard racing up the Opernring. The noise and the sudden appearance of flashing red lights were all most of the crowd knew of the incident.

With the smooth, quiet efficiency expected of the emergency services in any great city the man was gently laid on a stretcher and placed in the ambulance. The front of house manager enquired in all directions, 'Did anybody know him?' 'Was anyone with him?' No one could identify him nor remember seeing him before. Within two minutes it would have been difficult to get any consensus as to what he looked like at all. About his early thirties. Thick black hair. Swarthy face. Well, anyway it didn't matter. He would be well looked after. Wonder what was wrong with him?

In the back of the ambulance as it sped down the Ring toward Lorenz Bochler Hospital the senior medical orderly raised his ear from the man's nose and mouth and dropped his right wrist.

'He's dead,' he said to his mate.

On arrival the body was taken straight to the autopsy theatre in the Emergency Ward. It was laid gently on its back and two nurses started to remove the heavy serge overcoat, the back of which was now rapidly becoming a gooey mass of blood. They rolled the body over and stripped his coat and shirt. A quick swab of cleansing alcohol to clear the blood revealed a hole in the left side of his back so small it looked as though it had been made by a sail-maker's needle. The examining doctor's experienced eyes immediately appreciated the essential fact, a sail-maker's needle strong enough and long enough to go right through into the lung. The man had literally drowned in his own blood.

'Call Kriminalpolizei.'

That section of the crowd who left the Opera by the back and side doors were completely unaware of the drama that was played out in front. On a filthy night like this there were not many who cared to dispense with the services of the cloakrooms at the front of the building. Those who did were mainly students who didn't much mind getting wet anyway; the knowing who realised that the wait for a taxi would be a long one and therefore proposed to spend it in the comfortable luxury of the bar of Sacher's Hotel immediately across Philharmonicastrasse; and the very knowing who knew how to arrange that a taxi should be waiting at exactly the right moment and exactly the exit from which they intended to emerge. Amongst this last, small, group of sophisticates were two middle aged couples in evening dress who collectively made the dash from door to taxi in under thirty seconds and were promptly whisked off to a reception being given at the residence of the Israeli Ambassador, Jacob Doron.

The leader of this expedition was just six feet in height, no more than comfortably overweight for his fifty-seven years, with a thickish head of brown hair that tended to curl behind his ears, and a pronounced limp in the right leg. Although constantly referred to as 'an Englishman' (he looked and talked like one) he had in fact scarcely any English, or for that matter Anglo-Saxon, blood in him being the progeny of a very Celtic Welsh father and an Austrian/Hungarian/Jewish mother. A series of odd turns of fate had left him washed up in Vienna at the end of World War Two doing a highly specialised military job. His very English and very lovely young wife had died there, so he stayed. A highly successful art business kept his life full, interesting and comfortable. His name was Rupert Conway; or, in the records of his old regiment in Cardiff, Acting Major, the Hon. Rupert Conway, M.C., but that was a long time ago.

His partner for the evening was the ageless and lovely Julia Homburg; now semi-retired, which meant she retired nearly every year when she felt like it, and returned to the Burg Theatre company to play a starring role when they really needed her and her own restless energy sought an outlet. Since she had been with the Burg from the age of fifteen, and was an extremely nice person as well as a great actress, she was allowed such liberties.

The other couple were Manfried and Liësl Foglar, same age group, same general style of life; that is to say they were also natural and integral parts of that lively society which sparkles, without being pompous or brash, in contemporary Vienna. These are highly cultured, talented people, whose education included the horrors, not only of disastrous military defeat, but the infinitely more personal and scarring experiences of brutal occupation by both the Nazis and the Russians. Manfried held a senior editorial post on *Die Presse* which he combined with a budding career as an artist, while his gentle spoken, auburn-haired wife was one of Vienna's top dress designers. The four were friends of long standing and deep mutual sympathies.

The Dorons' residence on Starkfriedgasse presented a warm and welcoming refuge from the sodden gale outside. About a dozen people were already there, the usual mixture of local opera buffs with a wide variety of backgrounds, and representatives of Vienna's corps of diplomats and assorted experts accredited to the incessantly increasing number of missions representing new countries nobody had ever heard of and new bureaucracies spawned by the United Nations. 'Where on earth is Papua-New Guinea?' 'Why Sao Tomé *and* Principe?' 'What in Heaven's name is WIPO?'

It was pleasant and the food and wine were delicious. Julia Homburg was rapidly surrounded by an escort of male admirers whose wives seemed to be out of town. Having no desire to spoil her fun Rupert meandered into the library to admire some fine oil paintings by a young Israeli impressionist who currently intrigued him. The only other occupant was clearly a soul mate. He was large and comfortable looking, with a huge head, and he was smoking a pipe. Rupert at once reached for his own, they mumbled good evening at each other, and the pictures formed an eminently suitable topic of mutual interest.

They exchanged pleasantries. Rupert quickly decided that the tall, distinguished looking stranger would be worth knowing.

'I'm sorry, I don't know your name, sir.'

'Ah, of course. Kleinhart. Dr Jacob Kleinhart. From Haifa. And yours?'

'Conway. Rupert Conway.'

'Herr Conway. Why, of course. I have heard a great deal about you.'

'Have you indeed? Who from?'

Dr Kleinhart laughed. 'My wife and I recently moved into a new apartment; our neighbour never stops talking about you.'

Rupert made a self-deprecatory smile. 'Good heavens! Sorry about that. Now who would your neighbour be?'

'An elderly Viennese lady, Fräulein Meulheimer.'

'Oh yes. I remember her well. I trust she thrives?'

'Indeed she does. Entirely due to you, so she says.'

'That's very kind of her. I was able to be of some help to her.'

'Something to do with a Fabergé elephant, I believe?'

'Belonged to her brother. The Nazis stole it. By a strange piece of luck I came across it a couple of years ago. I was able to arrange some ... um ... compensation for her.'

'Remarkable.'

'Not really. My last job in the British Army was tracking down stolen works of art. This one just happened to take thirty years to surface.'

'Well, she's certainly grateful to you.'

'She is very welcome. You interested in the art world?'

'Interested, by all means. Nuclear physics is my line.'

'Since you come from Haifa, I deduce you do research at the Technion. Am I right?'

'I wish you were.' Kleinhart made a shrug of resignation. 'I used to. Now I do what is called administration. I'm swamped in it.'

The conversation was interrupted by the entry of newcomers.

'Ah, Kleinhart, glad to see you.' The speaker was Dr Sigvard Eklund, the great Swedish scientist who has been Director General of the International Atomic Energy Agency in Vienna since 1961. 'Rupert, my dear fellow. You two know each other?'

Eklund had also been to the opera and the conversation moved to Mozart. Rupert was on his home ground again. He gave it as his opinion that in her rendering of Mozart's great aria 'Martern aller arten' tonight Hilda de Groote had reached the ideal of a coloratura singer for whom the composer had created the music. When it looked for a moment that Kleinhart might be about to enter some qualification on this esoteric point, the genial Eklund said, 'I must warn you, Kleinhart, Herr Conway is one of Vienna's greatest Mozart specialists.'

'You flatter me, Sigvard. Enthusiast, certainly. I'm strictly an amateur.'

Eklund moved off to chat with the American Ambassador's economic adviser, but some invisible strand held Rupert and Kleinhart together for one more fateful moment.

'I just got a fleeting impression that you are by no means ignorant of Wolfgang Amadeus yourself, Doctor?'

'True. In a sense. But I fear my interest is dull as ditchwater to any real music lover.'

'Being?'

'Being the odd fact that, as a scientist, I have always been fascinated by the remarkable connection between music and mathematics. It is at its purest in the composers from the time of the elder Bach down to Mozart.'

'God bless my soul! Now you're way over my head.'

'It's obscure, I agree.'

'Funnily enough, I acquired some rare Mozart manuscripts at an auction in Rome only a short while ago. We only just started to sort them out last week.'

'Another lost symphony?'

'Nothing quite so dramatic as that, I'm afraid. Interesting though. Only this afternoon I was puzzling through pages of fascinating annotations on *Seraglio* by Karl Reuben.'

Kleinhart looked as though a wasp had just stung the back of his neck and he spilled his glass down his trousers. He coughed.

'You said Karl Reuben?' he said falteringly.

'I did.' Rupert wanted to say, 'and what the hell is the matter with you', but politeness forbade it. 'He probably *was* Vienna's greatest Mozart scholar.'

Rupert's practised eye and alert sense of hearing left him in no doubt that the casual, relaxed Israeli scientist of the past ten minutes had taken on a completely new interest in their conversation. He appeared to be trying hard to suppress a perceptible degree of excitement.

'Indeed. Interesting. Interesting. Tell me, Herr Conway, may one see these, ah, manuscripts you mention?'

'Certainly. Delighted to show them to you. Come round to my gallery any time. 5B Stephansplatz, just behind the cathedral.'

'I will. I will.' Jacob Kleinhart carefully finished what remained in his glass and made a consciously visible effort to restore his composure. 'Tomorrow, afraid I'm fully booked with meetings. Would Thursday morning be convenient for you?'

'By all means. I'll be there all morning.' Julia's glittering smile and radiant hair style beckoned from the wide doorway. 'Good night Dr Kleinhart. Delighted to meet you.'

Which was true, though Rupert had no idea exactly why.

He deposited Julia on the doorstep of her apartment with a fond and friendly good-night kiss.

'Thank you, dear Rupert, for a lovely evening. It is so difficult for me to get out in the evenings now with poor Georgy so frail. You are kind.'

'Give him my love, Julie.'

'I will. I will.' She turned the key in the lock and was gone.

Rupert climbed back into the svelte driving seat of his beloved blue English Jensen sports model, and indulged himself in just one deep throttled wwwerummmmmph from that high-powered engine. He turned into the Schubertring and then took a twisting course through small one way streets that led eventually to the underground garage so conveniently dug just between his own front door and the east end of St Stephan's cathedral. He had cheered when the City authorities decided to place it there. Privately he would confess that the banning of all vehicles from Karntnerstrasse was a vast improvement, but could not help nursing a small personal grudge against the City authorities that it deprived him of the pleasure of driving home at night down one of the world's most glamorous boulevards. It was the sort of change which makes any sensible person in their fifties begin to wonder whether they were really so keen on 'progress' after all.

He parked the Jensen in its usual spot, climbed the steps back to street level. As he came into the street he carefully looked round for any signs of people about. Vienna has long been one of the most peaceful capitals in Europe, but his early training as a soldier and his years of close association with police work, amongst other things, had long since taught him to be cautious. It was less than two years since there had been a gun battle on his own roof in which a policeman and a Palestinian terrorist had both been killed. The sound of a few late revellers carried from the other side of the great church; this part of Stephansplatz was deserted. He quickly crossed the street and went through his ritual performance with the two keys which were always secured round his waist by a stainless steel chain. The arrangement of small monitor lights visible through the large bullet proof glass window of the gallery assured him that all was normal within. He deactivated the burglar alarm system, opened the strong mahogany covered steel door and was inside in two quick movements. The spot lights which at present shone down on two superb renaissance paintings in the window always made him feel welcome. He walked to the end of the long showroom, climbed the stairs to his private apartments and reached for the next key.

There was a scurrying of feet, a thump on the other side of the door as a small, wiry body of self-generated fury hurled itself against it. Rupert turned the key fully and chuckled to himself.

'All right, Charlie. All right, old chap. Relax, it's only me.' The Welsh terrier greeted him with his usual unrestrained leaps and squeals, his sawed off stubby tail gyrating like a windmill. 'Thought I was never coming home, eh? Sorry I'm so late. Come on then, street's all yours this time of night.' Charlie hurled himself down the stairs and Rupert dutifully followed. This habitual routine was one all dog lovers know, and usually somehow manage to enjoy. The only words Rupert uttered from start to finish were, 'For the two thousandth time, you little devil, not on the Cardinal's doorstep!'

Some five hundred miles south of Vienna along the ruggedly beautiful Adriatic coast of Yugoslavia the weather was markedly different. In fact it was so warm and gentle that the late tourists lingered on, storing up the last few days of zest-giving sunshine, the last sybaritic delights of some of the world's finest still un-polluted beaches. In a seaside hotel just south of the small town of Ulcinj the proprietor pondered over a telegram which had just been delivered by way of a friend's car all the way from Titograd, nearly seventy kilometres northward. The local tele-phones had been out of order all week. The request posed a problem for him and he sat on his front veranda seeking guidance from the breeze floating lazily up from the south; so lazily that it scarcely rippled the silver moonpath on the softly yielding purple surface that stretched in front of him right across to the clearly discernible sparks that were the Italian shore a hundred kilometres away. How much longer would this idyllic weather hold?

Draǧa Janszcowicz thoughtfully rubbed his grizzled old chin and sipped his slivovitz with approval. The telegram was from a travel agent in Stockholm: would he stay open another two weeks to accommodate a package tour? The party of thirty-five would be from one of Sweden's 'most reputable health clubs'. Draga knew what that meant; they liked to come way down here because the local coves and tiny islands harboured beaches so secluded that the authorities continued to allow nude bathing. Being a devout Communist of the old Partisan school, that is to say about as unreconstructed a conservative as could be found, Draga didn't approve of that sort of thing. Still, money was always tight in this remote corner of Montenegro, and thirty-five sure customers who would pay in advance were mighty tempting.

Draga decided the weather would hold.

A thousand miles east in Beirut the evening was hot and sultry. In the battle scarred towers of concrete that had once been the luxury apartments of rich Arab businessmen and oil rich desert chieftains, the warm moisture laden air rolled down from the coastal hills cloying at the throats of the motley assortment of people who now lived in them. All traces of former elegance, and most of the comfort, had long been blasted away. The electricity worked seldom, the elevators never. There were few buildings whose walls were not pock-marked by bullet holes and mortar shells. Some were merely empty hulks of twisted metal and crumbled stone work. The obsequious uniformed porters and doormen had long since been replaced by a polyglot crew of ill-kempt and undisciplined soldiers, penniless and possessionless refugees, and gun slinging terrorists who arrived and disappeared again God knows where or why.

On the third floor of such a building that had once been the private hideaway of a group of bankers from the Persian Gulf states, three men sat by oil lamps amid the tawdry and ruined grandeur, deep in discussion. One of them was George Habash, head of the most notorious Palestinian terrorist organisation, the self-styled Popular Front for the Liberation of Palestine. Yasser Arafat's pseudo-Palestinian government constantly denied any connection with this desperate gang of assassins and thugs. No one who knew anything about Arab politics believed a word of it. With him was Wadih Haddad, the Front's 'external operations controller'; the advocate, trainer and planner of many of the most bloody and brutal outrages which have sent hundreds of innocent people to a useless, premature and mangled death in the last twenty years.

It is Haddad who runs the training camp for terrorists near Aden, Champ Khayat it is called – he also runs an 'exchange student' system with 'Patrice Lumumba University' in Moscow – something the 'Third World' enthusiasts for *détente* prefer not to talk about. *Détente*, after all, is only a French word for appeasement. It was Haddad who master-minded and trained the operators who shot up the El Al aircraft at Zürich airport in 1969; hi-jacked the SwissAir plane at Dawson's Field in Jordan in 1970; turned Athens airport into a charnel house in 1973; repeated the slaughter at Rome airport late the same year, and Tunis in 1974. His only known major set-back to date was the grisly affair at Entebbe in 1976 when the genius and courage of the Israeli airborne forces killed five of his star pupils while carrying out the most spectacular rescue up till that time.

The third, a slightly older man, was always just called Abdullah. He was a rather different type; a lifelong criminal and loyal supporter of the Front, but killing was not his speciality. He had lived in Paris for many years, a quiet and apparently respectable music teacher with a peculiar talent for getting himself into buildings, like banks and government offices, without being caught; and, even more important, getting himself out again. In his own quiet way he had provided the PFLP link men in France and Germany with vast sums of money received from the sale of stolen jewellery, pictures, works of art, and occasional hauls of large amounts of cash. Abdullah had been one of their most reliable sources of funds for years, and in the course of his operations had got to know his way into and out of many European police forces. He might have been still at it, living peaceably in his Left Bank apartment, if the whole team had not been blown by Carlos when he killed three men shooting his way out of a girl friend's apartment in the Rue Toullier.

Since his forced return to the Middle East, Abdullah had been used by Habash on jobs which required more refined techniques than just pulling triggers and hurling hand grenades at defence-less people. His presence that night was to finalise just such a delicate operation.

'There is no doubt young Reuben must still be in Austria. All our sources agree on that.' It was Habash who did the talking. Haddad was only interested in the killing. 'And we must have him alive. Dead, he is useless to us.'

Abdullah's heavy eyelids showed no sign of feeling of any kind. They seldom did. He spoke slowly, deliberately. 'I under-stand. Haddad's plan is skilful, but I must tell you frankly, I am far from happy with my team. This girl, Moda, whose sister was Reuben's lover, she has no experience.'

Habash said quietly, 'She has the experience you will need. She was three years studying in Vienna. She speaks fluent German; she knows her way around Vienna. And she knows Karl Reuben. She's a pretty girl too. Knows how to use her body when necessary. You can't do without her.'

'Very emotional girl. She's obsessed with her sister's death. No telling how she might react in a tight corner. I'll get Reuben for you all right, but I won't guarantee Mlle Moda won't put a bullet through him before I get him to Libya.'

Haddad said, 'She'll be all right. I trained her well.'

'And this young man, Yali. Some experience, not much. Once more, I ask of you, why can't I take Akache? If this job is so important he is the best man to help me.'

Habash looked pained. And very tired. 'It's no good, old friend. Not possible. You know our resources are stretched to the limit. We lost too many good operators at Entebbe. At the moment the Communist countries are refusing help. Nearly all our German friends are either in jail, or on the run. We will repair that. I can only tell you that Zohair Akache is engaged on such a task right now. That's why he can't be spared. It will be two or three weeks before Andreas Baader and Gudrun

Ensslin and their friends are able to join us. That is Akache's present task. Carlos is sulking in Aden; anyway, you wouldn't want him on a job like this. He's too impetuous. If you need help our Czech friends will give it, they know Vienna's underworld well enough.'

'And what about these two unknown Japanese?'

'You have your instructions how to pick them up in Athens. They are good gunmen, but disciplined. They won't shoot without your orders. While you are in Europe they will be your bodyguards. After you have Reuben on the boat, well, they are expendable.'

To these men all others are 'expendable'. After they have served their purpose.

CHAPTER TWO

By Thursday morning the north-west winds had exhausted themselves and the rain clouds were petering out somewhere in the Hungarian plain the other side of Lake Balaton. In Vienna it was a bright, crisp, perfect late autumn morning. Rupert breakfasted well, skimmed the morning papers and had a quick look at yesterday's *Times* from London. Nothing much caught his attention. Mr Carter and Mr Bresznev were still arguing about cruise missiles, and he presumed it didn't really matter whether one called them miss -iles or miss -uls. Ethiopia and Somalia had just torn up their friendship treaty and started fighting each other, but since no one could possibly make racial mischief out of that one the General Assembly of the United Nations seemed not to care how many people got killed. Apparently by their rules, a war is not really happening so long as the antagonists both have the same colour skin. Syria and Iraq, who only last year had sworn to be eternal blood brothers, were once again calling each other fascist hyenas and rattling sabres. What else is new? *Die Presse* and *Kurier* both carried rave reviews about Tuesday night's opera. A short paragraph mentioned an unknown man dying in the lobby; no details were known.

Rupert finished his coffee, lit his first pipe of the day, and called out his customary thank you to Frau Kröner in the kitchen. He went downstairs into the gallery and said good morning to the girls who worked there. He stopped to talk to Heinz, his irreplaceable man of all work ever since the last war in which they had both been badly wounded while fighting, on opposite sides, in the bloody freezing horror of Montecassino.

He picked up an auction catalogue from the hall table and ambled happily up to his own office on the second floor. American 'second', British 'first' floor. Without looking up from the folder in his hand he announced, 'Charlie, get off that chair.'

In one corner of the office stood a rather scruffy old brown leather chair which was clearly understood by all to be Charlie's property. It was also understood that whatever the house rules laid down Charlie preferred the more elegant velvet upholstered Gainsborough chair of his master whenever he could sneak into it. Which was always after Heinz had given him his morning airing and before Rupert came down from breakfast. Seven years ago, when Charlie arrived from the kennels in Wales, where both he and Charlie the first had been sired, Rupert had made a feeble effort to stop this breach of etiquette by clouting him with the morning newspaper. It hadn't had the slightest effect.

His desk, as always, was meticulously arranged for him by Martita Hauptmann, his secretary; the day's diary on the left; letters and notes for immediate attention in the centre; catalogues, art advertisements and papers for browsing on the right. He noted with pleasure he had no appointments for the day, there was nothing urgent in the middle pile, and nothing new amongst the catalogues that particularly interested him. He rumbled through his pipe contentedly and tossed a grateful smile somewhere in the general direction of St Stephan's towering spire which stared straight down on him through the big window opposite his desk. Being part Celt and part Jewish Rupert had a highly developed imagination, especially in spiritual matters – he never had any difficulty in picturing somewhere about the top of that spire was where his guardian angel constantly hovered.

'Going to be a nice, peaceful day, Charlie; who knows, might even get some time to think.'

The telephone buzzed on his desk.

'Yes, Mini?'

'There is a gentleman down here asking to see you, Herr Doktor. A Dr Jacob Kleinhart.'

'Ask Heinz to bring him up, please.'

'Jawohl, Herr Doktor.' Mini was probably the highest paid and most over-worked telephone operator in Vienna; she worked all hours of the day and night and she did it in four different languages. If she had a fault it was only that she could never forget she was a soldier's daughter. There were times when she barked 'Jawohl, Herr Doktor' down the telephone with such vigour that Rupert wondered whether she stood up and saluted.

There was a discreet knock on the door and Heinz ushered in the enigmatic Dr Kleinhart. From Haifa. On second sight Rupert decided his visitor's head was even larger and more distinguished than he had thought. He could not recall seeing a scientist who looked so exactly what a scientist should look like. Even to the gold rimmed glasses arched over that enormous beak of a nose. After the usual pleasantries about their meeting, the delights of the opera and the excellent quality of Madame Doron's hospitality, Rupert and Kleinhart were seated comfortably across the big Chippendale desk, puffing contentedly at each other. Rupert picked up a well worn document case and extracted a sheaf of papers, many with crumpled and torn edges, occasional ravages of mildew, and some, obviously far older than the rest, carefully laid between sheets of clear polythene to preserve them from disintegrating entirely. They were sheets of manuscript music, covered with notes, corrections, and explanations; old concert programmes and reviews torn from newspapers and magazines.

'Old Karl Reuben's papers. Or some of 'em.' He handed them across the desk.

'Most interesting, Herr Conway. How did you come across them?' Rupert noticed Kleinhart did not pick them up.

'They turned up recently in an auction room in Venice. A Rome dealer, friend of mine, knew my interest in Mozart, bought them and . . . ah . . . let me have them; for a consideration. Strictly business.'

'Interesting. Venice? Hm . . . yes, that fits.'

Rupert could never resist a mystery. 'Fits what?'

'Fits with what little we know of Reuben's movements during the war.'

'All I have ever been able to find out here in Vienna is that when the Nazis expelled all Jews from the Conservatory of Music Reuben disappeared. Even the people in the Mozart Library here, which he practically founded, have no trace of him after that.'

'He survived. God knows how. He spent most of the war in Venice.'

'Teaching music?'

'Waiting on tables, and sweeping floors.'

'This is fascinating. Do go on.'

'He was captured by the Gestapo. Late in 1938. Finding he was one of Europe's greatest cellists they broke his fingers. Somehow he managed to escape, and got to Venice where his sister and brother-in-law ran a small restaurant. He spoke perfect Italian, of course. They got him a new identity, false papers, all that sort of thing; as Venice was well off the track of all the fighting the Germans paid little attention to it. The Italian administration was generally too busy surviving to waste much time on little people. Reuben survived. In 1945 he got across to North Africa and eventually made his way to Israel.'

'I never knew that,' Rupert said with feeling.

'There are over a million of us in Israel who got there in more or less similar ways.'

'Which is just another reason, if I may say so, why Israel is such an amazing country. I'm part Jewish myself, you know.'

'No, I didn't.'

'My Viennese grandfather was one who did not escape from the Gestapo. But tell me. You knew Karl Reuben?' He was becoming a bit puzzled that his visitor paid no attention to the fascinating papers he had professed to want to see.

'Not the one you're concerned with. I know his son.'

'Good Lord! I never knew he had one.'

'Yes. He married in Israel, and produced one son, young Karl.'

'The old man is not still alive?'

'No. He died when the boy was six.'

'Is the boy a musician too?'

'No. A scientist. An exceptionally brilliant scientist.'

'In Israel?'

'He should be. At the moment we think he is in Austria. That is why I am here, Herr Conway.'

Rupert had long since mentally written off his day of peace and quiet. This was going to be too interesting to curtail.

'How about some coffee, Dr Kleinhart?'

'Excellent idea. Thank you.'

Rupert buzzed. 'Ask Frau Kröner to bring me in two cups of coffee, please, Mini. Milk and sugar, Doctor? Yes, both with milk and sugar. Thanks, Mini.'

Both men rose and stretched their legs. Dr Kleinhart glanced toward the door and said, 'May I . . . ?' to which Rupert replied, 'Yes, of course. Just down the passage. First door on the right.' Rupert took a phone call and Frau Kröner came in with the coffee, coughed disapprovingly at the smoke-laden atmosphere and opened a window. Rupert said, 'Yes, of course, Frau Kröner. You're quite right. Thank you very much.' He flicked the telephone switch and said, 'No calls until further notice, Mini.' Kleinhart returned as Rupert was selecting another pipe from the lovely 1778 Chelsea red anchor bowl on his desk and they both lit up again.

'Herr Conway, I will be perfectly frank with you. You saw, of course, that I was surprised when you mentioned Karl Reuben the other night. That name is never out of my mind these days. After you left I had a long talk with Jacob Doron who assured me I could trust you implicitly.' Rupert acknowledged the compliment with a faint smile. He valued the Israeli Ambassador's opinion. Kleinhart continued, 'We have a very . . .' he paused as though searching for the right word . . . 'delicate problem on our hands. So delicate, of a nature which could be so serious . . . for us, for many countries . . . we approached it at the highest level. I came here five days ago with a letter from Moshe Dayan personally to your Foreign Minister. From the Foreign Minister I was passed directly to your ex-cellent Police President, Dr Karl Reidinger. Eklund of the

Atomic Energy Agency has been fully informed. Everyone is being most helpful. But, so far, all results are negative.'

'You can't find Karl Reuben?'

'We can't even prove he is in Austria.'

'And why is this young man so important?'

Kleinhart took a deep breath, like a man signifying he had just made a vital decision.

'I don't want to appear melodramatic, Herr Conway. But what I now tell you is a state secret of the gravest importance. At the moment it is known only to the most senior people in my government, in the Hofburg, and to Eklund. Even Reidinger was not told why the matter is so important.'

'The only thing I do not understand so far, Doctor, is why you want to tell me.'

'What you told me Tuesday night about Karl's father set up a completely new line of thought in my mind. Somehow I think a freelance like yourself might be able to help us. Doron and I talked about it half the night. He phoned Jerusalem and got Dayan out of bed to secure his agreement to my telling you.'

'I have the greatest admiration for both Moshe and Rachel Dayan. I hope I was forgiven for disturbing their sleep.'

Kleinhart smiled. 'Like Dayan, you seem to know everybody, Herr Conway. They sent their regards to you. Now, I cannot tell you everything of course. If you are as bad at science as you insisted I doubt if you would understand it anyway. The gist of the story is simply this. Young Karl Reuben is one of the most brilliant nuclear physicists in the world. In his own line he is a genius. Socially he can be perfectly charming. If you met him I'm sure you'd like him. But, he is impossible. Neurotic, unpredictable, excitable, thoroughly unstable. His scientific insight is a generation ahead of mine but it was because of his personal weakness that David Erlik, our Dean of Medicine, assigned me to oversee his work; act as his father confessor. In the last three years that young man has taken ten off my life.

'Next, let me make it clear to you that we are not here concerned with bombs or weaponry of any kind. Whether the world believes it or not we at Technion and Rehovoth are solely concerned with what are called "the peaceful uses" of nuclear energy. There is little mystery about bombs any more, and little point in building bigger ones. Almost any intelligent physicist could manufacture an atomic bomb these days if he could lay his hands on the necessary fissionable material. That is what Eklund's agency is all about; trying to police the world's supply to prevent such dangerous substances falling into the wrong hands.

'But, and it is a terrifying but, the progress of scientific research into the peaceful uses has now reached a point where . . . if certain highly technical problems should be solved . . . well, the results could be vastly more harmful to humanity than building bigger nuclear bombs.'

'What a ghastly thought.'

'It is ghastly, I assure you. Fortunately, many of the best men working in the field of what is now recognised as nuclear medicine, are convinced that these problems are insoluble. Pray God they are right. But they may be wrong. They may be wrong.' He paused to let the awful implication of that play for a moment on Rupert's highly volatile imagination.

'Karl Reuben thinks they are wrong. He has been concentrating exclusively on such problems these past three years. Only I knew how close he was to a critical breakthrough. If the breakthrough comes in one way it could mean the greatest advance science has yet made in the treatment of cancer.' Another, longer pause. 'If in another way, it would mean that men could soon produce a weapon so terrible, so flexible, so easy to us. . . . The weapon of ultimate blackmail. I can tell you that amongst those in charge of fighting terrorism in all the major countries this possibility is their greatest single fear.'

'I have heard of that. Sounds like science fiction gone mad,' Rupert said.

'That's not a bad way of putting it.'

'And Reuben has found the answers?'

'For practical purposes, thank God, no. But how far his mind was running ahead of his calculations I don't know. Two months ago he had a complete mental breakdown. Ten days ago he disappeared.'

'You think he realised the implications of what he was doing?'

'Of that I have no doubt.'

'Terrifying thing to live with.'

'In Karl Reuben's strange life anything is possible. I must tell you that one of my greatest worries for long has been that he was also engaged in a passionate love affair. With an Arab girl.'

Rupert just raised his eyebrows.

'I fought for that boy's soul day and night. He would not give her up. She loved him, she knew nothing of politics, nor of science, he claimed. Their love was pure. He even imagined some kind of heroic scenario where the love of a Jew and an Arab would bring peace to Israel. When that dream blew up in his face he went completely berserk.'

'She jilted him?'

'Would to God she had. He was forced to face reality in the cruellest possible way. She was arrested. Along with five other members of a Palestinian terrorist team. As a group they had twelve murders to answer for. He insisted on giving evidence at her trial.'

'He gave evidence against her?'

'Worse still. *For* her. He made such a hysterical fool of himself his evidence completely damned her. He practically put the bullet in her himself. They were all executed. Then he disappeared.'

'And you think he came to Austria?'

'There are strong grounds for believing so. The only stable factor in young Karl's life was the love of his father. He worshipped him. When his nervous energy was dominant, appeal to his father's memory was the only rational thought that could influence him.'

'The immigration people must have a record if he landed here.'

'Unfortunately, they haven't. But all that proves is that he travelled on a false passport. Not a difficult thing to do these days.'

'Assuming he travelled freely. Suppose he was kidnapped?'

'That possibility is always in my mind. By sheer luck we have one tangible piece of evidence. The El Al agent in Cyprus saw him board the plane to Vienna. And he was alone.'

'So what's he running from? Or for?'

'We can only guess. There are several possibilities. My guess is that the PFLP would gladly murder him if they could get their hands on him. Maybe he's running from them. Maybe he's trying to get to Moscow. His political thinking was always in a turmoil. He might also think that Moscow is about the only place the PFLP could not get at him. The Russians shoot other people's terrorists on sight. Maybe he's just running away from life.'

'The girl. The Arab girl. Did she know what he was doing?'

'That,' said Kleinhart with slow deliberation, 'is the most ghastly possibility of all. We don't know, but if she did, and if she had passed on certain information into the hands of the PFLP, the possible consequences could be too terrible to contemplate.'

There was a gentle tap on the door and Heinz put his head round it. Rupert came back to earth and stared at the guileless, contented peasant face of his devoted servant with disbelief. It reassured him. Yes, there still really were plenty of decent kindly people in this troubled world.

'Yes, Heinz?'

'Sorry to bother you, Herr Doktor, but Dr Kuso of Kriminalpolizei is anxious to speak to Dr Kleinhart.'

'Freddy Kuso? Wonder what he wants? Thank you, Heinz, the Doctor will call him right away.' Turning to his guest he said, 'You know Freddy Kuso?'

'I don't think so.'

'He's the top man in Department Two. First class fellow.'

Into the phone he said, 'Mini, get Dr Kuso now, will you?'

They sat musing in silence for a minute, and then the phone buzzed.

'Dr Kuso on the line, Herr Doktor.'

'Put him on, Mini.'

'Jawohl, Herr Doktor.'

'Freddy, hello. You want Dr Kleinhart?'

'Please, Rupert, it's rather urgent.'

Rupert handed across the instrument.

'Kleinhart speaking.'

'Sorry to trouble you, Doctor. We have an unidentified body in the morgue. It doesn't quite tally with the description you gave us, but we think it's close enough to make sure. Could you come over and try to identify it?'

'Yes, of course. You would like me to come straight away?'

'I'll send a car round for you.'

'Thank you, that's most kind.'

To Rupert he said, 'They have an unidentified body for me to look at.'

'It may be the end of your search,' Rupert commented.

'In view of what we have just been discussing, I find myself in the unhappy state of, almost, hoping it is.'

They met again later over lunch in the most select hideaway in Vienna, a private room on the third floor of the Rennverein, the only place in Austria an American or Englishman would recognise as a club. The waiter opened a bottle of Kremser red, served veal cutlets with red cabbage and boiled onions, and withdrew.

'And was it?' Rupert opened.

'No, it wasn't. Close resemblance in many ways; age and general physical appearance. The bone structure of the head was clearly Semitic. The man was an Arab. He couldn't possibly have been born a Jew, but the pathologist evidently forgot to look in the obvious place.'

'No progress, then?'

'Not really. But there may be a connection somewhere. Did you know there was a murder at the Staatsoper Tuesday night?'

'Good Lord no! Never heard of it. When? How?'

'Apparently in the crush around the main doors someone

pushed a stiletto right through this chap's back, and then completely disappeared in the crowd. So far they've not a single witness.'

Rupert whistled. 'That's pretty cool. Must have been a real professional job.'

'No doubt about that. A favourite Arab technique.'

'Arabs killing Arabs is a new line, surely?'

'Not really. They do it all the time. Many of them hate each other almost as much as they hate us. The PFLP crowd couldn't care less who they kill. Sometimes I think they just do it to keep in practice. Still, that's your police's problem, not mine.'

The waiter came quietly in, refilled the glasses and as quietly disappeared again.

Rupert said, 'I've been thinking about this ever since you left me this morning. What you said about young Karl and his father. The music angle, I mean.'

'Any ideas?'

'Possibly. Let me think this through. Although there is no proof, you are certain he is in Austria, right?'

'Right.'

'His description has been circulated to the police all over the country, right?'

'Right.'

'And he's now been here nine or ten days and nobody has seen him.'

'Right.'

'So, wherever he is, he's well hidden.'

'Seems logical.'

'Now, if his terrorist pals have got him they'll probably kill him; or, conceivably they might try to smuggle him out of the country for their own use.'

'All airports and border crossings have been alerted to such a possibility.'

'Border crossings to our Communist neighbours are few, far between, and well patrolled. To the west and south there are hundreds of mountain paths where you can cross a border without even realising you've done it.'

'Reuben has never been in Austria before; in his present mental and physical condition I doubt if he could do it without attracting attention.'

'So let's proceed on the hypothesis that he is hiding here.'

'That's what I think.'

'So, the other side of that coin is that somebody here must be hiding him. He's got to eat, have a place to sleep. The police can't go searching every private house in the country for a man they're not even sure is in Austria.'

'So who would be hiding him?'

'Had he any friends here?'

'None we've heard of.'

'You see where we're getting then? Let's guess that he made contact with someone who was a friend of his father's.'

For the first time Kleinhart let himself look just a little bit hopeful. 'Sounds worth pursuing.'

'But how?' Rupert rang for the waiter who returned with biscuits and cheese. 'But how?' he repeated. 'My next guess is that you are just wondering if we could use my Mozart papers as bait?' Kleinhart made no attempt to disagree.

'Cast a fly, that is,' Rupert continued.

'A fly?'

'You a fisherman?'

'Not really. How do fish help?'

Rupert chuckled. 'Well, you see, when the fish hides at the bottom of a pool you have to entice him up to catch him. That's called casting a fly over him.'

'Have to be a pretty big fly to cover all of Austria.'

'That's it! That's the clue.'

'You're going too fast for me.'

'What covers all of Austria? Only one thing, *Die Presse*.'

'The newspaper! Interesting idea.'

'Let me think a moment. Here. Try this. We get *Die Presse* to run a story about old Karl's manuscripts, we hint there is far more in them than appears. Personal things. Details about

31

his past life. Things that would play on young Karl's imagination. You said he worshipped his father.'

'That's right.'

'It's a long shot, to mix the metaphor, but it's the best I can think of at the moment.'

'I've nothing better to offer,' said Kleinhart. 'How do you get *Die Presse* to publish it?'

'That's the least of our problems. Freddy Foglar is always after me to do him stories about mysteries in the art world. Leave it with me. I'll cut the phone off and dream up something. It's worth a try.'

Rupert worked hard at it all afternoon and went round to see Freddy Foglar just as the working editors were arriving back for the evening's principal tasks. They sent for coffee and worked on the story for another hour.

Friday morning's *Die Presse* carried the news of Rupert's musical discoveries on the third news page under the deliberately misleading headline, 'Vienna art dealer unearths mystery of world famous cellist.'

CHAPTER THREE

Friday was a more than usually lively day in the gallery, and with his partner, Max Kallendorf, and his indispensable archivist, Sandra Fleming, both away Rupert was as busy as the proverbial one armed paper-hanger with the itch. And loved every minute of it.

Max was in bed with a badly sprained ankle. 'Playing football with the grandchildren at his age!' his devoted but sorely tried wife, Pauli, had screamed down the telephone. 'He can't even see as far as his feet. Crazy old man!' Rupert was duly sympathetic but in no way surprised; in all the years they had worked together, since 1945 to be precise, he had seldom seen his dear old friend and partner without a break or a bump on some part of his battered anatomy. It always seemed a miracle that a man with such genius for self-destruction was still serene and happy at 82.

Sandra's absence meant that Frau Hauptmann was left to handle all the paperwork alone and it was beyond even her dedication to duty. The new Chicago gallery was still locked in unending argument with City Hall over their tax assessment, both sides were threatening to sue. The London gallery was up to its eyes in an authentication dispute over two works attributed to the obscure fourteenth century Florentine painter Andrea di Giusto about whom even the great Berenson had been known to change his mind. Since the buyer was a Persian gentleman who lived in Luxembourg and had learned his English in the oil business in Indonesia it frequently required many conferences just to decide what it was he was making all the fuss about.

33

During lunch it was discovered that a letter of credit for eighty thousand dollars from a Greek buyer had been directed to the wrong bank and if it could not be sorted out before the banks closed all sorts of awful complications would arise.

By half past eight Friday night Rupert was still in his work room poring over microphotographs of a painting of debatable origin which he had taken at a series of acute angles, a technique which throws the irregular surface of the picture into light relief thus allowing a more detailed study of the artist's brush work. After two hours with the microscope he was of the opinion that all these tests tended to affirm the work was what it claimed to be – which would not please the insurance company who paid highly for his expert advice on these matters. And they had a point, the texture of the canvas in no way matched up with the date the picture was supposed to have been painted. The fact that three quarters of its surface was badly damaged by smoke and water didn't make the problem any easier. The strain was beginning to affect the cunning of his eyes, it would have to wait till Monday. Rupert carefully locked up his papers, ate the cold steak and kidney pie Frau Kröner had left for him, drank a bottle of Batailly 1963, and took Charlie for his nightly constitutional – 'not on the Cardinal's doorstep, Charlie!' – and went to bed.

Saturday was a perfect autumn day. The business was open, but quiet. He and Charlie made a lazy start and then drove down to his country house near Semmering, where the hours were divided between walks on the misty pine-scented hillsides, and the huge, happily cluttered library. Charlie chased innumerable rabbits and put up two deer which was the fullness of happiness for him. Rupert never saw another living soul except the Erhoffers; Anna kept house for him, and Fritz was a woodsman on a neighbouring property of one of the Habsburgs. They were of the old school, looked after him, but didn't fuss him.

Sunday morning he drove over to the little Catholic church in the valley. This would have horrified his staunchly Methodist Welsh grandfather, but Rupert and his elder brother George had been brought up in the Anglican church, and he was a total ecumenist. In the late afternoon he and Charlie drove back to town where he had arranged to dine with Jacob Kleinhart at Sacher's.

When he arrived at his apartment the answering service informed him that Sandra had phoned from America and would call again at eight o'clock local time. He made arrangements to have the call transferred to Sacher.

They met at seven, each had a whisky and soda and they ordered dinner. They quickly drifted into mutual confidence and first name terms, which is far from automatic either in Austria or Israel. Jacob accepted Rupert's enthusiastic recommendation of Sacher's justly famous täfelspitz and the *maître d'hôtel* left them to their conversation.

Having nothing new to contribute Conway opened with the simply query, 'Any developments?'

Kleinhart shrugged. 'Possibly. Indeed, probably. And if so sinister.'

'Sinister?'

'Hmm. You know what is Mossad?'

'Your secret service people.'

'Hmm. Doron called me to the embassy this morning. He just received a message that on Friday afternoon a Mossad agent in Istanbul reported three Arabs boarding a plane for Vienna. Through Turkish contacts he was able to check the names under which they were travelling. Obviously false. We have asked Kuso's people to process the arrival here of such names. We should hear something tomorrow.'

'All Arabs are not necessarily sinister?'

'Indeed they are not.' Jacob sighed. 'It sounds so pathetic now, but it is true nevertheless, as a kid in Galilee many of my friends were Arabs. We all played together perfectly happily. In those days.' He shrugged. 'There were two men and a girl. The older of the two men our agent recognised. He's not a terrorist, but a known PFLP sympathiser, with a record of criminal associations in Europe. Been living recently in Beirut.

Our agent got photographs of them all. They're being checked in Jerusalem now.'

Rupert munched his beef thoughtfully and said nothing.

Jacob asked, 'How do you think the West will react to the next terrorist outrage?'

'Depends who's involved.' Rupert swallowed. 'America and Britain, alas, both still playing ostrich. France is unpredictable. Germany? Dunno. I'm told by friends in Bonn that this new German anti-terrorist unit, what do they call it . . . GSG 9 or some such . . . I'm told they're really good. They work closely with the British SAS, who have all the skills but are hamstrung by politics.'

'And would the Germans not be hamstrung by politics too?'

'Hard to say. The German people are really worried about terrorism. The kidnapping of that industrialist in Cologne last month, Schleyer, four people killed in a gun battle. After all the precautions Schmidt's government claim to have taken. The Christian Democrats really have him over a barrel on that one. Don't know, hard to say. My own guess right now is that Schmidt might surprise us by how tough he could be.'

'Hope you're right.'

A waiter interrupted them.

'Excuse me, Herr Conway. There is a long distance call for you.'

Rupert made his apologies and went into the phone booth.

'Yes. This is Herr Conway. Put her on, please. Sandra, darling, where are you?'

'I'm spending the week-end with Susan at New Canaan.'

'Wonderful. And how is that great lady?'

'Full of vim and vigour, as usual. She sends her love.'

'Please give her mine. When are you coming back?'

'I'm leaving tomorrow night.'

'Thank God for that.'

'Any troubles?'

'Not troubles. But Max is in bed again; sprained his ankle. Silly old man. We're up to our eyes in work.'

'I'm coming on SAS via Copenhagen. Flight 673 due in Schwechat Tuesday morning at 11.35. Can you have somebody meet me?'

'Yes, of course. I'd come myself but I know I'm going to be tied up all morning. You won't mind if I send Heinz?'

'No, of course not. What are you doing out on a Sunday night, is the redhead from Bucharest back in town?'

'No, worse luck! I'm dining with a man.'

'OK, OK. I believe you.'

'Honestly, my dear. You'll soon see. I'll send Heinz, he's completely reliable. See you Tuesday. God bless.'

When Rupert returned to the table Jacob had finished his fruit and was loading up his pipe. They ordered coffee. He decided to proffer an explanation; anyway, he liked talking about Sandra. As hard as he tried to keep their relationship strictly platonic, there were moments when he found it a bit of a strain. Especially since Commander Tommy Thompson, United States Navy, had left the embassy for the Pacific fleet without anything definite developing between them.

'That was my Hungarian cousin from New York. She's coming back Tuesday. You'll enjoy meeting her.'

'I'm sure. Tell me about her.'

'Her mother and mine were sisters. We were the lucky ones; my mother went to England; hers went to Hungary. Married an Andrassy. They had a foul time during the war. Lost everything. Four of them died. Sandra spent the first five years of her life being chased across the Balkans by the bloody Gestapo.'

Jacob understood. He had many friends and relatives who shared that awful fate. And few who had lived to tell the tale. He murmured sympathetically.

'Anyway. She and her mother finally got to the States. She grew up in New York. Did brilliantly in art and history at Cornell. Worked in the archives of the Metropolitan Museum. Then made a brief and disastrous marriage. So, she was miserable, I was desperate for a qualified archivist. She joined my firm ... what ... nearly two years ago.'

The doorman called a taxi for Kleinhart. Rupert was happy

to meander down Karntnerstrasse to home; so much more pleasant since they made it pedestrians only.

'I'll phone you as soon as I have news about the Arab visitors. Think we'll have any bites to your piece in *Die Presse*?'

'I hope so.'

'I do too. Time may be getting shorter than we know.'

CHAPTER FOUR

The only memorable event at 5B Stephansplatz on Monday morning was when Rupert advised everyone that Mrs Fleming would return Tuesday morning. The news was warmly welcomed, especially by the harassed Frau Hauptmann. Pauli phoned to say that Max was up and hobbling about on a cane. He insisted he would be well enough to come to work tomorrow. Rupert, anticipating inevitable disaster, instructed Heinz to stand by at the front door and be ready to catch the professor at any moment thereafter. He knew from experience there was no point in trying to persuade Max to stay home any longer.

It was not until mid-morning Tuesday that he received the anticipated call from Jacob Kleinhart.

'I don't know whether it is sinister or not, Rupert, but the tangle unquestionably moves closer to Reuben.'

'Found your terrorists?'

'No. We have still no real evidence that they are. Our intelligence people processed the pictures the agent took at Istanbul airport. The older man I told you about, confirmed. We know he has some association with the PFLP. That's about all we know. The young man we have no trace of at all. He has no record on our files. Nor has the girl for that matter. But we have found out who she is. Her name is Moda Tablishi, and she is the sister of Reuben's dead girl friend.'

'That sounds ominous.'

'It just couldn't be coincidence. Furthermore, she studied in Vienna for three years. That means she knows her way around. Has friends here. We've go to act on the assumption that they are here for the same reason I am. And it's a fine chance which of us gets to young Reuben first.'

'You've told Kuso all this?'

'I've just come from there. They are being wonderfully helpful; and I must say, I'm impressed by that computer record system, but it's going to have to be awfully clever to turn up anything on this crowd. They're all newcomers in the game.'

'Did the Istanbul flight come direct to Vienna?'

'No. It stopped in Athens, but the airline's computer readout is clear this lot got off here. But, of course, their papers are false, so all we know is that three people whose photos we have are now somewhere in Austria.'

'Along with forty to fifty thousand other visitors.'

'That's about it. Hotel checks, and so on, yield nothing. Police records on all known terrorist connections and sympathisers may help. Reidinger tells me his men are stretched to the limit, they're working closely with the Germans on the Schleyer kidnapping, but he's assigned two very experienced men to sift through all that material. With a little luck it may put us on the track of the Tablishi girl. At the moment it seems our only chance of heading them off. Any reaction from your *Die Presse* story yet?'

'Telephone's been ringing all morning. Plenty of fish biting. Soon as I spot a salmon I'll ring you.'

When Kleinhart rang off Rupert buzzed his secretary.

'Got those notes on the phone calls sorted out yet, Frau Hauptmann?'

'Just checking one more item, Herr Doktor.'

'Bring them in soon as they're ready, please.'

Rupert's concentration on the morning mail was broken by a frantic scratching noise from the other side of the room. He looked up over his glasses.

'Charlie! You little brute! How many times do I have to tell you not to bury your filthy bones in my best chairs. Get out of it!'

Charlie gave him a withering look, and then wagged his stump of a tail. A minute later he was at it again.

Frau Hauptmann came in and deposited a sheet of neatly ordered notes on his desk. There had been five phone enquiries about the Reuben papers story, of which four were easily eliminated from the main problem. One from *Die Presse*'s own music editor, one from the secretary of the Mozart Institute expressing the hope that Rupert would present these treasures to them, and two from music lovers whose names, addresses and bona fides had been easily checked. The fifth was from a Polish gentleman whose name was unspellable and accent so thick it had been difficult to identify his interest. He had promised to call in person. One possibility only in that lot.

In a dingy attic over a warehouse in the Ninth District Abdullah and his team were holding their first conference with their hosts and allies, the local representatives of the Czech Secret State Police. Ever since 1949 when the Russians decided that backing terrorism would be bound to make additional trouble for the West, and therefore must be good for Communism, all the various factions that make up the Palestine Liberation Organisation had had their own particular working partners. The actual combinations changed from time to time as they periodically squabbled, jilted, double-crossed and occasionally even murdered each other, but the masters in the Kremlin didn't mind that; it helped to keep the democracies stumbling over themselves chasing defunct networks, and the satellite countries always had to accept their orders anyway. In 1976, when there was a general game of musical chairs in the terrorism business, Habash's assassins, the Popular Front for the Liberation of Palestine, had been assigned to Czechoslovakia. It suited both parties.

The senior of the two hosts, they always travel in pairs so they can also spy on each other, was a heavy set, sallow-skinned Slav of middle years who looked and dressed like a small time gangster in a B picture of the 1940s. He did the talking.

'Here are the addresses for your escape network, the passwords, and a detailed map. You have till tomorrow to memorise them, then I want them back. Don't copy them and don't attempt to take them out of this room. Only two pieces of hard information for you. Neither we nor the Austrian police can find any track of your man here in Vienna nor in Salzburg. Here is an item from Saturday's newspaper.' He handed across a clipping of Rupert's story about the Reuben papers. 'It might help.'

Abdullah needed Moda's assistance with the translation. They discussed it briefly between themselves in Arabic, then Abdullah turned to the big Czech.

'Do you know anything of this Conway?'

The man handed over a xeroxed sheet. 'This is the information from the Soviet Kommandatura file on him. Our police would like to get their hands on him for border crossing irregularities, and the East Germans suspect him of being some kind of British agent. Nothing positive. Our opinion is that he is just an art dealer with a talent for making a damn nuisance of himself.'

Abdullah's wily mind circled round the news story.

'This appeared on Saturday. We arrived on Monday. Strange coincidence, isn't it?' He checked the exact meaning of some German words with Moda, and continued: 'Could be a signal of some kind. Who to? Young Reuben, maybe?'

The Czech said, 'This Conway is part Jewish. He has done business in Israel. He is some kind of expert on Mozart. We don't know enough about your man Reuben to evaluate this. You'll have to try that yourselves.'

'Which means one of us will have to visit Mr Conway. Is it safe?'

'If you don't attack him and provoke trouble with the police, I don't know why not. At the moment he is our only link.'

'And time is short,' Abdullah said, in his usual almost expressionless voice. 'Moda here is the only one of us who knows her way around Vienna. I should think we'll have to watch Conway. Probably have him shadowed. Can you help?'

'Those are my orders. I will. But I can't risk my men being involved in any shoot-outs.'

That suited Abdullah.

The Czechs stood up to go and the headman said, 'One of you better come with me. I'll show you the secret exit, and where the car will be kept.'

Soon after lunch Max arrived at 5B Stephansplatz and Rupert was glad to see that Heinz was keeping close watch on him in case of need. They discussed the news of the sale of the Rosebury family treasures in England which had art dealers around the world in a frenzy, but it left the old man quite un-moved. About three thousand years B.C. was Max's period; he understood and appreciated the renaissance masterpieces which were the firm's speciality, but could never quite help regarding them as modern, commercial stuff. To one of his fatalistic temperament there was little difference between four hundred years ago and last week. They chatted amiably for a few minutes then Rupert went to the front window to admire the view.

His eyes wandered leisurely from the soaring spire of St Stephans down to the unorganised bustle of the street. What he saw caused a split second transformation. His adrenalin count jumped as though he had heard a shot. A girl, sloppily dressed in jeans and sweater, with unmistakably Arab features, was heading straight for the door of 5B. It took him less than one second to make up his mind who she would be. He turned quickly and shouted, 'Heinz!'

Heinz jumped like the well-trained soldier he had always been.

Rupert said quietly, 'The moment I get that girl in my office phone Dr Kuso and say "the Arab girl is here". Got that?'

Heinz looked puzzled, but repeated, 'The Arab girl is here,' and at that moment she opened the door and stepped into the gallery.

Rupert adjusted his best professional art dealer's welcoming smile and addressed her in German, 'Good afternoon, can I help you?'

The girl's German was perfect. Three years studying in Vienna Kleinhart had said. She seemed a bit tense, a bit self-conscious, but quite in control of herself.

'Is it possible to see Herr Conway, please?' she enquired.

'I am Herr Conway, what can I do for you?' he said quietly.

'I understand you are a scholar of Mozart.'

'I'm an enthusiast of Mozart, yes indeed.'

'I am only a student,' she said, 'I am starting to work on my thesis. For my degree. I read in the paper that you have some of the famous Karl Reuben's documents. I hope you don't mind . . .'

Rupert had already imperceptibly ushered her halfway down the gallery in the direction of his office.

'Why, of course. I'd be delighted to help. Won't you please come into my office?'

Rupert opened the door for her and stood back. He said, 'Heinz, ask Frau Kröner to send down some tea . . . you would like some tea of course . . . Yes. And, oh, Heinz, make that phone call for me, will you, please?'

The heavy mahogany door closed behind them.

For the next hour Rupert plied Moda with tea and cigarettes and a drenching flood of words. Constantly on the alert not to give herself away, Moda struggled by every ruse her fertile brain could devise to get this extraordinary man off the, to her, utterly unintelligible maze of technical details of Mozart's cadences, his arpeggios, his cadenzas, his figured bass structure, his early experiments in syncopation and everything Reuben had ever written about them. He showered her with music manuscripts and printed first editions, which nearly drove her to distraction as she tried vainly to pretend she understood what he was talking about. Every time he stopped to draw breath, which wasn't often, she tried to divert the subject to the Reuben family and friends and connections. Always he came straight back with some new oratorio or concerto for string quartet and flügel horn. He asked her opinion on everything and never once asked a question she could answer coherently.

Her friend and teacher Wadih Haddad had never trained her to deal with an assault like this. She could not afford to lose her temper. She was stuck with the naïve student approach.

44

And she had to keep on the alert for the shafts which rained down on her incessantly when what she was trying to think about was, what does this man know? Could he possibly know? Is he just playing with me? Or is he genuinely some kind of music nut? How can a person think straight when he won't stop talking for a second? She took a deep breath and determined to try a frontal attack.

'Herr Conway, you are terribly kind. All this information is most helpful. But, please, I know you are a very busy man . . .'

That was a mistake. Before she could get the next word out he cut her off . . . 'Not at all, my dear. Always happy to help any young person who is so obviously really steeped in the tradition of the great master . . .' She exploded and cut him off.

'Please, please. I beg you. My time is limited too. Before I go I must know something about Karl Reuben himself. The man.'

Rupert stayed the torrent of words and was actually silent for nearly a minute while he loaded and lit another of his interminable pipes. The refreshing quiet came as a shock of relief to the harassed Moda.

'Of course, my dear. Karl Reuben,' he said slowly and deliberately. 'Which one?'

She stared at him almost dazed.

'Which one?' she stammered.

Rupert repeated very quietly, 'Which one? The father, or the son?'

'You know where is the son?' she blurted out.

His voice dropped another two tones.

'I have heard he is in Austria. Why do you ask?'

She struggled to get back on course, and Rupert could not help admiring her mental toughness. He knew perfectly well he had been driving her to the edge of distraction. He had tried hard enough. Quite calmly now she said, 'It would be so interesting to talk to him. To learn something at first hand about his great father. And his work.'

Rupert put on a new, but gentler, burst of enthusiasm.

'Oh, indeed it would. I should love to meet young Reuben. If you find him, please promise you will let me know.'

Moda realised her gamble had failed.

He saw her out with the same effusive courtesy, talking a blue streak again about the great work Reuben senior had done in interpreting Mozart for modern listeners, and repeatedly insisting she promise to get in touch with him, let him know, if she found young Karl.

As the front door closed behind her Max looked up at him enquiringly through his thick glasses. Rupert smiled. He said softly, 'I showed her the B flat minor concerto and told her it was the G major. I'm afraid she'll fail her thesis. She doesn't know Mozart from Louis Armstrong.'

He watched through the big glass window as the determined figure marched off toward Rötenturmstrasse, and a trench coated man leaning against a workman's hut by the cathedral nodded gently to another man at the corner. As Moda turned into the busy street the man at the corner stamped out the cigarette he had been smoking and leisurely followed after her.

Freddy Kuso had understood the message.

Moda Tablishi came out of the snack bar of the Franz Josef Bahnhof in a foul temper; with herself, with the world in general, and with one Rupert Conway in particular. She had now completely made up her mind about him. And her thoughts weren't nice. Somehow he had known from the beginning she was acting. How did he know? Almost as important, what did he know? He wasn't a fool. He acted like one deliberately. He had made a fool of her. Her memory on the critical point was quite clear. She had not brought young Reuben into the discussion. He had. The clearer the trick became in her mind the angrier she got. That devil must know where the young pig is! She stumped off through the grimy, dingy streets beside the railway tracks, her body a seething mass of anger and hate.

Being lost in her own bitter thoughts and, as Abdullah had early observed, being inexperienced in the terrorist business, she was totally unaware of being followed. She crossed the Doblinger

Gurtle and turned into a grubby alleyway leading to the backs of warehouses and down at heel tenements. It was getting dusk, the streets were crowded with people going home from work. She did not notice a man dressed in mechanic's overalls sauntering along sucking a cigarette a few metres behind her. Moda entered a building on the left side of the alley between large garage doors which stood open; without a turn of the head she went straight to a rickety wooden staircase and started to climb. The mechanic strolled unconcernedly on, having carefully noted what was written on a grease stained signboard beside the doors: it read 'Technoexport Elec Agence of the People's Republic of Czechoslovakia.'

Moda climbed three flights past decayed and decaying wooden doors painted, a long time ago, a bilious green, each with a shabby sign saying something unintelligible in a strange language. At the top the staircase came to an abrupt end in front of a locked door. She knocked impatiently, and there was a muffled reply from inside.

'It's Moda. Let me in.'

There came the sounds of more than one heavy lock being turned, bolts pushed back, and eventually the door opened cautiously inward. Moda pushed herself against it resentfully and brushed a young man out of her path without a word. She stalked across the long, gloomy garret built into the roof timbers and lit by four deeply inset dormer windows, which wouldn't have let in much light even if they were clean. They were filthy, and covered with cobwebs. As a human habitation it was obvious no one had been in here for years. The atmosphere of the place did nothing to improve her temper. Haddad's Czech 'friends' had promised to hide them; they hadn't said the hiding place would be a rat hole.

Abdullah was sitting under one of the two bare lights, reading, which was how he spent most of his time. He lifted his heavy eyelids and they stared at each other. After a studied pause, Moda advanced slowly toward the table and said deliberately, 'Conway knows where Reuben is.' She wasn't going to explain how she knew, nor the humiliation she had suffered.

Abdullah nodded. 'Good. Then we know where to start.'

The young Arab came over to the table and sat down looking at her resentfully. The two Japanese sitting on their uncomfortable beds stopped cleaning their arsenal of assorted guns, which was how they spent most of their time.

Abdullah looked round slowly at them all. 'Our time for action draws close, comrades.' He always addressed them all as comrades, and the word made Moda wince every time she heard it. Calling the toiling masses one was dedicated to liberate 'comrades' had been fine at university, but, like most comfortably born middle class terrorists the more she saw of simple, less educated human beings the more she despised them.

'Tell us about the lay-out, Moda,' he said quietly.

She described the location of Conway's gallery. Abdullah unfolded a map of central Vienna and laid it on the table under the light. She drew an enlarged diagram of the area around the cathedral. 'Plenty of cover, lots of people about, tourists, students. It won't be difficult to keep watch.'

'We'll need help from our Czech friends.' He reached for the internal, military style field telephone that had been installed, dialled two digits and waited. 'We might get one of their men inside too. Wonder if they can produce any Mozart enthusiasts?'

They could.

CHAPTER FIVE

Heinz met Sandra as planned, the plane was only four hours late. During the drive home he kept up a constant stream of apologies that the Herr Doktor was so busy and so sorry he couldn't meet her himself. What he was up to Heinz didn't know, and if he had wouldn't have said. It was after five when they reached Stephansplatz where she received a warm welcome from everyone present, especially Charlie. Heinz took her bags up to her apartment on the top floor and brought her a strong vodka and tonic. Frau Kröner took a tray of supper up to her sitting room. By half past six everyone had left and Sandra was fast asleep.

She slept like a log, but inevitably had the usual problem adjusting to the six hour time change between New York and Vienna. She was down in the kitchen before Frau Kröner arrived and made herself coffee and toast. Rupert appeared punctually at eight as always, they embraced in their customary affectionate cousinly fashion. After breakfast Sandra went to Rupert's office and gave him a full report of her American visit. It had been her first trip 'home' since she had fled from the agony of a bitterly contested divorce trial just a little under two years ago, and the experience had not been without its unhappy memories. When her mother died she had married Alex Fleming, a handsome, athletic, college type, six years younger than herself, who had almost immediately taken to the bottle and in two years became a hopeless alcoholic. In his sober moments he had become even more morose and unbearable than when he was drunk. This, and the family tragedy of her childhood from which only she and her mother had survived, inevitably left deep scars, even on one who had inherited both the Magyar and the Jewish primeval genius for survival. Her classic head and long, lovely face still retained a strong trace of the aristocratic Andrassys and Esterhazys from whom she had been bred; but when her dark brown eyes were in repose a strained, hunted look crept back into them, and the lines of suffering round her mouth were inclined to distort an otherwise warm and eager smile.

She stuck strictly to business and did not mention whether or not she had seen or heard anything of Alex. Rupert did not ask. She had spent two days in Chicago at the new gallery on Michigan Avenue, sorted out all the artistic side of the paperwork and arranged their systems to be compatible with those in Vienna and London. She was reassuring that Rupert had been right in sending a very English Englishman in the shape of Nigel Coleman to run the operation; anyone who thought that middle western millionaires were not sophisticated about their art buying these days misjudged his market. Rupert was pleased to hear that Nigel's lovely wife, Amy, for whom he had a real soft spot, was happy in her new home and a big help to the business. He was also much relieved to hear that the new regime at City Hall seemed to bark worse than it had any intention of biting, Nigel hoped to get a reasonable solution to their tax problem before the end of the year.

At eleven-thirty Rupert left for the Italian embassy to keep an appointment with the Cultural Attaché. He had been given a commission, for a suitably handsome fee, to advise on and translate into German the catalogue for an exhibition of art treasures from Rome they were planning as part of an 'Italian Week' to be held next spring. His friend, the Attaché, insisted on taking him to lunch which Rupert thoroughly enjoyed. The chef at the Imperial Hotel excelled himself, and they sat contentedly over coffee and strega just five minutes too long.

At the same moment that the black Alfa Romeo bearing the insignia of the Italian embassy deposited Rupert in front of the archway to the courtyard that formed the back entrance to Stephansplatz, the door of Conway Vienna opened and a frail old man, wearing a moth-eaten, old-fashioned, broad-brimmed brown hat and a shabby tweed coat wrapped around his emaciated, bird-like body, stepped into the street. He stood trembling for a moment, as though startled by the noise and bustle which engulfed him; then he darted across the street and disappeared through the little courtyard by the entrance to the chapel of the Teutonic Knights. A second man came out just behind, and hurried after him.

Rupert had enjoyed not only his lunch; the Italians had accepted his judgement about how they should describe their own pictures as though it was pontifical. He had early in life learned how to switch his cares and problems on and off at will. He sauntered across the courtyard at peace with the world, and smiled at two pretty girls who smiled back; he had no idea who they were but knew they worked in a shop or office somewhere nearby. He paused outside his own massive window to admire the effect. It was part of the ritual that the window was changed every week. The scene gently massaged his ego; it pleased him. He had for some time felt that a certain change of pace would be timely, and had acquired a particularly lovely Dutch still life from the estate of a member of the Schwarzenburg family. It was by Nicolaes Van Verendael and he intended to get twenty thousand dollars for it. The girls had lit it beautifully, and someone had had the genius to accompany it with a solitary ochre coloured velvet wing-back chair. The total ambience was perfect.

Then he opened the door and went inside. The distress of the devoted Heinz was written all over his face, and was pitiful to behold.

'Herr Doktor! Herr Doktor! You just missed them. There were two gentlemen here . . . about the Reuben papers.'

'Did you get their names, Heinz?'

'No Herr Doktor. Neither one. They ask questions but tell me nothing.'

'All right, Heinz. Can't be helped. Come up to my room and tell me about them.' 'Damn that second coffee, my own fault,' he thought. They climbed the stairs to his sanctum, he threw his coat absent-mindedly over Charlie's chair, with Charlie in it, and himself into his own. 'Sit down, Heinz. Relax. Not your fault.' Between puffs and relights he said, 'Now, tell me all you can. Two men you said. They came together?'

'No, Herr Doktor. Not together. The first man came just after you left this morning. Then he came in again while the other one, the old man, was here. Just a few minutes ago,' he added sadly.

'OK. Let's take it in order. The first man?'

'The first man asked to see the Van Verendael. He stayed some time. Asked many questions about the picture. About you. Then he said he had read the story in *Die Presse*. He said he would like to talk to you about the papers.'

'But he left no name?'

'No, Herr Doktor. I asked him twice, but he said you would not know him, and he would come back.'

'Can you describe him?'

'Difficult, Herr Doktor. I think he was a foreigner. Maybe Polish. Or Czech. Could have been a tourist. About forty; as tall as you are. Not so fat, I think.' Rupert, who struggled to keep his weight down, winced. 'Dark hair; moustache. He was not well dressed. Not Viennese, Herr Doktor.'

Heinz was unquestionably a snob about things like that.

'And the second one?'

Heinz looked happier. 'The second one was distinguished-looking, Herr Doktor. Definitely a gentleman. Seventy-five, maybe more. Tall. Very thin, I think. He kept his coat wrapped round him, and an old-fashioned wide, brown hat on. But his hands, his neck, I remember, very thin.'

'Can you describe his face, Heinz?'

'Jawohl, Herr Doktor. Large nose. Many lines. I think as a young man very handsome. Definitely an officer type.'

'An officer type? Hmm. What about his voice?'

'Definitely, Herr Doktor. An officer type. Viennese.'

'Anything else strike you about him?'

'I think he was an aristocrat, Herr Doktor. An aristocrat who now has no money,' he concluded triumphantly.

'No money?'

'No Herr Doktor. His clothes were very worn.'

Rupert gazed out of the window at his favourite source of inspiration. He mused. 'An aristocrat. Over seventy-five, and a poor man. You're sure, Heinz?'

'Jawohl, Herr Doktor. I am sure.'

'OK. Thanks, Heinz. Thanks a lot. That's most helpful. And these two men were not together – did they speak to each other?'

'No, Herr Doktor. I don't think the old man even saw the other one.'

Heinz had gradually lost his air of having been guilty of some grave dereliction of duty, he hurried out and Rupert continued to stare at the magnificent vaulted roof of St Stephan and addressed his ponderings to some obscure saint perched up there.

'First man may have been the Pole who telephoned yesterday,' he was addressing Charlie and St Stephan as though they formed an exclusive group of conspirators. 'Or he may not. Nothing to go on there. Neither of them would leave a name. Was there any connection between them? God knows. The second one? Not what I was expecting at all. An aristocrat? Officer type? An old regular army sergeant like Heinz is as good a judge of that breed as still exists. What would his interest be in old Karl Reuben's papers?' He got up from his desk and prowled round the room. Came back to the window. 'Come on, Stephan! You've got nothing else to do but sit up there all day. You must have seen them. Who was this lean and hungry aristocrat? Who was he? Wait a minute.' His smile lit up. 'Got it!' The smile disappeared. 'Or have I? Yes, yes. That must be it. He's about the right age. Must be one of Karl Reuben's old pupils. Just the sort of man young Reuben might go to. Must have been especially close to his father.' He stopped and sat down at his desk.

'And how many aristocratic officer type cellists were there in Vienna in the nineteen thirties? Worth a try.' He buzzed the phone button for Mini. Half an hour later he left a note of apology for Sandra and hurried out.

After the opera came out that night Rupert had a date in a small café in the Neuer Markt with two men and a lady. They were all cello players, the lady had white hair and did not come from Bucharest. He only knew one of them personally, and he could not give them a clue to the real reason he had suddenly become so interested in their late revered teacher and maestro. The story in *Die Presse* was enough to arouse their interest in him, and there was no difficulty making conversation. Before the coffee and the brandy ceased to flow that evening Rupert had elicited the information that the only aristos any of them could remember amongst their band of disciples at the Academy were Count Andrew Polanyi and Graf Manfried von Eck. No one had heard of von Eck for years. They were reasonably certain that poor Polanyi had been killed by the Gestapo. That narrowed the field.

First thing next morning he called Freddy Kuso at the Police Praesidium and told him about Manfried von Eck. Kuso promised to have the information fed into their computers to see if they could trace him and phone back as soon as he had any news. They went on to discuss the problem of the mysterious Arab visitors and Kuso emphasised that even when they had been located he had no evidence upon which to base anything except a surveillance order. Their presence certainly strengthened suspicion that the equally elusive Mr Reuben was probably somewhere in Austria, and it seemed reasonable to suppose that the Arabs entertained nasty designs on him, but he couldn't arrest anybody on those flimsy grounds. As a good democrat Rupert could not argue with that.

Rupert next phoned Jacob Kleinhart and reported his news and his hopes concerning von Eck. Having dealt with the morning mail, which meant that it was now all on Frau Hauptmann's desk, he decided to spend the rest of the morning with the Reuben papers. He went upstairs and put up a card table by the piano where he spent two blissful hours in what he called 'research'.

For the first fifteen minutes he browsed happily over the whole range of sheets, lifting and moving them with tender care. His eye for value led him quickly to the oldest and the most authentic-looking amongst them for closer study. He picked out fourteen sheets, yellowed with age, but mostly undamaged; they were in manuscript and at the bottom of the last sheet in the sequence someone had written '10 March 1776'. From a glance at other notes it certainly appeared that the date was written by the same hand which had transcribed the music. Which was interesting, because it was the Sonata in F, catalogued by Köchel as number 280, and while it was generally accepted that Mozart had written it in 1774, no one was certain. The hand-writing certainly looked like Mozart's, but a lot of study was necessary before any decision could be made on that point. Even if these sheets should prove to be written by the master himself it still left a lot of questions unanswered: was it an original or a copy; perhaps a revision of a previous version? Was the date necessarily related to the completion of the work, or was it related to the notes which may have been added later? He held the paper to the light and examined it through his jeweller's glass; it would need careful checking, but at first sight it appeared to be fairly typical mid-eighteenth-century German, which fitted both the date and style of transcription. Art dealers had learned, to their cost, even that was not con-clusive any more; there was a still untraced genius at work in Belgium who had somehow acquired reams of untouched eighteenth-century German paper and was making himself a small fortune producing 'antique' documents. Another, modern, hand, presumably Reuben's, had written a note about melodic cadence figures which was quite new to him. Only thing to do was play it and find out. Once he started he was lost to the world until Frau Kröner marched into the room and un-ceremoniously informed him that his lunch was getting cold.

As he finished a quick lunch he received a phone call from

Herbert Spitzer, Kuso's number two. Spitzer gave him the welcome news that a print out had just come up from Records regarding his enquiry about a certain Manfried Eck. In 1920 the first republican parliament of what remained of Austria after the Versailles Treaty had forbidden the use of all titles of nobility, and officialdom had to maintain the practice, even if nobody else did. There was no doubt this was the same man; farther down the page Records had carefully noted that the subject of the file, 'had previously been known as Graf von Eck'. He lived quietly in retirement in what was left of his old family property east of the little town of Zurndorf, in the Burgenland. Only a few kilometres from both the Czech and the Hungarian borders. The local police had been instructed to 'have a look round', and get an up-to-date report.

Rupert was pondering what to do next when Sandra came in about the problem of the eighty thousand dollar letter of credit from the Greek client. It now appeared there was some further complication before it could be cleared. She took a cigarette from the exquisite Fabergé case which had been made for their common grandmother, and sat watching with amusement while Rupert wrestled over the telephone with an unhelpful bank clerk. 'Then put me on to the manager.' The manager was busy. 'Well, have him call me back as soon as he is free. It's urgent.' He put down the phone and muttered, 'Balls!'

'What did you say?' Sandra smiled.

He looked up from making a note and said, 'Sheer obstructive bureaucracy. The absolute quintessence of balls!' There was nothing to do on that matter but wait till the confounded manager phoned back.

Heinz put his head round the door.

'Excuse me, Herr Doktor, but there is a gentleman downstairs. From Washington, he says. He insists you would like to see him.'

'From Washington? Not expecting anybody. Did you get his name, Heinz?'

'I found it a bit difficult, Herr Doktor. He gave me this card.'

He handed it across to Sandra who was nearest. She looked

at it quizzically and snorted, 'Only in Washington could a man get a name like this.' She read out, 'Thornhill J. Biddle, Junior.'

'Good Lord,' Rupert said. 'Young Thorney!'

'I suppose that was inevitable,' she sighed, 'but why young?'

'Well, it's obvious. His father was Old Thorney. Not to be confused with Old Horney, when we were schoolboys in Washington that term was reserved exclusively for President Harding!'

'You couldn't have been more than five years old!'

'Ah, but schoolboys grow up fast in Washington.' Then he noticed Heinz still standing looking puzzled in front of him. Rupert rose abruptly and went downstairs to the gallery, hand extended eagerly to greet his old friend. Through the open door Sandra watched; interested, amused, thinking how men in their fifties suddenly coming upon each other unexpectedly react like schoolboys. It was obvious that their friendship was a continuing one, Rupert's father had been Third Secretary at the British embassy in Washington way back in the twenties some time. Then she began to take stock of Mr Biddle. The first thing she noticed was that he was lean, grey-haired and elegant; no master of ceremonies could have resisted calling him distinguished – he didn't have to do anything, he just looked it. The second was that he carried a cane and had a most unusual stoop; he didn't limp exactly, but his back and his legs didn't seem to join up properly. They certainly seemed to be enjoying themselves, laughing heartily, at their schoolboy jokes, no doubt. The jet lag was beginning to catch up with Sandra and she was feeling matronly. No, she quickly checked herself; that's not the right word. Bitchy. I must stop it.

Thornhill J. Biddle, Junior, waddled to the door with Rupert's friendly arm on his shoulder, they wrung each other's hands once again, and he was gone.

Rupert came striding back into the office. 'Isn't that fine? Great character, Thorney. Great character.'

'Where did he drop from?' she asked.

'Been staying with friends near Salzburg. He's coming to

dinner. This is one of Frau Kröner's nights in, I hope?'

'Thursday? Yes. Unless anything changed while I was away.'

'No. That's all right then. You'll be in to dinner? You'll get a kick out of Thorney.'

'Yes, I'll be in. Tell me something about him. How did anyone get a name like that?'

'Well, about a hundred years ago there was a man called Biddle, who was not rich, and did not come from Philadelphia; and he married a girl called Thornhill who was and did.'

'I see. Is there a Mrs Thornhill J. Biddle, Junior?'

'No. There isn't, alas. Young Thorney never married.'

'He's not one of those, is he?'

Rupert chuckled. 'No. He's very much not one of those. Thorney was in the U.S. Navy. At the landing at Okinawa he stopped a machine gun burst right bang in the testicles. Poor devil. Miracle he lived at all.' He looked at his watch. 'God bless me. Look at the time. What a fascinating day we're having!'

CHAPTER SIX

He spent the rest of the afternoon trying to get on with his normal work. He found it difficult to concentrate and became increasingly frustrated as none of the numerous phone calls were the ones he wanted. He tried to get Kleinhart to tell him they had traced von Eck, but he was out and the Israeli embassy could not trace him. The ambassador was attending some highly obscure committee of the United Nations and was not expected back before six. The police at Zurndorf had been asked to make a discreet examination of the von Eck property, was the old man there, and was there any evidence of anyone staying with him. To Rupert they seemed to be taking a devil of a long time about it.

At five o'clock Sandra had gone off to visit a friend who lived out at Grinzing and who had had a baby while she had been away. She would be back in time for dinner. Everyone else went home and Heinz locked up, having turned on the front door intercommunication equipment and switched it through to the hall of Rupert's apartment upstairs.

One of the few things that disturbed Rupert's easy going temperament was delay. He was impatient to know whether his little stratagem concerning von Eck had worked or not. Twice he thought of trying to get hold of Thorney and put him off dinner. He had a feeling he should go down to Zurndorf to-night, now, to see for himself. But he had no idea where Thorney was staying. Anyway, he wanted to see him. He wanted Sandra to meet him. And Thorney to meet her, for that matter. At five-thirty Heinz came in to say good-night, and Rupert gave up the pretence he was working. He had smoked too many pipes all day and didn't want another one. He got up and wandered around the office moodily, picking up art catalogues and magazines and putting them down somewhere else. He went upstairs to the drawing room and drifted moodily over to the grand piano. He played a few bars of a Mozart *étude*, but it didn't work. 'Corn,' he said out loud to the empty room. 'That's what I need. A little old-fashioned corn.' He got up again and helped himself to a whisky and soda. For the next half hour he ploughed through some old-fashioned Fats Waller favourites. He then selected a bottle of Château Branaire Ducru 1966, a very special favourite, and by the time Thorney arrived at seven his mood was quite restored.

During the afternoon the small, lugubrious troup in the attic over the Czech Technoexport warehouse had their spirits lifted to high heaven. Not once, but twice. A radio news bulletin gave the world the first information of the skyjacking of Lufthansa's Boeing 737 from Palma, Majorca, to Frankfurt. So that's what Habash was being so mysterious about. Zohair Akache and his team have done it! Abdullah hugged his Koran. Moda cheered as though it was a football game. Eighty hostages in their hands! Revenge for the débâcle inflicted on them by the Israelis at Entebbe. And release for their badly needed allies, the Baader Meinhoff gang from Germany. The international network of terrorists for which so many Palestinians had worked so long was in action at last; its first operation a spectacular success! What a triumph for Haddad! How delighted they will be in the Kremlin! If the Patrice Lumumba University were anywhere except Russia they would have declared a half-holiday.

Only minutes later the phone rang to announce that their enigmatic host was on his way over for a conference. The news he brought took them a big step forward in their own mission: he had found an agent who could talk intelligently about Mozart, it was a common enough trait in Vienna; the agent had hung around Stephansplatz all morning keeping close watch on Conway's gallery and been inside twice. His second entrance

60

had been occasioned by the sudden appearance of a strange old man who had intrigued him; playing a hunch he went in right after the old man and overheard him having an agitated discussion with one of Conway's assistants about the Reuben papers. It appears that Conway wasn't there but the old man was so concerned and agitated about something to do with Reuben that the agent thought it worth finding out who he was. He followed him; all the way to his home in a small village in the Burgenland. The agent had arranged to spend the night in a nearby hotel, some of the night anyway, and they were sending another man down in a car to assist him.

With that the Secret Police officer abruptly departed with a curt reminder, 'Don't forget, you do your own watching at Conway's tonight. I haven't any more men to spare.'

Abdullah nodded, he understood.

At five o'clock Moda and the young Japanese left the warehouse by the secret exit leading into another street. The Czechs had cut a door through a third floor wall which gave access to a grimy apartment in the adjoining tenement, and thence down a staircase leading into the street behind. They got into a shabby black saloon car with CD licence plates obligingly provided by their hosts, and drove off. They were still unaware that the hideout was under police surveillance, but the police were still unaware of the clandestine exit. Kuso had asked permission to search but had been refused; the building was covered by the Czech embassy's diplomatic immunity and in neutral Austria such action was more than normally delicate; it could not be challenged without much stronger evidence than was in Kuso's hands.

It was nearly half past five by the time Moda had navigated through the evening rush hour traffic and found a parking place on Domgasse, just across from Stephansplatz. They sat quite still for a couple of minutes, as instructed, and then two men wearing the proverbial slouch hats and raincoats which were the uniform of their trade walked over to the car. One of the men went for another walk round the square keeping his trained eye in the general direction of 5B, while the other three entered a small bar where Moda and her escort were briefed. These two agents had taken over just after lunch and had made good use of an uneventful afternoon by studying their territory in detail. They had reconnoitred the garage and deduced, correctly, that the blue English Jensen would be Conway's car. They had even managed to search it but the only item of note they discovered had been an old bone stuffed down behind the back seat. Their conclusion had been corroborated when at five o'clock they had seen a smartly dressed woman, whom they assumed, incorrectly, was either Conway's wife or his girl friend, come out of 5B and drive off in the blue car.

The news of the woman in the fancy English car made a particular impression on Moda; if it were possible, she believed she hated bourgeois women even more than bourgeois men. Like Andreas Baader, Gundrun Ensslin and all the rest of the most experienced and hardened female terrorists, the reason was simple. Any competent psychiatrist could have told her it was because that was an exact description of herself. Self-hate is as blinding as self-pity. The difference in Moda's case was that she was neither experienced nor hardened. She was a neophyte terrorist on her first mission. Her mind at that moment was anything but hardened. It was in a turmoil. The discovery that controlling her emotions under stress conditions was turning out to be much more difficult than Haddad and his instructors in the mechanics of murder had led her to expect was worrying. She was still smarting from what she thought of as the humiliation Conway had inflicted on her. She was elated by Akache's triumph in the skyjacking, but, on second thoughts, what were they doing in Bahrein? Why weren't they in Libya as Habash had said they would be? Had something gone wrong? To add to her confusion she and Abdullah had had another flaming row just before she left, with him giving her one of his interminable lectures on the importance of being calm and patient, and she ending up screaming at him, 'The pigs didn't kill your sister!'

Traffic had now dwindled to nearly nil around the cathedral and Moda went out and moved the car to a handier spot, just east of the archway where Schulerstrasse runs into Stephansplatz. Just in case of emergency. In her present mood an emergency was exactly what she was busting to create! By half past six the area behind the great cathedral was deserted, and the frequency of police patrol in this quiet backwater appeared to be less than once per hour. Moda and the Japanese boy discussed the best routine to remain inconspicuous, and decided to sit in the car for the first hour. It gave them a good view of 5B and the garage to which the woman, Mrs Conway, might very probably return before the evening was through.

In fact they had rather less than an hour to wait. Moda sat fascinated, excited, feeling like a feline huntress as she saw the blue English sports car, unmistakable from the Czech's description, slide smoothly up to the entrance to the underground garage and disappear down the ramp. The adrenalin raced through her body which was literally quivering as every nerve answered some primitive call. This particular situation had not been foreseen. There were no orders given to cover it. On the spur of the moment it seemed like a heaven sent opportunity. Moda was in no mood to stop for second thoughts. She gave the boy beside her a nod which told him all he needed to know. 'No guns,' she whispered and he just smiled back. She reached into a deep pocket of her raincoat for a vital item of 'emergency equipment'. She took out a small polythene bag and a sharp penknife. Then she shed the coat from her shoulders and they both slid noiselessly out in to the street. There wasn't a soul about. The night sky had clouded over and a slight drizzle of autumn rain was gathering momentum. The floodlights high above on St Stephan's enormous roof cast no more than an eerie glow at street level. The lights of the last shop window in the street had gone out ten minutes ago.

Moda and the youth stood for a moment in the shadow of the arch; then the glow of light from the garage exit splashed the shadow of a woman on to the wet pavement. She was walking up the ramp. As Sandra entered the street and unsuspectingly crossed it Moda and her escort strolled arm in arm out from under the arch. Sandra reached the sidewalk by the gallery's front door and put one foot on the step. It occurred to her that

63

she had not thought to enquire whether the alarm would be on or not. In view of a guest coming to dinner, probably not. The monitor light confirmed her view. She looked down to open her handbag and get out her key. All she felt was two strong hands grasp her arms and pin them to her side. Before she could muster the beginnings of a scream the suffocating fumes of some powerful anaesthetic stifled her nose and mouth.

The Japanese boy was strong, he had no trouble in throwing Sandra's inert and helpless body over his shoulder; Moda ran ahead and opened a door of the back seat. They had just finished roughly pushing the body into the car and laying it across the seat when two men came round the corner. Moda let out a girlish laugh and said loudly in her best Viennese German, 'If we hurry we have time for a meal before the cinema starts.' The men walked on, paying no attention, and the car drove quietly away.

In the drawing-room upstairs Rupert and Thorney were fully preoccupied enjoying their reunion. They had not met for some five years and had plenty of catching up to do. Did you ever buy that pineapple farm in Hawaii? Why Chicago? Is that the same Coleman who was up at Cambridge with you? Did you see Terry Rattigan's new play while you were in London? How could a man write so brilliantly when he is suffering the way he is? Brave man. You've never seen my place at Semmering, why not come down this week-end? What on earth do you want to go to Dubrovnik this time of year for?

An otherwise thoroughly kindly fellow, Thorney's passion in life was shooting ducks. 'Met a man up in Canada who told me the Baltic teal fly right down the Dalmatian coast in mid-October every year. They winter up the Nile somewhere. This chap said if you get there just the right time the marshes between Dubrovnik and the Albanian border offer terrific duck hunting.'

Rupert rose to pour them each another whisky. 'What were you doing in Canada?' he asked.

'Just amusing myself. A bunch of us who were in the U.S.

and Royal Canadian navies, during the early Atlantic convoy runs, we have a sort of old boys' dining club. One year we go up to them, then they come down to us. It was in Toronto this year. Had a wonderful week-end's golf, and a great booze up at the York Club.'

'Sounds like fun.' Rupert handed Thorney the glass and sat down again.

'Was. Heard quite a bit about you in Toronto, by the way.'

'I tried to sell the Royal Ontario Museum a Guardi last year, but they didn't like my price.'

'No, wasn't to do with that, I shouldn't think. They told me some wag in a Toronto newspaper wrote a piece about you recently. He's dubbed you "the cultural James Bond". I rather like that.' Rupert sent him a small prayer of thanks, and hoped he may be right.

It wasn't until seven-forty-five when Frau Kröner shuffled in to announce dinner that Rupert realised to his surprise Sandra hadn't come home yet. They decided to wait another fifteen minutes. He couldn't phone the house in Grinzing because he couldn't remember the people's name. Her absence put a damper on the dinner, and Rupert kept looking at his watch and wondering what could have happened to her. When he let Thorney out just before ten o'clock it occurred to him to walk across to the garage to see if the Jensen was there. When he found it was he went straight in and phoned the police. For the first time in many years he was really frightened.

Moda and the Jap had returned to the warehouse by the same back door, leaving the Czech's car parked in the darkened street, and humping the still unconscious Sandra into the building, without being seen by anybody. They dragged her roughly up the three flights of stairs, through the dingy apartment, then two more flights to the attic, cutting and bruising her badly on the way. When they carried the motionless body into the garret and dumped her down on an iron bed Abdullah exploded in wrath.

'You fools! What in the name of Allah do you think you're

doing? Blind, stupid fools.' He cursed and swore and yanked at his hair and beard as though he would tear them out by the roots. His consuming, frustrating rage brought tears to his eyes and set him off in a coughing fit as though his lungs would burst.

The Japanese just stood there and said nothing. He didn't speak much Arabic anyway, and he knew the old man wouldn't dare attack him physically.

Moda fought back with all the fierceness of which her fiery soul was capable. They all accepted that this was Conway's wife.

'A hostage of course!' she screamed back at him. 'You find a better way to make this bastard Conway lead us to Reuben!' They shrieked at each other for ten minutes till both were exhausted. The fact that none of the din even roused a flicker from Sandra was evidence of what a powerful overdose she had been subjected to.

Both Abdullah and Moda needed a pause to recover. Yali and the two Japs just sat in brooding silence never saying a word. Abdullah sat hunched morosely in his chair fingering his beloved Koran. Moda smoked two cigarettes in quick succession, lighting the second off its half smoked predecessor. As she at last began to calm down she felt the first, jarring doubts about the wisdom of what she had done.

Sandra's bruised body quivered and she let out a groan.

Yali spoke for the first time.

'She's coming round.'

Moda walked over to the pathetic, blood-stained figure sprawled on the bed, and looked down.

'No she's not. I gave her enough dope to keep her out for two hours. We learned how to use that stuff in Aden.'

Abdullah spoke quietly.

'Just be careful, you can't be sure.'

'Oh yes I can,' said Moda viciously. 'Haddad taught us how to be sure.' Without hesitation she leaned down and tore the front of Sandra's dress open, slip, bra and all. Then she took a long draw on her cigarette and thrust the burning tip hard between her breasts. The red hot ash made a sickening, sizzling sound on the moist flesh. Fortunately for Sandra, she was still deeply unconscious.

Abdullah hissed at Moda, 'What a disgusting exhibition of futile brutality. Another of your friend Haddad's Gestapo tricks!'

Moda screamed at him. 'You lie! Wadih Haddad was never in the Gestapo!'

'He was trained by the two most brutal of that gang of sadists who ever reached Palestine. You know that perfectly well,' he said icily.

Moda realised she had gone too far. They all knew about Haddad's Gestapo connections. She began for the first time to feel a bit frightened. And a bit sick in the stomach. Acting tough did not come as easily as she had expected.

Abdullah said to one of the Japs,

'Bring me that Walther.'

The Jap laid the high velocity nine millimetre on the table. Abdullah picked it up, checked it was loaded, cocked it, and laid it down in front of him, keeping his hand on the butt.

'Now. Listen to me,' he said in quiet, firm tones. 'I am in command here, and you will do as I say.' He looked straight at Moda. 'I don't like these methods, they are crude and unnecessary, but you leave me no choice. We are on an important mission. Amongst our enemies. You will take that woman out of here and leave her, anywhere, not too close to here. And you will do her no more harm. That is an order. Do you understand?'

Moda stood and glared at him.

'Or,' he said quietly, 'I shall shoot you.'

Just before midnight, as Rupert paced his drawing-room in a state of rising anxiety and fear, the phone rang. It was the duty officer at the Inner Staadt, First Precinct, police station, to tell him that Sandra had been picked up lying on the grass in the Staadtpark, badly bruised and sick from an overdose of some drug, but otherwise apparently unharmed. She was in the emergency ward at Lorenz Bochler hospital. They had not attempted to get a statement from her yet, and had no evidence of what had happened.

Rupert spent the rest of the night in the hospital waiting-room. Just after five a.m. she woke up for a few minutes and he was allowed to see her. For the first time since he had opened the telegram informing him that his dearest friend and elder brother, George, had been killed at the battle of Alamein he broke down and sobbed like a child.

CHAPTER SEVEN

Abdullah had ordered Yali back to continue the night watch on the Conway ménage. He had managed to secrete himself with some degree of comfort amongst the piles of building supplies and rubble which had almost permanently adorned the back of St Stephan's for years now, and was undisturbed by the police all night. He had been bewildered and miserable when Rupert emerged so suddenly and unexpectedly just after midnight, hailed a taxi and drove off at frantic speed while Yali was still trying to think of a plan of action. It was with intense relief that he saw him come in again just as sunrise was breaking through a soggy sky. At six the two Czechs arrived to take over again.

The fitful sleepers in the garret above the warehouse were wakened by a gentle tapping on the heavy door which was the welcome signal announcing the daily visit of their courier. The cadaverous, slow moving Czech with dour Slav features was, in theory, foreman of the warehouse downstairs. Since, in practice, very little electric machinery actually passed through the Technoexport Elec Agence it left him plenty of time for his multifarious other duties, nearly all of which consisted of activities for which those with diplomatic status are automatically deported if caught by the host state. He brought them food, cigarettes, and news when there was any.

He handed several rumpled slips of paper to Abdullah who looked at them sceptically. 'Sorry,' said the Czech, 'there have been translation problems.' They were in garbled French and had obviously passed through many hands. No doubt even their 'friends', the Czechs, had studied them for hours in the hope there might be some pickings in the messages for themselves: in this demi-underworld everybody preyed on everybody and dog ate dog whenever convenient; after all, the intellectuals never could entirely make clear the difference between the new 'class loyalty', and the discredited old-fashioned kind; however clear it may have appeared in the university, it was too subtle for ordinary mortals. Basic human instincts for survival rejected all revolutionary fervour to change.

'The car will be in the usual place when you want it,' the Czech said, and shuffled out.

Moda put the rusty kettle to boil on a small gas ring to make tea, while Abdullah studied the slips of paper trying to re-assemble their garbled, often mis-typed and frequently amended contents.

'The agent in Corfu confirms that the boat will be available from the sixteenth,' he said without looking up. That was an-other successful piece of Wadih Haddad's operations planning and he did not wish to let Moda score any points on behalf of that butcher whom he loathed. He had no desire to antagonise the girl, however, and the next message would give her some legitimate satisfaction.

'You will be glad to hear that Saleb completed his mission successfully. Achram Assad is dead,' he read out.

'Good,' she said laconically. 'Where, and how?'

'Right here in Vienna, apparently. They don't give any de-tails.'

'Those who betray the revolution must die,' she intoned with as much feeling as if she were repeating the jingle from some television commercial. To her, very probably, it was. She was fated never to enjoy the relish of knowing that the devil Conway had spent most of the night in a room almost on top of the marble slab where Assad's still unidentified body was lying.

Abdullah painstakingly interpolated the contents of the last message until he could make coherent sense of it.

'Zohair Akache and his German friends plan to land in

Libya – that's a little out of date – on the thirteenth. But our instructions must stand, I suppose. Habash says it is important for us to reach Libya before the twentieth. Only another six days.' He looked across at Moda and said, 'From then on the success of this operation seems to lie entirely in your hands.'

She liked the sound of that. For the first time since they left Beirut Moda was able openly to indulge her own sense of importance at Abdullah's expense. He would no longer be in command then. The Israelis, who suffer from the same gentle weaknesses as other civilised states, had allowed her to visit her sister before she was executed; she had received a full report about the nuclear work on which Reuben was engaged, and where his most secret thoughts were leading him. Habash, having been trained as a doctor himself, instantly understood the full significance of that report. He had hugged her with delight when she repeated it all to him. 'Vastly more effective than bombs. The weapon of ultimate blackmail,' he had called it enthusiastically. Moda's life from that moment had been dominated by the idea that revenge for the death of her sister would be one of the most spectacular in history.

'Yes,' she said gloatingly; 'the Libyans can afford the facilities for Reuben's work much easier than we can. That's why Gaddafi is paying the PFLP so much for this operation. I have to stay with Reuben to see that he works.'

She was well aware Abdullah knew all that, but this was the first chance she had had to say it. She liked the sound of it too. His leathery face registered nothing. It usually did.

After only two hours' sleep Rupert had a hurried breakfast and took a taxi to Polizei Praesidium where he met Kleinhart in the lobby. Luckily for his shadows there had been another taxi right behind and one of the Czechs was now standing leaning against a tree in the Schottenring right opposite. After a brief wait a young police officer appeared and ushered Rupert and Kleinhart upstairs to a conference room where they were welcomed by the enormous, genial bulk of Oberpolizeirat Jozef Liebmann, number two man in the Staatspolizeiliches Buro, Department One.

They dealt with foreigners, security and allied matters. Liebmann was Rupert's closest friend in the Vienna police, they shared enthusiasm for pictures, food and wine, and Jo was probably the only man in that organisation who could exhale more smoke in less time than Rupert did. He was puffing heavily on one of his museum collection of meerschaums. He had already been at his desk for over an hour reading the various files of apparently quite unrelated events all of which for some reason still unknown, had entangled themselves around Rupert Conway. He had read the reports of the young Detective Sergeant who found Sandra in the Staadtpark last night, and greeted Rupert with the requisite sympathy and friendship.

Liebmann took the chair at the head of the big table and introduced those gathered round it. There was a security officer from the Israeli embassy, Yitzak Sokol, who was Kleinhart's official liaison with the Vienna Police dealing with both the Reuben disappearance, and the arrival of the dubious little group of Arabs and Japanese. Sokol was a classic Sabra; tough, intelligent, cultured, dedicated to the survival of Israel, and with no illusions. There was Hubert Spitzer representing Criminal Investigations, Department Two. There was an officer from the computer section with his print-outs on von Eck; one representing Wolfram Triska, the Precinct Captain of the Innere Stadt in whose area Sandra had been found; another representing Walter Büchgraber of the Dobling Precinct who was charged with surveillance of the Czech warehouse. Finally there was an assistant from Liebmann's own office who arrived at the last minute with a typescript of a long phone conversation he had just had with the local Inspector at Zurndorf.

Just before calling the meeting to order Liebmann took a phone call. He put the receiver down, signalled for silence and, turning to Rupert, he said, 'That was the Inspector from the hospital. He says Sandra has taken a little light breakfast and is resting quietly. He had a few words with her but unhappily, so far, she remembers nothing from the time she took her key out at your front door, until the patrolman found her on the grass in the park. She was able to check her handbag and is sure there is nothing missing from it, so we can eliminate robbery as a motive.'

He turned to Triska's representative.

'You don't get many muggings in your district, do you?'

'Very few, sir. We've never seen an anaesthetic used before.'

'Do we know what it was?' Liebmann looked round the table.

'Yes, sir,' his assistant replied. 'I have the pathologist's report here. He writes he is satisfied it was some derivative of pentathol. There are plenty on the market. Probably in suspension in a neutral gelatinous base of some kind and released automatically when the air got to it. He says the victim received a massive overdose. He comments the lady has strong heart and lungs or the dose might easily have killed her.'

Rupert felt fainter than he had since his leg had been shot up in the assault on Montecassino in 1944.

Liebmann turned back to the Precinct man.

'Anything else to tell us?'

'Yes, sir. Our forensic people have carefully examined the lady's clothes. The marks and tears on them generally seem to match up with the abrasions on her person. There are several smears of blood, her own, and mud together; and small splinters of wood embedded in the fabric of her dress. Soft, badly worn wood. The deep burn on the lady's breast was from a cigarette. Her injuries don't indicate actual beatings, with fists, or kicking or anything like that. It looks more as though she was dragged quite a long way.'

'How far from her home did you find her?'

'The patrolman reported he saw the body, begging your pardon, sir,' he said with an apologetic nod to Rupert; 'the lady was lying on the grass some two metres from the pavement near the north-east corner of the park. She would appear to have been driven there and just left. There were several footprints around where she was lying, but the rain has left little one can identify.'

'That's only six blocks from Stephansplatz,' Rupert said.

'Yes, but they couldn't have dragged her that distance. And she was missing for at least three hours.' Liebmann turned to the man from Dobling Precinct. 'There is, of course, nothing we know to connect this unfortunate incident of Mrs Fleming, with our, ah, visitors, living in the Czechs' electric machinery warehouse, but what exactly do you know of their movements last night?'

'Not a lot, I'm afraid, sir,' the officer said candidly. And a little defensively. 'We only received the order to keep the place under watch at nineteen-seventeen Wednesday night.'

He consulted his notes and continued.

'We had two men installed in a vacant apartment of the building opposite by twenty-fifteen. Two of the men left the building at seven-o-five yesterday morning. There were several exits and entries during the day of the other three. The two returned at eighteen-ten. Nothing after that. After our men were in position in the apartment the man on the street was relieved. And, I must remind you, sir, up till now we have no orders to follow these people. Only to keep the building under observation.'

Liebmann nodded, not in approval, but acquiescence. He said, 'How well do you think you have the building covered?'

'Not as well as we should like, sir,' the officer said frankly. 'It's a huge, rambling old place; it has three doors of its own, and we just learned this morning there is an entrance into the tenement next door on the third floor, with access on to two separate streets. We can only cover them with patrols. Besides that anybody really trying to give us the slip could get out of one of those attic windows at night and come down into one of four streets half a kilometre away.'

Liebmann asked, 'How many men would you need to do the job properly?'

'At least ten, sir; and working eight-hour shifts, which the men's union are very adamant about these days, that's a total of thirty. Captain Büchgraber instructed me to make that very clear, sir. He just hasn't got the men.'

Liebmann knew the problem only too well. All modern police services suffer from it, it forms an item of permanent anxiety at all Interpol meetings, and no democratic government has

74

yet been able to break out of the strangleholds of wage restraint and anti-inflationary manoeuvres with their trades union movements to solve it.

After nearly half an hour of discussion around the table Jo Liebmann said, 'Well, gentlemen. There seems no point in dragging out this unfortunate business. We must face the fact we have no firm leads at all. In particular we have no evidence linking the Arab delegation with the attack on Mrs Fleming.' He paused for a moment and then said, 'It almost looks as though whoever was responsible for the grab, later decided they had made a mistake and just dumped her in the nearest convenient place.'

He turned to Triska's man, 'Those bits of wood from Mrs Fleming's dress. Did forensic get sufficient samples to make a comparative study?'

'Yes, sir, I should think so. There were five small splinters extracted which should be easily identified under a microscope.'

They all looked at Liebmann expectantly. He rubbed his huge hands together, hesitantly he said, 'The Czech warehouse, Inspector. Pretty old and dilapidated you said in your written report?'

'That's right, sir.'

'And the Arabs are on the top floor?'

'Yes, sir.'

'And the staircase in an old building like that would almost certainly be wood. D'you think that's likely?'

'Almost certainly, sir.'

'So,' Liebmann was thinking out loud; 'if the forensic boys could compare their splinters with bits of that staircase, they might just possibly be able to prove that Mrs Fleming had been dragged up and/or down it?'

'We could check that easily, sir,' the Precinct Inspector said eagerly.

Liebmann grunted sadly, 'Yes, I'm sure you could. Technically, easiest thing in the world to do. Trouble is the damned building comes under the Czech's diplomatic immunity, which means that before we can get inside it – without creating one hell of a great rumpus – we've got to clear it with the Foreign Ministry, and they would insist on seeing the Czech ambassador, and he'd protest and make every possible difficulty, during which time they'd move out.' Everybody's face fell again. He turned to his assistant and said, 'I'll have to see the Minister of the Interior personally; we can't move in this field without political authority. Go and see how soon you can make an appointment for me.'

The young man got up and left the conference room.

'In the meantime, gentlemen, we have nothing but hunches to go on, and no evidence to connect this unfortunate incident of Mrs Fleming to anybody at all. Until you hear from me about government's attitude all you can do is proceed with routine enquiries as best you can. Oh, and tell Büchgraber to phone me as soon as you get back to your station, we'll have to find him some more men somewhere.'

They turned their attention to the report from Zurndorf, which was equally full of insoluble, and apparently inconsequential little mysteries. His assistant having left the meeting Liebmann picked up the typescript of the local police's report and read it out to them. The position was that old Manfried Eck lived in a small part of his family's ancestral country house; another part of it had been divided into separate apartments which currently housed five different families; one whole wing had been abandoned for years and was uninhabitable. The old man lived alone but there was a part-time housekeeper who came in by day to look after him. She knew nothing of a visitor. The only regular visitor who ever got inside was the local doctor who called every few weeks to deal with the ailments and bodily deterioration of an old man who had suffered the appalling hardships of three years in a Russian prisoner-of-war camp.

From the description given of him Rupert was in no doubt at all that he was indeed the agitated and shivering visitor to 5B Stephansplatz. One of his neighbours had described exactly the battered, broad-brimmed, old felt hat which seemed to be his only known headgear. Of seven people asked if there was a visitor staying there none had seen anybody; three said they thought there might be, and four were sure there was not. The only positive indication that might mean something was that the genial, gossipy lady who ran the village grocery store said that old von Eck had been buying rather more food lately than usual. He had also bought several pads of note paper, which she could not recall him having done for years.

They kicked that around for twenty minutes. The police could get a search warrant, but the local Captain had stressed that the Graf was a most peaceful, kindly old gentleman, well liked in the village, and in view of his delicate health he was reluctant to cause him unnecessary distress. Both Rupert and Kleinhart volunteered to go down and try to talk to him. After a lot of discussion it was decided that Rupert's knowledge of the Reuben musical documents was probably the best way to get close to von Eck, and he might stand a better chance if he went alone. Liebmann offered a police escort but Kleinhart opposed this; he was deeply concerned that, if Reuben was hiding there, and pray God he was, they still had no real insight as to why. Was he seeking sanctuary from Palestinian terrorists? It seemed unlikely that Reuben knew about the strange collection of people shacked up in the Czech's warehouse. If he knew he was in danger from terrorists which, frankly, seemed doubtful, why had he chosen to come to Vienna? America would have seemed a safer haven. And was there significance that he had chosen a hideout right on the Hungarian border?

'Do you think he's trying to defect to the Russians?' Jo Liebmann asked.

'No, I don't,' replied Kleinhart. 'But it is possible. His political views have always been as unstable as everything else about him.'

'From what we know of old von Eck he'd be unlikely to help him in that direction.'

And so they went on, round and round the possibilities, and with less and less solid ground to tread on. Since they had got away from the subject of Sandra's sufferings, for which Rupert felt a miserable sense of responsibility, he had begun to feel more like his usual ebullient self. He had lost a few hours' sleep, nothing worse than that. Finally, just before twelve o'clock, he said positively he would like to go to Zurndorf himself, and alone; he thought he had a better chance of gaining von Eck's confidence. No one presented any strong argument why not.

At almost the same time another conference on the same subject was being held in the attic off Doblingerstrasse. Their Czech ally had arrived with two of his top men and the pregnant news just received from his agents in Zurndorf. During the night the two men on the spot had made a careful and completely unde- tected survey of the old man's residence; it seemed a number of families lived in the rambling old building, but what had attracted their attention was a light showing in a tower window in part of the mansion that appeared to be completely derelict. Over several hours of observation they had twice caught a glimpse of a man who seemed to be occupying the room. Could this be the one they were looking for? Abdullah produced photographs of young Karl Reuben, features which every one of his team had etched on their memories, but the Czechs had no means of identification one way or the other. Moda, Yali and Okana must go to Zurndorf with all haste to find out. He and the young Jap would await developments here.

And if it was Reuben? What little information they had gave no clues as to whether a snatch on the spot would be practical or not. The Czech was adamant that his men would guide the party in but if there was any shooting or rough stuff to be done they were strictly on their own. Abdullah had no anxiety about accepting the terms. In half an hour alternative plans were worked out and they were on their way.

CHAPTER EIGHT

Rupert had a snack lunch and left immediately after. He drove the Jensen cautiously through the thick of the early afternoon traffic, making a circuit of one way streets to cross the Ring into Weiskirchnerstrasse. The traffic lights turned green and he surged across the tram tracks to the handsome tree-lined avenue opposite; his stomach gave a protesting lurch as he realised he was passing within a few metres of the spot where poor Sandra's battered and drugged body had been picked up only a little more than twelve hours ago. The feeling was only momentary; he had been able to speak to her on the phone before leaving the office and she sounded almost cheerful. The effect of the powerful anaesthetic agent had worn off leaving her with only a mild headache and occasional slight bouts of nausea. The burn on her chest was a little painful, but she had the heart to put it, in the old stiff-upper-lip phrase, 'only when I laugh'. The doctors had said she could go home tomorrow. Rupert's usual resilient spirit was having small difficulty in reasserting itself. 'Spilt milk,' he murmured to Charlie who was enjoying the sights of the ride as he usually did, sound asleep on the luxuriously pig-skin upholstered seat next to Rupert.

The traffic moved in fits and starts, plodding southward up the gently sloping hill to the Gurtle and then down the long, dull, shop-lined suburban sprawl of Simmeringer Hauptstrasse, past the Vienna Cemetery, Schwechat airport, and then into open country following the ancient Roman road to Budapest. Rupert's mind was chiefly engaged with trying to work out a series of possible scenarios for his, hoped for, interview with Graf von

Eck, and to plan his counter-responses to a range of likely reactions. His thoughts were temporarily interrupted, as they always were, when he passed the enormous, ornate cemetery, and the same two faintly ridiculous ideas always obtruded themselves; one was the thought that no plot of ground on earth contained the relics of so many people who had brought him so much pleasure, starting with Mozart, Schubert and Beethoven; and the other, the good-natured but faintly contemptuous comment which all Viennese taxi drivers make to foreigners coming in from Schwechat, 'That's the biggest cemetery in Europe – it's half as big as Zürich – but twice as much fun.'

Traffic was reasonably heavy as the broad, low-lying highway swept eastward into the rich farming plain of the Burgenland and on to the Hungarian frontier. It seemed a very pleasant, ordinary afternoon in late autumn to enjoy a drive into the countryside.

The only hold-up along the route was in the centre of Bruck where repairs were being undertaken to the main bridge over the little river Leitha. It only lasted fifteen minutes, and it was not quite three-thirty when Rupert drove into Zurndorf. He had no difficulty in finding his turning, left at the far end of town, a gas station on one corner and a bank on the other; it is signposted to Deutsch Jahrndorf. The area surrounding the turning was cluttered with traffic. Two huge Berlei forty ton trucks on the Romania to England run were parked in the street in front of the gas station; this was obviously the drivers' first stop west of the supervision of scowling, gun-slinging soldiery and the peculiarly unattractive breed of frontier police which all Communist countries find essential.

Zurndorf was a typical country town in a good to average prosperous farming district; the road was well paved and cared for; on each side squat, neat houses were surrounded by tidy gardens; as one got farther from the main highway the number of barns and chicken runs and vegetable patches noticeably increased. There was a well advertised farm machinery sales and repair depot, a small grocery store, and then the little bridge over the Leitha. Across the river the grain fields and occasional vineyards began to give place to more wooded areas, and the road curved between shadowed stands of poplars, birch and pine trees. Another mile farther on Rupert came upon a cluster of houses, a small general store, and another garage obviously catering to the farming industry, with the usual tangle of fierce looking farm implements lying about. At the other end of this scene of rustic peace and harmony there appeared another bridge, over the Leitha canal, and running along the near side of it the dirt road which he had been instructed ran to the gate of the von Eck property.

As the Jensen emerged from the tree shrouded lane he got a good view of the old house and its surroundings. It was a scene common enough in the central plains of Austria and Hungary. It was what the English call 'a manor house', and was surrounded by the same rustic clutter of attached buildings whose original uses had gone with the houses. Like so many of its genre all over Europe it was built in the middle of the eighteenth century by a moderately rich man who had probably acquired most of the farmland for miles about. Like many ambitious men before and after him, the founder of the von Eck family fortunes took as his model the best and the fashionable within his knowledge; in this case the contemporary baroque grandeur in which Johann Friedrich von Hohenburg was finishing Schönbrunn for the Empress Maria Theresia. The main body of the house was four storeys high, with an octagonal tower at each end, and at least twenty bedrooms in between. It must have looked grand when the clean, lofty lines of white pilasters, each topped by classical statuary, had set an elegant framework for the long rows of arched windows which interlaced the background of smooth mustard yellow plaster with such perfect symmetry.

Today it was a romantic, but sad, sight. The plaster work of the whole façade was cracked and crumbling. In the odd places where some crude attempt at repair had been made in order to prevent rain and rot from permeating the main beams, the resultant scars were bigger and more blatant than the cracks they sought to hide. None of the Roman gladiators, saints and demi-gods who had once inhabited the roof-top parapet remained intact, and the forlorn figures lacking arms or heads made a macabre skyline from down below. The fact that every one of them was decapitated was no coincidence; the Russian Army officers who were billeted here during the Allied occupation of Austria used to amuse themselves after dinner on summer evenings by shooting the heads off. When the last of the von Ecks finally got his property back he had run out of money, sons and health.

The north end of the buildings was clearly the part he had heard described as uninhabitable; most of the windows were boarded over and the lawn in front of it had been allowed to go completely to seed. The enormous double front door heavily carved with heraldic designs also appeared to be sealed up, but along the south side a number of windows on the ground level had been converted into doors, and these were clearly the 'apartments'. In front of them the driveway petered out into a patch of badly worn grass, where only fragments of paths and large lumps of stone remained to commemorate what had once been an elaborate ornamental garden. An old lady sat sunning herself and knitting before one of the unlikely placed doors. A shiny new Volkswagen was parked next to another. Just in front of him three small children were chasing a cat, while two older boys were mending a broken bicycle. None of them gave the approaching car more than a cursory glance.

Rupert parked the Jensen in what seemed as likely a place as any, and eyed the cat with apprehension; Charlie was bound to wake up as soon as he opened the door, and if he got sight of his hereditary enemy all hell was likely to break loose. By happy chance at that moment the cat eluded its small pursuers and disappeared around the corner of the building. Rupert got leisurely out of the car, picked up his document case and adjusted both the door windows to give Charlie sufficient space for ventilation, but insufficient to allow him to hurl himself out should some unforeseen chance suddenly catch his wanton fancy. He tapped out his pipe on the heel of his shoe and ambled over to where the old lady was doing her knitting. He doffed his hat and said in his most courtly manner, 'Guten tag, gnädige frau.' All elderly ladies in Austria love being addressed like that, even if their pretensions to be 'gnädige' had been few and long ago. She looked up with a welcoming smile and Rupert enquired where he might find Graf von Eck. The old lady indicated that around the southern corner of the house he would find another, lower, wing which connected the main building to the stables behind. The door to the Graf's apartment was about halfway down this wing. She was not at all sure that the Graf was well enough to see anybody.

The wing she had described was a long one-and-a-half-storey affair which had originally been designed to cater for the comfort of gentlemen before and after the hunt. It had a steeply sloping gabled roof, the wooden windows were badly worn but clean and tastefully curtained. Here, at least, someone kept up an effort at a simple, but formal, garden. The path was weeded; rose bushes happily advertised the loving care and attention someone expended on them. As Rupert approached the door he noticed a pair of gardening gloves lying on the path beside a trowel and an old wicker basket full of dead leaves and flowers. At that moment the door opened and a man came out. He was very much as Rupert had pictured him; tall, gaunt, stooped of shoulder, and painfully thin. His distinguished, skeletal head, with the carefully clipped military moustache, the few wisps of grey hair, and the careworn, sunken deep blue eyes spoke eloquently of the Army background, and the too many years of suffering and failing health.

He was wearing a pair of well-worn and shapeless brown corduroy trousers and an equally ancient grey sweater. He stood looking down at the path for a moment, trying to locate where he had left his gloves and the trowel. He seemed quite unconscious that he had a visitor. Rupert advanced a little closer, shuffling his feet on the gravel path to attract attention; he didn't want to risk giving the old man a fright. When he did look up and see Rupert advancing slowly and smilingly toward him his lined face registered total blank. Rupert had decided in the car that he would break the ice gently, but directly.

'Graf von Eck,' he said, 'my name is Conway. I am so sorry I was out when you called at my gallery.'

The frail figure looked at him, vaguely, nervously. He almost seemed not to comprehend the stranger at all. Rupert tried again.

'Rupert Conway, Graf von Eck. I was out when you came to see me in Vienna. So I came to see you.'

The word Vienna seemed to open some small door.

'Vienna. Vienna,' he said haltingly. 'I never go there these days . . .' His voice trailed off. It was clearly going to be heavy slogging.

'You came to my gallery, on Wednesday, sir. I believe you wanted to see Karl Reuben's papers.'

The old man's eyes showed some animation for the first time. The mention of Reuben pushed the small door a fraction wider.

'I'm sorry, sir,' he said, speaking a bit more distinctly now. 'I don't think I know you.'

Rupert held up the document case.

'Your old cello teacher, sir. Karl Reuben. I brought his papers to show you.' He moved closer and by sheer will-power imperceptibly edged his reluctant host a step closer to the still open door. Patience, patience, he said to himself. Mustn't rush him. He eased back the zipper on the leather case and indicated the papers it contained. He got his first blush of encouragement when he noticed the sad, old eyes were staring intently at him. At last something seemed to register. It was the moment to press the attack.

'I know how devoted you were to Dr Reuben, sir. I would love you to see them. Please, may I come in?'

The old man put his hand hesitantly on the door and Rupert was through it before he had time to change his mind.

The door led directly into a large stone walled room that was a veritable museum of the old regime. At one end was an enormous open stone fireplace with a carved overmantel going right up to the vaulted and oak-beamed ceiling; through the accumulation of years of smoke and soot one could still just discern the emblazoned coat-of-arms of the von Ecks. The sombre walls were covered with weapons and hunting trophies: the heads of stags, elks, wolves, wild boars and lesser denizens of the Hungarian forests over which the owners of this old house had roamed freely until the Treaty of Versailles had split their land between three newly created and helplessly unstable countries in 1919. Against one wall was an old-fashioned roll-top desk, entirely practical and unlovely; like the famous one used for nearly seventy years by the Emperor Franz Josef, and by thousands of editors of small-town American newspapers. Along the opposite wall was a scarred oak refectory table fully five metres long and standing on eight legs of massive gargoyles. Its surface was a litter of books, gardening magazines, and a dozen faded photographs in tarnished silver frames; nearly all of strong, aquiline faces in long extinct uniforms, be-booted, be-spurred and be-sworded, covered with medals. Rupert noted with intrigued amusement that three of them were wearing the coveted red and white sash of the Order of Maria Theresia. Whatever these men had done they had served their Emperors as a way of life and duty. The only non-military and un-Nimrodic form of decoration visible was a large gesso crucifix which hung directly above the worn velvet armchair into which von Eck immediately collapsed.

Rupert walked slowly towards him and took the first folio of carefully selected and arranged sheets out of the leather document case. He gently held them out to the pathetic figure slumped in the big chair in front of him.

'Please,' he said, 'I'm sure you will find these interesting.'

Slowly, painfully, the old man's spider-like arthritic fingers took a grasp of the proffered sheets. He fumbled for a pair of gold-rimmed spectacles lying on the table beside him. Rupert quietly withdrew to the nearest chair and instinctively took out a pipe. He loaded it, lit it, and sat in silence for fully five minutes watching intently while the old man's curiosity gradually generated the energy to read, and then attempt to comprehend, these strange echoes from a world he had loved, and long since lost. After an agonising silence von Eck slowly looked up and stared across at Rupert. It seemed almost too great an effort just to take his glasses off and adjust his eyes to focus the farther distance. When he started to speak his voice was so faint it seemed as though it took every spark of energy left in him.

'I am an old man now, sir. Very out of touch with the world. I live alone here.' His voice trailed off, he breathed heavily and tried to concentrate his thoughts for a further effort. 'These are interesting papers. Karl Reuben was a great teacher. A great teacher. And a dear friend. He was treated disgracefully. Horribly. I heard the Nazis broke his fingers.' For one awful moment Rupert feared he was going to burst into tears. His inherent pride and military discipline only just won the day. 'It is very good of you . . . good of you to bring these papers to me. I am grateful to you, Herr . . . Herr . . .'

'Conway, Graf von Eck. Rupert Conway.'

'Of course. Of course. Forgive me. I've heard of you. Memory not very good these days. I've heard of you. My . . . ah . . . my aunt, I think . . . Princess Marie von Hohenstein. . . .'

'That's right, sir. I found her Veronese for her. Just after the war.'

'So you did. So you did.' He subsided into another exhausted silence.

Rupert decided the critical moment had arrived. Rising from his chair he said gently but firmly, 'So will you help me find young Karl Reuben, sir?'

For a few seconds there was no reaction whatever from the emaciated figure slumped in the big velvet chair. Then there was a nervous quiver, almost of fright. His voice took on a new, agitated, pitch. It seemed two tones higher.

'Young Karl! No, no. I know nothing about . . .'

Judging his timing like a skilled advocate cross-examining a reluctant witness, Rupert pressed his point.

'Graf von Eck. You can trust me. I know Karl is in grave danger. He needs help. I want to help him. Please let me do so.'

Again there was a reaction indicating alarm, agitation, even fear.

'No, no. I don't understand what is happening. You must forgive an old man, sir . . .'

Rupert said with heavy emphasis, 'I *can* help him, Graf von Eck.'

He walked slowly across the room.

'I *can* help him,' he repeated.

The old man mumbled to himself in a shaky whisper, 'You can help him. You can help him.'

Rupert stood right over him and said with slow deliberation, 'I *can* help him, Graf von Eck. If *you* will take me to him.'

The old man shook his shoulders feebly.

'I can't. I can't,' he stammered.

Rupert decided this was the moment to play the emotional card he had thought out during the drive down. It was a gamble, trite, even naïve, but there was little left to try. 'As one old soldier to another, sir. It is your duty to take me to him.'

Then he stood back for what seemed to be endless, pregnant, emotionally draining moments. Had the ploy worked? Or had he offended beyond hope of redemption?

As the adrenalin started to pump and the horrible prospect of failure started to mount inside him, the conflicting commands of some dimly remembered thing called duty fought themselves to some kind of muddled conclusion in von Eck's troubled mind. Then he said, 'I must ask him.'

Rupert's heart leaped.

'Then he *is* here,' he challenged the old Graf's honour.

There was another, terrible silence. Then the old man looked up at him and with great weariness he said, 'You are a clever man, Herr Conway. But, if you can help young Karl, well, God grant you can. I'm sure I can't.' He struggled to his feet. 'Please wait here, sir.' He squared his haggard shoulders, like a man who has just taken an unwelcome decision, and seeks the strength to act on it. 'Please wait here, sir,' he repeated and walked feebly to an inner door. Rupert listened eagerly as he heard the shaky footfalls disappear down a long, echoing corridor.

87

There was nothing he could do but wait.

At the same moment that von Eck was wrestling with his conscience, painfully approaching the point of decision to break what was clearly a vow of secrecy, the man to whom he had given that vow was pacing the octagonal tower room at the northernmost end of the building in a state of high nervous tension. For many days he had not set foot outside this dilapidated, mildewed, long disused hiding place, except to descend the rickety stairs to an even more improbable but barely functioning lavatory beneath. This tower eyrie into which he had thrown himself in a mood of wild romanticism, self-persuaded that at last he had found sanctuary from the nightmares of recent weeks, a haven where he could pursue his researches in peaceful solitude, protected by the smiling ghost of his adored father; this unlikely elysium had now become a strangling, suffocating prison, the results of his work a nightmare.

Young Karl Reuben looked, not just like a man who had recently suffered a severe nervous breakdown, but one who might well be stumbling through a short intermission before the next one. His appearance was in awful harmony with his surroundings; his tangled hair was dishevelled and uncombed for days, as the ceiling above him was cracked and unplastered for years; his eyes were sore, careworn and sulky like the ramshackle clutter of odd bits of board, cotton, and glass which served as windows. His clothes were shambling and shapeless; as was the unmade bed, the motheaten old plush chair and the litter of papers, papers, papers that covered everything in the room like a snow storm in an old Charlie Chaplin movie. The room's solitary reminder of human affections and strivings only added to the melancholy, the faded and worn photograph of his father in white tie and tail-coat, the famous Stradivarii cello resting against his knees, which was Karl's only personal possession, looked grotesque under an ancient sheet of yellowing celluloid surrounded by a cheap, torn plastic frame.

Karl stood for a moment gazing down at the paper-strewn

wooden table at which he had been working uninterruptedly for days. He made an effort to restore some kind of clarity into his self-tortured brain by tidying and sorting the extraordinary mass of sheets into some kind of order. Any casual observer would have been baffled by what they saw; he appeared to work on mathematical problems and musical exercises simultaneously. It was only a matter of minutes before his attention was diverted from the task in hand. For a second only, and not overly loud nor officious, he heard a sound that rekindled some of the most violent, emotive instincts which dominated his tired, over-strained brain. The unmistakable, high-pitched wail of a police siren. He dropped the papers in his hands as though he had been shot. He rushed to one of the few windows that had a pane of glass in it, and faced the dirt driveway leading up to the house. His excited and uncomprehending eyes did not see the large brown cow which sauntered off the middle of the driveway registering bovine indignation at the unwelcome hooting which had disturbed it. All he did see was an accelerating police car apparently racing for the house at speed. To Karl's uncritical, weary brain it was menacing speed. The police had arrived like this at the little bungalow outside Technion City which he had shared with Kaled Tablishi. They had taken Kaled away. Kaled had been shot. Now they were coming for him! Something inside him snapped.

The horror of his lover's trial and execution, the searing memory of his recent mental collapse, the excitement and tension of his secret flight from Israel, and the bitter disappointment of the new reality he had created suddenly overwhelmed him. He panicked. Like a man possessed he flew to the door and hurled himself recklessly down the stairs, stumbling, slipping and sliding as he went. Three floors down the rest of the staircase was blocked by a locked door. He turned blindly into the first corridor that presented itself, and rushed at the first door he saw. He fumbled for the handle which gave easily to his grasp. The big room in front of him was almost in darkness, the only light filtering in through a few cracks in the boards which covered the glassless windows. All he could make out in his hyper-excited condition was large piles of furniture covered with long undisturbed dust sheets. As he tried to pick his way through the maze spider webs enmeshed his eyes and his hair wherever he turned. These sticky, invisible threads added a new dimension of bizarre fear to his panic. He tripped over an unexpected carpet and went sprawling across the floor, crashing his head against some particularly solid item of furniture. He staggered to his feet, now quite hysterical, driven only by a primitive, animal compulsion to flee.

Somehow he reached the other door leading out of this chamber of horrors, and found himself on a wide gallery facing a staircase of monumental proportions which descended to the great baroque front hall. At this very moment he passed over the head of the old Graf, heading in the opposite direction along a back corridor one flight below. If the Graf heard anything his numbed and pain-racked old brain never registered it.

By the time the Graf had clambered up the first flight of the tower stairs and was fussing with the key in the locked door Karl Reuben, now sweating and panting like the hunted animal he believed himself to be, was thrusting his way through the abandoned wing of the old kitchens projecting back from the centre of the big house, and ultimately joining the barns and stables at the far end of an internal courtyard, which in its great days could accommodate sixty mounted huntsmen with grooms and stableboys in attendance.

On the lawn in front of the house one of the young policemen who had arrived in response to a frantic phone call from the mother of the three small children had just completed his rescue of the cat from the top of an old pine tree, returned it to the grateful and effusive old lady, and was quietly putting his coat and cap on again. Compliments and thanks were exchanged all round, and as they drove off the young driver playfully hooted his siren again at the cow now contentedly chewing its cud by the bank of the canal.

Back in von Eck's sitting-room Rupert anxiously looked at his watch for the fourth time. The old man had been gone six minutes now. Rupert heard the second siren, and was uneasily conscious that some commotion was going on somewhere. His instinct was to go and investigate. But in this vast, rambling place, it was impossible to know even in which direction to start. Supposing the old man had fallen and hurt himself? Supposing there was nothing he could do maybe it was better to be patient. For a few minutes longer anyway.

Reuben's progress through the kitchen and scullery wing was as frenetic as it had been upstairs. Twice he cracked a shin on malicious bits of furniture. He knocked over a pile of old glass jam jars which crashed splintering on the stone floor and sent two cats scurrying through a broken window. That in turn set off the unmistakable bark of an Alsatian in the barnyard the other side of the wall. It was inevitable that Reuben was petrified of Alsatians; and that the next door he staggered through opened right into the barnyard. He tumbled off the stone ledge into the middle of a flock of enraged chickens who ran, flew, and clucked an angry protest. The Alsatian barked menace and defiance at the world in general, but it was obvious even to a man in Reuben's state of agitated excitement that it was securely chained to a stone post. He looked wildly round and his eyes fell upon what appeared to be the only hope of flight. The big solid barnyard gates on the other side stood half open. Somewhere, out there, outside these imprisoning, crushing, agonising great walls, somehow there might be a moment of respite. The view of well-tended, open fields, and the late afternoon sun glistening across the little pond made by the junction of the river Leitha and the canal, gave Reuben the first glimpse of something approaching calm he had felt since that fatal siren had sparked off this bout of uncontrolled, irrational frenzy.

He picked himself up out of the muck and straw of the barnyard, with a muddy hand rubbed some of the sweat from his face, and ran for the gate. As he reached it his strength just about gave out; he leaned exhausted against its outer side, fighting to get his breath. The warming rays of the sun glancing over the top of the poplars on to the water danced in his eyes. He breathed deeply, heavily; the fresh, rich smell of country air was like fine wine in his throat after the drear, thin damp of his tower cell. The race in his mind, like his body, was beginning to subside. He remembered his father's picture. Well, he would have to go back, but now he would walk back, calmly, in the front door, careless of whether anyone saw him or not. In some strange way this bout of hysteria had acted like a catharsis. He had committed no crime. The terrifying nature of his research was now only too appallingly clear to him; he now had no doubt where it was heading. It would be better abandoned. Someone else might some day stumble on it; he could not prevent that. He would make a new start, somehow or other, here amongst his father's people. There were myriad other fields of medical research to be explored. For a few moments, in that peaceful autumn farmland, young Karl Reuben was as close to experiencing contentment as he had ever known.

One man, casually but meticulously keeping watch on the whole back wall of the von Eck property, saw Karl leaning heavily against the big wooden barnyard gate. By radio he quickly summoned another. Karl gradually came out of his reverie and started to move, limping along the path, away from the gate, toward the main house. The men came at him from in front and behind. He was too weak, too dazed even to struggle. Someone strong and ruthless pinned his arms. Someone ripped the sleeve from his torn sweater and shirt. He felt the sharp prick of a needle in his bare arm. That was all.

The men picked him up and ran back past the gate to the far end of the barn. There was a black Opel four-door parked there with the engine running. A girl was at the wheel. The men threw Karl's limp body into the trunk, slammed down the lid and clambered in. Yali said, 'No one saw us. Just keep your eye on the road and take it gently. With luck we may get back to the highway without attracting attention at all. When we find a clear piece of road I'll use the radio.'

The car drove down the farm lane along the edge of a wheat field and turned right along the river bank. Just before they hit the sideroad leading back to Zurndorf, a man drove out of the field on a tractor. He took no notice, but he undoubtedly saw them.

Yali was studying his map. He said to Moda, 'We'll make straight for the safe house at Wiener Neustadt. East at the main road, just before Nickelsdorf there is a lane off to your right, it rejoins the main road southwest of Parndorf. It will be at least two hours before the police have a general call out for a black Opel four-door. By that time we'll have ditched this one and should be nearly to the frontier.'

Rupert looked at his watch for the sixth time; he noted the old man had been gone for eight minutes, and started to debate yet again what he should do when he heard hurried, stumbling footsteps coming down the corridor. Von Eck literally fell into the room and leaned heavily against the wall as though he were about to fall.

'He's gone!' the old man gasped.

'Gone!' Rupert echoed, horrified. 'Where? Show me!'

The old man shook his head, and slumped into his chair.

'I'm sorry. I can't,' his voice sounded a long way off, and Rupert thought he would faint at any moment. 'Brandy,' he said abruptly and von Eck raised one hand feebly indicating an oak corner cabinet near his chair. Rupert found a bottle, and a glass, and thrust it into the old man's quivering hands. His impatience was held in check by the thought, 'God help us if he passes out.'

The old man took two gulps and with agonising slowness a little colour came back into his emaciated cheeks. He rested his drinking arm on the side of the chair and managed to stammer, 'Karl is not in his room. You can find it. That corridor, top of the tower, at the far end.' Rupert gave the dazed old man a quick glance and decided he would live for another hour or two anyway. He raced along the stone floored corridor, the pounding clatter of his heels echoing and re-echoing as though ten men were running down it. It went the whole length of the house with innumerable doors and passageways running off it and through it. When he reached the other end there were more

93

corridors going off both to left and to right. He made a momentary calculation that the tower was on the front and turned left. He went through a series of doors and found himself at the foot of a staircase. He thanked Heaven he was fit for his fifty-seven years and took the stairs three at a time. On the first landing a door was standing partially open. To his intense relief he saw the staircase continuing to ascend just the other side of it. By the time he reached the fourth flight he was down to single steps but still running.

At the top the door was wide open and suddenly Rupert realised he was in the room that had been Karl Reuben's hiding place while both the Israelis and a band of Palestinian terrorists had been looking for him. The photograph of old Karl caught and held his eye for a moment. He moved closer to the crude wooden work table. There was still sufficient light in the late afternoon to make a cursory study of the disorganised mass of papers lying there. He was at once seized of the fact that there must be significance in this indiscriminate jumble, so it seemed, of sheets covered with mathematical symbols and others with musical symbols. He hesitated only an instant to consider the alternatives, and their consequences. Reuben was missing from this room. How far had he gone? Would he come walking back in any minute? Rupert had too much sense of the dramatic to persuade himself that was likely. If he was not coming back? His friends in the police don't take kindly to amateurs interfering with what obviously must be vital evidence. His acquisitive instincts got the better of him. Looking round he spotted a cheap little canvas and cardboard suitcase. He scooped every paper in the room into it and raced back down the stairs again.

Wherever young Karl had gone the time had definitely arrived for reinforcements. Rupert ran, starting to puff a bit uncomfortably, back down the long corridor to the Graf's quarters. The old man was still sitting motionless in the big, worn chair, but he was perfectly conscious and seemed to have recovered himself. Rupert shouted as he came through the door, 'Telephone,' and von Eck said, 'In the kitchen. Through there.' Rupert dialled the police emergency number and said in his loudest most commanding voice, 'Police Praesidium, Vienna, urgent, it's a matter of life and death.' This left no room for argument nor even a polite request for further information. The policeman on duty in the Zurndorf station connected the call to Vienna. 'Hofrat Liebmann's office, direct, it's very urgent.'

By sheer good luck Liebmann was in his office. Breathlessly Rupert explained what little he knew had happened; Reuben had been hiding here; he had been here less than an hour ago; for reasons unknown he had disappeared. There was no point in fogging the issue by mentioning that suitcase full of papers now. Liebmann took him seriously enough to say he would get on direct to the Police President of the Burgenland at once and ask him to put every man available on a full scale manhunt. He did. Then he gave an assistant instructions to alert all border crossings and to have Records computer telex all information they had on Reuben to all stations. The man must be intercepted at the earliest possible moment.

Rupert then phoned the Israeli embassy where Jacob Kleinhart had spent an anxious afternoon waiting to hear from him. Rupert went through the story again and Kleinhart's heart sank. They could do nothing further at present but hope and pray the police net would find Reuben. Alive? Alone?

Rupert took his farewell of the disconsolate and dazed old Graf. He asked the lady in the apartment at the corner of the house to call the Graf's doctor and say a visit as soon as possible seemed urgently necessary. Then he got into the Jensen, put the key in, pressed the starter button. The car started all right, but there was something wrong. Rupert's preoccupied thoughts burst like a bomb! Charlie! Where's Charlie? He switched off. Charlie's been dognapped! No, that's ridiculous. He ran across to the old lady. Yes, she had seen the children playing with a strange dog. She had never seen one like it around here before. Where were they now? Oh, she hadn't seen them for some time now. Rupert looked anxiously at his watch. He had to get back to Vienna. And quick. Charlie was a tough character, and resilient. Little devil! What a time to run off. Rupert drove back to Vienna with another problem on his mind.

CHAPTER NINE

The rush hour traffic entering and leaving Vienna was heavier than usual. It was half past six when Rupert brought the Jensen to a halt in the underground garage. He started to run up the slope and immediately made another unhappy discovery; for a man of fifty-seven with a badly wounded leg he had already done more than enough running that day. His right leg nearly collapsed under him and he grabbed at the concrete wall to prevent himself from falling. A quick stab of pain caused him to catch his breath, and cough. He knew the feeling of old, it hurt, but it was nothing serious. 'A mere boy of fifty-seven,' he muttered to himself; 'bloody ridiculous!' He limped up the slope and across the street as fast as he could.

Heinz, loyal and painstaking as always, was watching from the big show window for him, and had the door open before he reached it. They went straight into Rupert's office and Heinz told him he was to call Jo Liebmann's office the moment he arrived. Liebmann had left headquarters but it took the switchboard only a few seconds to locate him; in a car heading home to a much-tried wife. His news was threefold, and not quite all of it bad. The Arabs and their Japanese cohorts had slipped out of the warehouse in the Ninth District before the police reinforcements were in position – 'seems certain they actually left during the morning – while we were sitting talking about them' – no word nor trace of them had been reported since. Nevertheless, whether the Foreign Ministry were helpful or not he intended to have a first class forensic man inside that warehouse tomorrow.

His second item was that just a few minutes ago a farmer whose property adjoined von Eck's had told the Zurndorf police that at about four-thirty he had seen a black Opel four-door saloon driving out of the lane behind the barn. He had thought it a bit odd at the time, but being busy with his own work had not paid much attention. He had not noticed the licence number but he was adamant he had a good memory of the occupants; there were three people in it, a girl driving and two men; they were all 'foreign looking'. Liebmann's computer brain took less than seconds to put two and two together and from that moment on he was never in any doubt about the true sequence of events. He told Rupert in his usual, clear, unexcited and monosyllabic way the orders Police President Riedinger had immediately authorised him to issue. Within another fifteen minutes every policeman on duty in Austria would be alerted to a description of the car and its occupants and under orders to report instantly with a code word reserved for Anti-Terrorist operations: they didn't want some nice young country policeman to get his head blown off while in the act of innocently enquiring, 'May I see your licence, please, sir.'

Rupert just grunted, Liebmann made a long sigh, and then with a chuckle, he said, 'Rupert, old friend, I think there is one bright star on the horizon for you.'

'What's that?'

'Have you seen Charlie, lately?'

'Has someone found him?'

'The Burgenland Police have done a very thorough job of combing the area north of Zurndorf. We had a report about half an hour ago they found a hell-hound of a breed nobody in Zurndorf had ever seen before. He was prowling suspiciously around old von Eck's garden. It took three men to catch him and he bit two of them before they could get him in the van. They're processing his licence tag through the usual channels but if there is another Charlie Conway loose in this country we'll have to put our men in armoured cars.' Jo enjoyed his joke and chortled happily.

'That's the best news I've heard today, Jo. Thank you so much, old man.'

The mystery of how Charlie had got out of the car was one they never solved: kids, probably.

Rupert phoned the hospital and had a brief, very reassuring talk with Sandra. Yes, she would be home tomorrow all right, none the worse for wear except a few bruises and a burn scar which would preclude the wearing of low cut dresses for a while. He did not worry her with his news. It could wait. He next called Kleinhart and they agreed to meet for a quiet dinner at a little restaurant just off Karntnerstrasse and come back to 5B for discussion, and drinks, afterwards. Rupert said good-night and thank you to the faithful Heinz and climbed the stairs to his apartment. On his way through the drawing-room he helped himself to a strong Scotch and headed for the bath tub.

Just after half past nine two pipe smoking middle aged gentle-men, deep in discussion, reached the bottom of Karntner-strasse, strolled leisurely around St Stephan's great cathedral and down Stephansplatz. Rupert, now alert for any unexpected danger, was relieved to see that there were more than the usual number of police about, especially in the vicinity of 5B. Two of them watched attentively from a discreet distance while he went through the lock and burglar alarm routine and entered the gallery fully assured by the alarm monitor lights that all was in order, at least within this temple of culture and orderly living. They went upstairs, repeated an alarm check at the door to his apartment, and made themselves comfortable in the elegant, but determinedly masculine drawing-room. While Rupert poured the Scotch, with ice, Jacob Kleinhart browsed about the silver framed photographs on the piano.

'Anthony Eden, Yehudi Menuhin, Duke Ellington, and an English lord and lady in full regalia,' Kleinhart said with amuse-ment. 'You have a wide circle of friends, Rupert.'

'My godfather, the classics, jazz and my parents,' he replied with a smile. 'All part of the great loves of my life.'

'And this beautiful girl, in English uniform?'

'My wife,' Rupert answered simply. Kleinhart looked surprised. 'The greatest love of my life. She died many years ago.'

'I am sorry.'

'That's all right; you couldn't have known. Enough ice?'

'Fine, thank you. Who's the handsome fellow in the uniform?'

'My brother, George. God rest his soul. That was taken on his last leave. In London. He was with Monty, Eighth Army. Killed at Alamein.'

Kleinhart murmured another 'sorry', and they sat down. He went on, 'I'm impressed by the very thorough security precautions you take, Rupert. I always thought Vienna was an especially peaceful city.'

Rupert put his glass down and thought a moment.

'You're right, Jacob. It is. It still is. But an awful lot has happened here in the last few years. For a long time Vienna was a bit of a backwater. Not now. There is no east and west Austria, you know. These people got the Communists out of their country, and one of the ways they did it was to write perpetual neutrality into the constitution. They're as western orientated as anyone could be, but if they deviated from the constitution the Russians could, in theory at any rate, come back in again. So, in a funny way we're becoming another Switzerland. Austria doesn't threaten anybody, and we have more darned international organisations and committees than a dog has fleas packed into this city. The United Nations are scheduled to pack in a whole flock of new ones, worse luck.'

'You don't approve?'

'Oh, I approve all right. This process of becoming a new world crossroads is very interesting. Intellectually stimulating. But it plays hell with traffic, inflation and our taxes,' he said ruefully. 'And, as you well know, it has made us a stamping ground for many brands of bloody-minded terrorists,' he said with deep feeling. 'Oh. By the way. Have you heard any news of that fellow who was killed at the opera last week? It's strange, there has been almost nothing in the papers.'

Kleinhart replied, 'Yes, we have been following that very carefully. I discussed it with Dr Kuso only yesterday.'

'Haven't Criminal Investigation picked up anything?'

'Oh yes, they have. But it is a long, tenuous thread. The reason there has been little in the papers is that very little has happened that makes news. All they have is an unidentified body. Nobody recognises it, nobody has claimed it. Nobody resembling it has been reported missing. The police traced the make of the suit the man was wearing to Rome. It was a needle in a haystack operation. The Rome police finally found the shop that had sold it. To a stranger, a Middle Eastern looking sort of gentleman, so they said. He had paid with American Express traveller's cheques. They traced the cheques and found they were part of a haul from a bank robbery in Turin which was known to have been done by Palestinians. So, as they say in the official statements, investigations continue.'

'What does Freddy Kuso think?'

'Very interesting. His theory is that it was a PFLP revenge killing; they're just as brutal with each other as with anyone else. That hideous creature known as Carlos shot his friend and colleague Michel Moukarbel right through the face when he thought Moukarbel had betrayed him. And boasted about it. Then their head killer in Europe, a certain Mohamed Boudia, one of Arafat's El Fatah henchmen by the way, he was blown up by one of our Wrath of God squads, but we got the tip-off from the Palestinians.'

Which brought them to the events of the day.

Rupert said, 'Tell me more about young Karl Reuben. Naturally I feel sorry for him, but just why is he so important?'

'It's not easy to explain. How much do you know about radiation sickness?'

'Very little. Some connection between the atomic bomb on Hiroshima and the treatment of cancer, is there not?'

'You wouldn't pass any exams by putting it that way, but, crudely speaking, yes, there is. What we call ionising nuclear radiation is part of life. We live with it every day. We know a lot about it. There is an abstruse argument about whether the sun is the sole source, or a main source amongst others, but that's by the way. The buildings in which we live give off microwave emissions. Medical X-ray equipment does. Modern high energy radar does. And so on. The limits are well understood and in small, more or less continuous doses are as harmless as sunshine.

'But the slightest overdose creates conditions in the body which are pretty new to science. We are well aware of the strange things that happen to human blood when the body receives any serious physical trauma. If you suffered a big loss of blood, say in a motor accident, a blood test would find that the cell count of your body had altered. And it can alter in many different ways. Very roughly, that is caused by the blood acting as a kind of fire brigade, rushing around trying to heal the injuries the body has suffered. The action of what we call histamine in allergies is similar. Nature tends to overdo things. Now, for reasons we don't fully understand yet, radiation has exactly the same effect. In lab conditions you can actually watch the results of an ionising radiation beam setting blood cells into something that resembles a spasm in a nerve, or muscle; they go quite haywire. The movements become unpredictable. But, the big difference between your accident and your receiving radiation is this: radiation is in no way detectable by the body while it's happening. You can't see it, hear it, smell it. You can't even feel it.'

'And what happens when the blood cells go haywire?'

'The pathology of it is too complicated to explain. Very roughly what happens is that the remaining healthy blood cells in the body signal a three alarm fire and start rushing about like crazy things trying to restore their stricken comrades.'

'And that kills you?'

'It isn't even as simple as that. It depends, first, on how much radiation. Different human bodies can absorb different amounts. A small dose might give you a headache, or an upset stomach. A large dose, forgive the mixed metaphor, pulls out all the plugs of the body's computer, it disrupts all the normal defence mechanisms of a healthy blood supply, the fire brigade are so busy trying to take care of the cells damaged by the radiation that they can't cope with the ordinary running of the machine. Just to add to the danger, you would also be suffering fits of nausea and vomiting either of which might kill you in this help-less physical condition.'

'Sounds perfectly horrible. For God's sake, have another drink.' He replenished their glasses.

'OK. I think I understand the horror stuff to date. What's all this got to do with master Reuben?'

'Patience; there is worse to come. You mentioned cancer. The most successful therapy so far developed is the use of radiation, under most carefully controlled conditions, to deliberately assault the diseased blood cells in the malignant tissues. All live blood cells, healthy or deformed, breed on themselves, so, the theory is that if you can kill off the diseased ones selectively you increase the chances that healthy ones will replace them. Within limits, it works. There have been many cures. But it's a cumbersome business; and a dangerous and unpleasant one too. The strain on the patient varies from one person to another, but it can be terrible.

'Now, we're getting to Reuben. The present limits of all this are pretty clearly understood. The total amount of active radiation you can get out of any given quantity of fissionable material is believed to have a theoretical limit. Nobody has quite got there yet, but we know within a pretty certain degree of mathematical accuracy what it will be. The new neutron beam research facility the British are building at Cambridge is expected to teach us a lot science wants to know. The other, purely practical, limitation is that all fissionable material at present known, and most people believe, pray God, ever likely to be known, is heavy, bulky stuff and by the time you have shielded it with an inch or more of lead and cadmium sheeting and a lot of plastic coating so that you can work with it without killing yourself, it's far beyond the ability of any normal human being to lift.'

'We should thank the good Lord for that, at least,' Rupert said in an awed whisper.

'We should indeed,' Jacob said. 'We should indeed.'

'So where was Reuben's research leading him?'

'I think I told you, when we first discussed this, that Karl

Reuben was brilliant, and he was not satisfied that our present theoretical knowledge of what might become possible was necessarily right. He believed the two limiting factors might turn out to be different, possibly very different. If someone could discover a method of producing a greatly increased amount of radiation, from a very much lighter mass of material, and could devise a means of controlling its operation; well, as the Americans would say, it opens up a whole new ball game.'

'In what way?'

'Two ways. The good one is that the use of radio-active materials in the medical field might become much easier, much cheaper; they could therefore be used much more widely for the relief of human suffering, the cure of disease and such like.' He paused.

'And the bad one?' Rupert asked.

'The bad one is almost too terrible to contemplate.'

'Like what?'

'Like,' Jacob said reluctantly, as though the words did not want to come out at all. 'Like the ultimate weapon for terrorising and blackmailing the civilised world. That may not be science fiction. If Reuben were right, if the rest of us were wrong, we would no longer have suicide squads of mad fanatics rushing into crowded airport waiting rooms and spraying them with machine-guns and hand-grenades. Theoretically, and I underline theoretically, all a man would have to do would be to leave something, the size of a small suitcase, something like a portable typewriter case, in such a place . . . the individual concerned could be on a plane and five thousand miles away before the first effects of the radiation being given off were even known . . .'

'And then?'

'Then, hours, one, two, even three days later, anyone who had passed through that airport waiting-room would start to vomit, to be overcome by nausea. To collapse and die from a host of different, apparent, causes. By the very nature of an airport waiting-room, hundreds of those people would by then be spread over half the globe. Many might be dead before the source was discovered. Can you imagine the panic that could start?'

Rupert felt sick just to contemplate it.

'No wonder Reuben was a nervous wreck.'

'Now you can see why David Erlik, our Dean of Medicine, made me Reuben's full-time watchdog. Up till a few weeks ago he had made little progress; his calculations were only just pushing on what I might call the limits of orthodox opinion. But, now? What was going on in his brain when he disappeared even I don't know. The one, awful thing we can deduce for certain today is that before his late girl friend was caught she knew what was in his mind, and somehow or other she conveyed that knowledge to her PFLP friends; we now know that evil genius, George Habash, who runs that conglomeration of evil, believes it is worthwhile to kidnap Reuben to find out.'

After a moment Rupert took another long pull at his Scotch and said, 'I think that is the most terrifying thing I have ever heard.'

Jacob Kleinhart said dryly, 'I'm quite certain it is.'

CHAPTER TEN

At five minutes to six, while the farmer at Zurndorf was giving his statement to the local police, Moda drove the black Opel into the respectable, but rather dreary eastern suburbs of Wiener Neustadt, made a left turn off the Neudorf road, three blocks farther down a right into a quiet street of small, innocent looking villas, each with its own high fenced garden, and turned quickly in at a gate where the house was almost completely hidden by trees. She had memorised her way to the house from every direction when she had reconnoitred it the first day they were in Austria; getting on to a 'safe house' network, and planning one's escape is an operation that precedes working out the exact details of a kidnapping, which so often turn out to be simply grasping an unforeseen opportunity. She drove the car right round to the back of the house where a garage and the thickness of the trees completely obscured it from the vision of any nosy neighbours, got out and knocked at the kitchen door. It was opened by a middle-aged woman with iron grey hair and an iron grey face.

She looked at Moda without registering any kind of emotion and said, flatly, 'You were supposed to telephone first.'

'Yes, I know,' Moda replied hastily. 'There just wasn't time. Things have moved faster than we expected. Are you alone?'

'Yes, all alone. Bring "him" in.' The emphasis on the word him made it clear that she knew a male victim of some kind had been the object of the operation. Moda turned and signalled to the men in the car who got out and walked quickly to the house, Yali and the young Japanese carrying Reuben between them by holding his arms round their own shoulders.

'You'd better take "him" in there,' the woman said, opening a door to another room where the shutters and curtains were apparently always kept closed. 'He's not dead, is he?' she said, showing a hint of anxiety for the first time.

Moda answered: 'No, he's not dead, but we'd better check his pulse and heart. And get a longer term sedation inside him.' At this moment Abdullah and Okana rang the front door bell having walked from the nearby railway station. Abdullah took charge.

They laid Reuben on a couch and Abdullah opened his shirt putting the palm of his hand gently over the heart. He felt his pulse; put his head down and laid his ear right against the mouth and nose to listen to the breathing. He whispered just loud enough to be heard, 'His condition is not as good as it should be, the heartbeat is irregular.' He looked up and raised his voice a fraction: 'Remember, all of you, if this man dies then our mission has failed. Moda, I think it is time for your new role to commence. I hope you can do it.' He got up and turned to the grey lady. 'Three things we need. A quick meal, your telephone, and another car. You are prepared?'

'Yes, I'm prepared. I'll make you some soup and wiener schnitzel. The phone is through there.'

'What about the car?' Abdullah asked.

'That wasn't so easy, but my son is away, you can take his station wagon. It's in the garage.'

Abdullah had not heard of this son before.

'Your son? We didn't know you had a son here. Is he aware of what you do?'

'No. He's away most of the time. The young woman said you were going to leave the same night, so if I report his car stolen tomorrow morning it won't do you any harm, will it?'

Abdullah thought for a moment, then said, 'No. That's not a bad idea. Protects your cover too.'

'That's right,' she said and went back to the kitchen.

Abdullah made his phone call, to a number in Graz. Yali

went out to the garage to transfer their weapons into the station wagon and make some adjustments to the Opel.

Moda started to try to enact her 'new role'. Until they had left Zurndorf with Reuben safely locked in the car she had scarcely thought about it since they flew out of Beirut and the final, exciting briefing from George Habash himself. All her natural instincts, and they were powerful, taught her to hate this particular Sabra with all the well-cultivated feelings of hatred she had been so carefully taught. It was part of the extraordinary genius of Habash, a man whose life was dedicated to murdering innocent men, women and children, that he had a talent to play on human weakness and passion with such startling versatility that he could, and frequently did, persuade people to do, and even to feel, things which were quite foreign to their nature. He had worked hard on Moda. Sure, any good young PFLP member could track down and kill Reuben, any time, easy; I could authorise you to do it, I'm sure it would give you great pleasure, my dear girl. That's the way he talked to them. But what a waste! 'Keep your mind concentrated on what your sister told you.' Yes, Moda could do that all right. Kaled had died for the cause. Kaled's spirit had to be reborn in her. Kaled had lived with this strange Jewish scientist, his head full of weird and terrible theories; lived with him and made love to him, for nearly two years. Her sacrifice and her death must not be in vain, Moda swore to herself vehemently.

Left alone in the comfortably furnished but ill-lit room she approached the inert body, breathing heavily and erratically on the large sofa. She knew he should be coming round any time now. She knew the first act of her new role was to be his nurse. How would he react, in another day or so, when they allowed him a sufficiently small dose of sedative that he could stay awake and start to think a little? There could be no doubt he would recognise her, they had met often enough when he and her sister lived together. She was only two years younger than Kaled; people often said they looked very much alike. How would she strike Reuben?

Right now the question was how did Reuben strike her? As

he lay there helpless in front of her, her first feeling was an almost uncontrollable surge of excitement quivering through her whole body; her eyes became glassy, the scene in front of her unreal; without realising what she was doing, as though from a trance, she suddenly awoke to the awful fact that she had her gun in her hand! The slightest move of the first finger of her right hand and this Jew against whom she had sworn vengeance could be killed. Just as simple as that. For the first time in a young life which had been moulded by refugee and terrorist camps, trained since a child to hate, Moda Tablishi found herself overwhelmed with horror. She started to cry. She stood there staring down at the drugged man whose head was no more than two feet from her trigger finger. She thought of her dead sister and cried. It seemed like a lifetime. Maybe it was.

The noise and angry words caused by Yali slamming the kitchen door brought her back to earth with a bang. She thrust the automatic back into its hidden holster, took a crumpled handkerchief from the back pocket of her tight-fitting blue jeans and rubbed her eyes hard. Reuben's body was beginning to twitch, and faint moans escaped his lips. She could look at him more calmly now. She went into the kitchen and got a glass of water. She took two dark red pills from the phial in her handbag and laid them on the table, and as she looked back at Reuben his eye muscles started to flicker. She stood there hesitating, motionless. Funny, it had never struck her before how she might feel the first time she actually had to touch him. At this instant it struck her as repellent, loathsome. This was the man whose insane testimony had led directly to Kaled's death. Kaled! 'Keep your mind concentrated on what your sister told you.' Moda picked up a small pillow off the nearest chair, raised Reuben's head and gently placed the pillow beneath it. As she did so he opened both eyes, and through the ebbing and flowing mists of the sea of post-anaesthesia he could feel rather than see that an attractive girl was bending over him. The serious, dark face and short cropped black hair stirred memories somewhere far back in his troubled mind.

He heard a girl's voice say very quietly, 'Here, take these.

Then you will sleep more comfortably.' He felt her hand prop up his wobbling, groggy head, and she placed a glass of something wet to his lips; when he opened them she gave him a pill, then another one. He swallowed more water and it made his parched throat feel easier. The girl moved her hand away and put the glass down. She shifted his legs so that his body lay in a straighter, more comfortable position. There she was looking down at him again. This time his barely conscious mind could just discern that she was smiling. He tried to speak, but the words simply refused to form themselves. If anything at all registered in Karl Reuben's wearied brain at that moment it was only that he was drained, exhausted physically and mentally. And he ached from head to foot. There was no energy available for any effort at arousal yet. He let his eyelids fall shut again and fell asleep.

When she went into the kitchen the men were already sitting round a table eating soup and large hunks of bread, while their colourless hostess was cooking the veal. Abdullah was going methodically through the next stage of the plan with Okana; discussing his exact role just so far as they intended him to know. They had so little of any language in common with the younger Japanese gunman that Okana had to explain everything to him anyway. It was a good thing that Japanese instructor at Haddad's school at Champ Kyayat spoke fluent Arabic; especially these days when so many Palestinians themselves had lost the stomach for terrorist activities. Moda sat down hungrily to a large plate of steaming hot vegetable soup and said to Abdullah, 'Did you get our friend at Graz all right?'

'Yes,' he replied, 'everything is in order for us to cross tonight.'

They ate their wiener schnitzel and noodles heartily and Abdullah allowed they could spare another ten minutes for coffee. The grey lady who made a comfortable living providing discreet services like this for those whose movements required secrecy had relaxed a little by now, becoming positively chatty.

'How's your friend Carlos these days?' she asked Abdullah. He looked surprised. 'My friend?'

109

'Well,' she said, 'he's one of your lot, isn't he?'

Abdullah gave Moda one of his most sardonic smiles; it was common knowledge the lecherous Carlos had tried to bed her down and been roundly slapped for his pains. It was well known that the same could be said about many women. There were two great sorrows in Carlos's life these days, first that there was almost nothing in Aden on which to spend the blood money Gaddafi had paid him, and second that pretty young Arab girls were not nearly as promiscuous as he had persuaded himself to believe.

'Yes, I suppose, in a way, he's one of our lot,' Abdullah said, 'but nobody has much use for him these days.'

'Never did like him myself,' the landlady said. 'Nasty, conceited brute he was.'

'How do you know Carlos?'

'Who do you think looked after him when he was here?' she said self-importantly.

'He stayed here when he was planning the OPEC kidnapping?' Moda asked.

'And other places. I arranged them all.'

This could have been an interesting topic of after dinner conversation, but that was not their business. Abdullah said they must leave by seven. Yali picked up the car keys he had been given and went out to the garage; he brought the big green Fiat station wagon up to the kitchen door. The two Japs very carefully carried Reuben out of the house with Moda fussing round as though she really was a nurse. Abdullah watched with amusement, enjoying a rather surprised sense of satisfaction. While Yali showed Okana the basic layout of the Opel the young Japanese and Moda settled Reuben between them in the back seat of the Fiat; Abdullah got in next the driving seat; Yali drove the Fiat, while Okana came behind, alone, in the Opel. The plan was to try to keep within sight of each other, but if that was not possible Yali would slow down to thirty kilometres an hour when he hit the new six lane highway they would pick up at Hartburg, which should give Okana ample time to catch up before they left it again at the turn-off for Furnstenfeld and the

Hungarian border. They took a roundabout route out of town, avoiding main intersections, and headed south. As they left the town they heard on the car radio that their colleagues who had skyjacked the Lufthansa 737 had now landed at Dubai. The German government refused to negotiate. Something had gone wrong.

Traffic was reasonably thin at this hour, the sky heavily over-cast, and about eight o'clock it started to rain. When they were approaching Helligenkreuz, one of the few places where it is possible to cross the thickly defended and ceaselessly patrolled Hungarian frontier, it was just after nine and the wind was driving the rain across the highway reducing visibility to no more than a couple of hundred metres. The road was quite deserted and just before reaching the lights of the town Yali pulled in and stopped at a spot where a small wood came right down to the edge of the highway. Okana drew up behind him. Yali got out of the station wagon, Moda whispered 'Good luck,' and Abdullah slid across into the driving seat. Yali got into the Opel with Okana and they drove off toward the border. Abdullah watched their rear lights disappear in the rain ahead of them.

Driving out of Austria on a minor traffic artery is pretty much the same casual process it would be in any other country in Western Europe, or between Canada and the United States. The buildings of the small town came to an end and gave way to farmers' fields. A hundred metres farther on there was a simple red and white steel barrier across the road and a small white painted concrete hut containing one lonely and bored young policeman. No one in the Austrian government ever felt any compelling urge to plant land-mines, watch towers and barbed wire along their borders; nor any cause to have them bristling with heavily armed soldiers. Their chief concern with border crossings was to make it as easy as possible for foreigners to enter the country and swell the revenues of Austria's vital tourist trade.

As Okana drove the Opel up to the hut the young policeman unconcernedly put on a heavy raincoat and walked over to the car. He saw it was a black Opel, hesitated for a moment, but there were clearly only two men in it. He proceeded to his duty. Okana put down the window and handed out a plastic pouch designed to contain passports and similar documents. The policeman turned to walk back inside to examine them. Yali shot him through the back. The gun had a silencer. There was no one about to see the victim fall face down in the mud. Yali was out of the car before the body hit the dirt, picked up the passport pouch where it had fallen from lifeless hands, opened the steel barrier, and climbed back in. They drove cautiously out into no-man's-land, more than a kilometre of scrub with a thin pine wood which gave out at a small stream marking the actual frontier. The car lights picked up a large red and white sign proclaiming in four languages, 'The People's Republic of Hungary.'

Yali said. 'Stop the car a moment. I just want to be certain the others got through all right.' He slipped out on to the muddy, rain soaked road and walked to the back of the car. As he passed the rear mudguard he quietly pressed a small, sticky glob of something against the cap of the gas tank. Then he walked on, counting his carefully timed steps. 'One, two, three . . .' At eight he was in the shelter of the pine trees. He kept on walking. 'Seventeen, eighteen, nineteen . . . now.' As he said 'now' there was a violent explosion behind him, a searing streak of flame blazed up into the night sky. 'Tough luck, Okana,' he said to himself, 'long live the Japanese Red Army.' Yali turned off the road to the north and started to run. In a few seconds there was another blaze of light as the Hungarian frontier post came to life, floodlights and searchlights combing the road toward the inferno that had been an automobile half a kilometre west of them. He could hear the sound of armoured cars starting up and officers shouting orders. He smiled to himself, he could afford to; the woods gave him good cover from all that activity, and he knew the Hungarians would not cross the stream. It would be at least five minutes before the Austrian police could be on the scene to investigate. Yali was tough and fit. And he knew exactly where he was going.

On the Austrian side another road ran northward parallel

to the border. Yali came out on it more than a kilometre north of Helligenkreuz and stood in the shadow of the pine trees. A police car came down from the north, light flashing and siren screaming. It raced past him toward Helligenkreuz. A minute later he saw the lights of another car approaching from the south, going very slowly. Yali was confident it would be the green Fiat, but he couldn't take a chance of showing himself until he had made positive identification. It was. It slowed down to a walk, Yali waited till it passed him then leaped from his hiding place, raced alongside, and slid into the front seat beside Abdullah. The car speeded up and they drove another six kilometres north till they turned westward at Güssing, and then doubled back on a series of carefully chosen country roads until they were once more heading south on secondary roads well away from the frontier. No one here would be concerned with the movements of a green Fiat station wagon. They headed for a little town called Radkersburg, a few kilometres south of where the borders of Austria, Hungary and Yugoslavia all meet together.

They sat in total silence for nearly fifteen minutes. Then the young Japanese could not contain his anxiety any longer. In his faltering German, he wanted to know where Okana was. When would he rejoin them? Were they in Hungary now? Abdullah reassured him in his soft, velvety voice. All would be well. All would be well. Okana would join them again very soon. Knowing the young Jap could not understand a word of Arabic he told Moda and Yali to speak in their native tongue. Moda examined her patient as closely as she could and reported his breathing seemed more regular. He was sleeping soundly.

Abdullah said, 'Sorry we had to do that. I was beginning to like Okana.'

Moda said, with evident pride, 'That was a brilliant plan of Haddad's.'

Yali said matter of factly, 'Yes, if it works.' Like all Haddad's best pupils the cold blooded killing of two men left him totally unmoved.

Abdullah lit a cigarette and took a long, contented drag. He said, 'If it keeps the Austrian police looking in the wrong direction for two, maybe three, days, that will be enough to get us through to friendly territory. In the meantime,' he added sombrely, 'we now have to get across Yugoslavia; there will be nobody looking for us there, but, we have no friends until we cross the next frontier.' He was silent for a moment while his eyes surveyed the dimly lit dashboard in front of him. Then he said, 'We'll have to stop for gas before we leave Austria.'

As they approached a main road junction ten kilometres short of Radkersburg he was relieved to see the lights of a service station loom up in the murky rain soaked darkness ahead of them. He approached the isolated patch of cold luminous brilliance which sparkled off the smooth wet concrete surface showing up the blue garage with its white roof and its three bright blue and white pumps standing rigidly like sentries in front of it. They pulled to a stop by the middle pump. A young attendant muffled up in a shiny white raincoat came across to them. Abdullah wound down the window, handed out the key to the gas tank, and said in his best German, 'Fill it up, please.' When the attendant finished his task he came to the window to collect the money; 'That will be a hundred and ninety schillings,' he said cheerfully. They were talking about the trip across Yugoslavia, but in German now for the attendant's benefit. As Abdullah was fumbling out his wallet and selecting the proper notes, he said in reply to a query from Moda, 'It will take us two days to reach the Yugoslavian frontier.' The attendant went inside to get the change. He returned with a slightly puzzled look on his face, handed over some small notes and coins and was about to say something when Abdullah wished him a friendly 'Good-night', wound up the window and the car moved off. The young man shrugged his shoulders and went back inside out of the storm. The car disappeared into the darkness.

They drove in silence into the little town until they reached the market square. The rain and wind were good friends for their purpose and the streets were virtually deserted; the cinema had closed an hour ago, and the only lights showing were from a small café bar, and the window of a drug store. There were two deserted cars parked across from the town hall. They drove slowly around the square and as they cleared the double row of plane trees autumn shorn of foliage on the opposite side they got their first view of a truck laden with milk churns parked there. As they went past it at a walking pace they could see a man sitting in the driver's seat idly smoking a cigarette. Abdullah went to the next corner, stopped, and turned around. As he moved very cautiously back down the street the truck driver flashed his lights twice, quickly. Abdullah did the same and instantly they heard the harsh throb of the truck's engine being started. They kept their eyes on him anxiously as they rounded the square a second time going in the opposite direction. The truck moved forward slowly and they had comfortable time to catch up with him just as he turned off a side street running to the north. They kept a respectful distance following him out into the country. After about three kilometres they came to a defile between two small hills, where not a light showed in any direction. The truck stopped and Yali ran ahead and jumped up into the cab with the driver.

The two men just looked at each other and the driver put it into gear. After a few minutes he turned off the main road to the east. For fifteen minutes the truck and the car wound through country lanes, over rolling hills, and then turned into a thick woods. Here they left the road altogether and took what appeared to be a lumbermen's track through the forest. They crossed two small streams, emerged from the forest and turned on to what seemed to be a farm track. Twice they heard dogs bark but there was no sign of any human stirring at that hour of the night in the hostile weather. They came out onto a main road and drove for another two or three kilometres until they could see the lights of a largish town casting a glow up into the sodden clouds some way ahead of them. The truck stopped and the Fiat pulled up close behind. The driver turned to Yali, held out an envelope and said, 'You're in Yugoslavia now. That's Murska Sobota ahead.'

Yali exchanged envelopes with the driver and each held what they had received under the dash lights to examine the contents.

The driver flipped his fingers over a package of thousand-schilling notes and appeared satisfied. Yali checked five new Austrian passports each containing nothing but the marks of an ink stamp recording their legal entry into Yugoslavia, and the visa necessary for their next border crossing. In the morning he would insert the necessary photographs and personal details which he had carefully prepared and ready. Without a word he got down into the road, the truck turned round and drove off. Yali climbed back into the Fiat, which went on into Murska Sobota and turned south again on the main highway sign-posted to Zagreb. The clock on the town hall as they passed it read five minutes to one.

They drove all night, Abdullah and Yali sharing the driving while the other one tried to get some sleep. The three in the back seat slept fitfully and Moda was tempted to try one of those red pills herself. They made good time on the deserted highways and as dawn began to reflect its own glory on the calm waters of the Adriatic drove up in front of a cheap waterfront hotel in the bustling, cosmopolitan seaport of Rijeka, the capital of Yugoslavia's extensive maritime industry. It was the sort of establishment accustomed to people coming and going at all hours, where nobody asked any questions. Somehow they got Reuben out of the car on his own two feet, with a lot of help from Moda and the young Japanese, but still in a state of docile semi-consciousness. They had no trouble getting two large rooms, one for the three men, the other for Moda and her patient. As soon as she had him behind a locked door Moda got another two strong pills down Reuben's throat, undressed him and put him to bed. Then she too collapsed exhausted on the other bed. She felt Kaled would be proud of her.

CHAPTER ELEVEN

Weary as she was from the long, uncomfortable night spent in the car, three of them packed tight together in the swaying back seat, Moda was only able to sleep for a couple of hours. By half past nine the hurly burly of the streets lining the harbour outside the hotel, the clanking of railway freight cars in and out of the docks, and the vainglorious screechings of a hundred tugs and assorted small boats as they bustled around the giant freighters and cruise ships, made sleep impossible. Her first reaction on being harshly awoken by a particularly piercing blast was, inevitably, irritation. Her back ached and her legs were stiff at the knees. She stretched and wriggled to try to relieve some of the kinks. The fresh cool feeling of cotton sheets touching her tired body brought on the consoling thought that this was the first time since they had left Beirut that she had slept in a clean bed. She looked round the bare room, dimly lit by the thin strips of light filtering in between the shutter slats. Spartan certainly, but clean, and a world away from that bug infested attic above the warehouse in Vienna. The Yugoslavian tourist authorities were sticklers for hygiene, even amongst third class hotels.

Then she looked across at the other bed only three feet away from her. The muscular lines of the lean back and shoulders, the short, straight rumpled hair, and one slightly hairy arm lying above the cheap coverlet were sufficiently illuminated by stripes of sunlight to leave no doubt that it was a man lying there. This was no dream she was living through. She tried to turn reality over in her mind. That man had been her sister's lover. Three months ago when a bullet from the rifle of an Israeli soldier had passed clean through that sister's head Moda's pent-up fury and passion had burst with a venom that for weeks had almost consumed her. There had even been moments when it frightened her. She had been born in a refugee camp on the southern slopes of Mount Hebron, where every day as a child grew up it could watch the waters of the Jordan moving idly, effortlessly down into the land one's ancestors had inhabited for thirteen hundred years, from which one was constantly reminded one's own parents had fled. For Moda, as for countless thousands of others, the natural happy-making instincts of childhood had been twisted and strained from birth. Many of the youngsters of her ill-fated generation had managed to grow up to face the world with some vestige of faith and hope, even if not much charity. Many had not. In one way she had long known she was luckier than most; in the years before the government of Lebanon had been the victim of mayhem by its own heterogeneous people it had been possible for a bright, hard working teenager to get scholarships to foreign universities. She had been both. Three years in Vienna studying European languages and history had forced upon her begrudging but lively intelligence the realisation that there was, after all, something more to life than everlastingly brooding on the blood feud between the Arabs and the Jews. It also sparked off that schizophrenic condition which so often tortures the clever student brought up in humble circumstances: one day, unprepared and unaware, that awful moment suddenly strikes when, for the first time, one's devotion and dedication to the lowliest and humblest of 'my people', 'God's people', the noblest most idealistic people in the world, are abruptly punctured by a burst of angry frustration upon discovering how dull and stupid and infuriating many of them are! It is a critical human experience, which has broken the hearts of earnest reformers since the beginning of time. Love, after all, is not enough. Nor is hate.

Her return to Lebanon in 1975 had not resolved those doubts, but it had allowed her to submerge them in the sea of violent activity into which she had enthusiastically plunged. In the three years she had been away the world of her childhood had been shattered, and grim though that world had been, it at least had had a simple stability which young people crave. Now, the country was torn with strife and bloodshed, everyone's hand against his neighbour. The anarchy which enveloped her led easily, without conscious thought, into recruitment to the PFLP, the most violent and militant of the many factions into which her own people had splintered. She was smuggled into Israel to make contact with her sister. It wasn't difficult, nearly a quarter of a million Arabs had never left Israel; providing they kept out of trouble the Jewish authorities made many efforts to befriend them. They had civil rights, they could vote. Neither side ever really got close to the other but there were plenty of pragmatic realists in both camps more interested in staying alive than fighting.

And then Kaled had been shot! If she hadn't met him she would still be alive. My dear, happy, carefree sister. That man lying there is my enemy! As the thought crossed Moda's troubled mind one hand automatically slid under the pillow and gripped the butt of her Walther nine millimetre. With silencer. That was one of the first lessons she had learned from Haddad, when you are on a mission never, never, never let your gun get out of your reach. Especially when you go to sleep. In the immediate impact of the horror of Kaled's death Moda had thrown herself into Haddad's horror training with such ferociousness it even scared some of her class mates. No fire was needed to stoke her capacity for hatred. She wanted to be taught how to kill. Quick. Often. She relished the idea of butchering the enemy. The deliberate indoctrination of enjoying inflicting suffering on others is a part of the Haddad curriculum. Innocent, are they? Weren't we? Needless suffering? Who have suffered more needlessly than the Palestinian people? And who have suffered for so long? The obvious answers to such questions, that countless millions of human beings have known similar woes since the beginning of time, especially the Jews, are submerged in a flood of carefully contrived emotional ranting that drives both reason and human compassion into the wilderness.

Haddad developed his techniques from study of the Nazi propagandist, Josef Goebbels; the incubator for so many of Haddad's teachings.

Last night in the car, as they drove twisting, undulating roads through the wild, rugged country across Croatia, for long weary hours her body pressed against that of this man on whom she had sworn vengeance, against whom she had these three months entertained such a hatred as she had never experienced before, she had the opportunity to think seriously for the first time about the extraordinary trick fate had played on her. 'Keep your mind concentrated on what your sister told you.' That's what Habash had kept repeating to her. 'The whole success of this operation depends on your doing exactly that. Never lose sight of it. You're special. This mission is special. You are not being sent out to shock the western countries with screaming headlines of sky-jackings and shootings. This mission will give us a chance, a small but a real chance, to lay our hands on a new, unique weapon of revenge and terror which can change the course of history. Gaddafi can supply all the money and the laboratories and the computers Reuben may need. Only *you* can ever make him work!' She could still hear Habash saying it.

And that meant that she had to persuade him, to nurse him, to live with him. However repulsive she might find him it meant she would almost certainly have to let him, help him, make love to her. Haddad even taught his girl pupils how to do that; the time-worn and cynical adage, when rape is inevitable relax and enjoy it, was just the starting point in the course. She was already safely over the first hurdle; the shock of first touching him had passed off quickly. She remembered only a few hours ago when she had actually undressed him and put him to bed. He was only another man. Yes, but he was unconscious. How will I feel when he's conscious? When he touches me? Moda's physical passions were not immature. She knew she must not let her mind dwell on such thoughts. Concentrate on what your sister told you! For an instant it flashed across her mind, there was always just a possibility that the very violence of her fury might burn itself out. She rejected it vehemently. I won't forget what my sister told me. I'll never falter in my sacred duty to the revolution and my people. If I have to love him I'll love him till it kills him. But I'll still hate him!

Reuben was still asleep. She raised herself and sat on the side of the bed looking at him. Her watch said a few minutes before ten; the sleeping pills she had given him should be effective till about noon. She tried to shut the street noises out of her ears to listen to his breathing as Abdullah had instructed her. She thought it was easier, more regular than last night. She had comfortable time to wash and dress and go about her business. In strict accord with training rules she reached under the pillow and picked up her gun. She stood there for a moment looking down at the drugged man lost in peaceful sleep his head a few inches from her thighs. And was suddenly struck by the bizarre thought that she was stark naked, holding only her gun. Like most Arab girls Moda still retained a strong streak of old-fashioned modesty; she went across to her small suitcase and hurriedly dressed. She had every desire to postpone the moment, the probably inevitable moment, when Karl Reuben would have to see her naked.

She slipped quietly out of the room, carefully locking the door behind her. She knocked at the door of the men's room and had a brief conference with Abdullah and Yali. Yali gave her her new passport which he had by now expertly doctored. They left their door open so one of them could always keep an eye on that opposite. The young Jap was sitting morosely staring out at the sea.

She stopped at the desk in the sparsely furnished front hall and spoke to the clerk in her best Viennese German. Fortunately he spoke good German. That was another hurdle over. She handed him her passport which the weary night clerk had obligingly not insisted on seeing when they had arrived just before dawn. She asked the quickest way to the shops she must visit, and to a bank. She noted there were several within a few blocks. The clerk happily answered all her questions. The thought that she might be anything other than an Austrian of

Slavic name and origin shown in her passport never crossed his mind.

She stepped out into the clear sunlight of a perfect late autumn day on the Adriatic coast. The ancient and historic harbour of Rijeka, which was known to the world as Fiume until as recently as 1945, is a fine sight, but hardly a beautiful one. It is Yugoslavia's most international city and sea port; which was why they had chosen it as their best possible haven along the journey south. The Croatian separatists having, for the present at any rate, been effectively crushed by President Tito's mildly authoritarian but efficient security forces, there was no network of safe houses to shelter them in Yugoslavia. The complex of docks and railway tracks was directly in front of her, the gently lapping sea only a few metres away. The scene was one of ships, large and small and no two alike, flying the flags of a dozen countries. There were two naval destroyers and some coastal patrol boats lying at anchor bearing witness to the care with which these waters were patrolled. Tito had years ago abandoned the *cordons sanitaires* with which the countries of the modern Russian Empire had been compelled to surround themselves, but the efficiency and incorruptibility of the police and immigration authorities had from the beginning ruled out the idea of trying to smuggle their prisoner across the Mediterranean from these ports.

She walked unconcernedly along the broad water-front, the jumble of ships and cranes and people and cargo on one side; on the other the shabby façades of the ornamented blocks of buildings the Italians had designed at the beginning of the century; a warren of commercial activity fronted by cafés, bars, and shipping offices. Just one street back from the sea lies Narodni Square and the Korso, the heart of Rijeka's shopping and entertainment district. She entered the first bank she came to, presented her passport, signed a form in the name of the bearer, Maria Sevcik, and changed five thousand schillings into dinars. She crossed the square and sat down at a sidewalk café where she breakfasted on cold ham, rolls and coffee. If Tito did not occasionally remember to use that amorphous word 'communism' one might easily think one was still in Austria. Or Italy. Which was logical; Rijeka had been a part of Habsburg or Italian domains for most of the last five centuries. From 1920 when the crazy dream of d'Annunzio's 'Free State' finally collapsed until 1945 when Tito annexed the city, the border between Italy and Yugoslavia had been nothing more than a wall along a canal only a few blocks from where Moda sat enjoying her breakfast. She paid her bill, and went shopping.

She had never shopped for a man before and the experience amused her. She bought him a toothbrush, soap, comb, a safety razor, brush and shaving cream. She went into several small clothing shops and bought him a sweater, tee shirt, socks, a pair of slacks which were probably a bit too big for him, and some underwear. She figured he could manage the few days before they reached Libya in the shoes he was wearing. She went to a grocer and got some fruit, bread and plum jam, and a bottle of milk. She hoped he liked milk because she had been instructed that the sedative powder she must now get into Reuben without him realising it was not easily detectable when dissolved in it. On the way back she passed another drug store and on impulse she went in and bought some basic cosmetics for herself. She had not worn make-up since she left university two years ago, but she remembered that Kaled had always worn it and it occurred to her it might make her more attractive to him. She knew that if she tried she could look as pretty as Kaled always did. She found this very feminine line of thought slightly amusing. At first. When she found herself actually enjoying it, she felt a little frightened. She must concentrate on her duty; not on Kaled's relationship with this man, but on what Kaled had told her.

Moda walked casually back to the hotel in a state of as near contentment of mind as she had known for a long time. She checked with Abdullah and agreed she would try to have Reuben ready to leave about one o'clock. Life suddenly seemed almost normal. Barring something totally unexpected, there was every reason to believe they would be safely out of Yugoslavia by tomorrow evening. For the first time in months the tension in her body seemed to be subsiding, and she felt a little more confident in her ability to keep Karl Reuben in a reasonable state of docility, at least until they got him aboard the boat. She was not yet ready to attempt to speculate beyond that.

She turned the key and let herself quietly into the room. From the look of him Karl Reuben had scarcely moved since she left more than an hour ago. She locked the door again and stood silently listening, and watching him. He seemed to gasp a bit from time to time, but other than that his breathing was steady. Has he got a bad heart? She didn't remember Kaled ever saying anything about it. Hopefully, that noticeable irregularity Abdullah spotted at Weiner Neustadt was only the temporary result of fear and a strong anaesthetic. She went over to the simple wooden table by the wash basin and started to unwrap her parcels; she wanted to make just enough noise to help him wake up. They had a long journey ahead of them. As she took the make-up she had bought out of the brown paper bag she looked at herself in the mirror nailed to the wall above the basin. Her hair wasn't a mess exactly, just black and straight and cut off short. It was hair, that was all. She remembered the way Kaled used to wear hers, long and wavy so that it swept off her shoulders; she remembered that when she was a teenager she used to think her big sister looked like a movie star. Then she was cross with herself for indulging such silly, selfish vanities. Haddad had lectured them about the dangers of soft thinking too. She could not remember much of what he had said because at the time she felt indignant that he should think it needed saying at all. Now? The only way to deal with such thoughts was to shut them out of her mind completely. She put the make-up in her handbag; she might use it later, if she felt it was necessary in her struggle to win Reuben's acquiescence.

She was laying out the clothes she had bought him on the dresser when she heard the sound of movement from the bed behind her. She turned her head and saw him lying facing her, his head propped up on one elbow. She had rehearsed this moment carefully and the response was simple; a reassuring smile and 'Good morning, hope you slept well.'

124

'Yes, quite well thank you.' That was the first time she had heard his voice since Kaled's trial. For the first time in a long while it came back to her in a rush that his normal speaking voice was gentle, with a deep, lilting timbre about it. Kaled had told her before she met him that his voice was seductive. She remembered that Kaled had lived with him for more than a year before she joined the PFLP. She really had loved him. Damn! Why do these sentimental, bourgeois thoughts keep popping up in my head? She had known she would have to face these moments, but they were coming quicker and more frequently than she had bargained for. Her instantaneous impulse was to throw something at him and scream, 'Damn you! Damn you! You killed my sister!' She bit her lip so hard she drew blood, and tears welled up in her eyes.

'You feeling all right?' he said, his voice giving every sign of genuine anxiety for her.

Damn you again! her mind exploded. This is idiotic! All the wrong way round. He's feeling sorry for me! Having surmounted the initial shock of touching him it had not crossed her mind that talking to him for the first time would be so emotionally disturbing. She was furious with herself. And with him. For one horrible moment she felt trapped.

She turned her face away from him and started to unwrap the food parcels. She had to get control of herself. It did not help that the total silence from the bed kept her conscious of the unwelcome fact that he was lying quite still, watching her. It was nearly a minute before she felt calm enough to say, 'Yes, I'm all right. Just tired. Didn't get much sleep last night.'

'I've been asleep since yesterday afternoon,' he said as though it were the most natural thing in the world. Then in the same gentle tones, without a trace of rancour or resentment, he added, 'You've been drugging me, haven't you?'

Another cell in Moda's self-composure blew! Damn again! He's not cross. He's not frightened. Well, what did she expect him to say? He's going to be nice and docile, isn't that what we wanted? Her primitive feminine instinct saved her. She picked up the toothbrush and selection of toilet articles she had bought him. She forced a smile and walking over to him said simply, 'Here, I bought you these.'

He sat up and held his hands out, not knowing what 'these' might be. Their fingers touched; he showed no sign of reaction of any kind, but Moda found herself clenching her jaw to stop it quivering. He looked them over quizzically, rubbed his chin, and said quietly, 'Thank you. That is kind. I look a bit of a mess, I'm afraid.' He started to get out of bed, then paused on the edge with the cotton coverlet rather coyly draped around his middle. He said, 'You undressed me and put me to bed last night?'

She had moved across the room and was opening the shutters. That was more like it, she could deal with that. With a slight smile she replied, 'Someone had to. You needed a good rest.' To which he gave the unexpected reply, 'Then you won't mind my being naked, will you?' and promptly got up. Moda saw the funny side of it and without a word threw him a towel. He just said, 'Thank you,' and wound it round him. As he walked across to the wash basin he saw the new men's clothes laid out neatly on the dresser.

'For me?' he enquired, still his speech gave not the slightest indication of anxiety, or even curiosity.

'Yes,' she said, 'the clothes you were wearing were pretty scruffy. You haven't been looking after yourself properly.' That little speech, carefully rehearsed, made her feel much better; it was the first time she had succeeded in getting their conversation into the track she had planned it should take. She kept the initiative she had won with such difficulty. 'I've got some food for you, when you're ready. You like fruit, I remember.' She was rather pleased with that line too; and she was becoming puzzled that so far he had given no sign of recognition at all. It was inconceivable he did not know who she was. Or was it? Had some shock caused him to lose his memory? Her brain spun again! After all this trouble, all this risk, all our hopes, have we got nothing but an empty shell of a man?

As if fate was again playing childish games with her, he

replied in the same even, gentle voice, 'Oh yes. I like fruit very much, thank you.' Moda's tormented brain notched up a new anxiety. During the shaving and dressing operation neither of them said a word. She was uncomfortably conscious that he was watching her closely, either directly or in the mirror. She packed his old clothes and her own few essentials in a rucksack and started to prepare some food for him. Then he created a situation that completely threw her.

'I have to go to the loo.'

They hadn't thought of that, and the consternation that showed in her face made it obvious. She stumbled with words for a moment and said, 'You'll have to use the one across the hall, but . . .'

'It's all right. I won't run away. I don't want to be shot.'

She went to the door while he stood quietly watching her. She showed him where it was and stood in the hall her hand seeking reassurance by feeling her gun. For some ridiculous reason she was too embarrassed to summon the aid of her male colleagues in this unforeseen emergency. After a moment he came out and straight back into the bedroom.

Reuben sat down at the table and the first sign of animation he showed was when he dug the spoon into a large, juicy orange. He wolfed it down, and Moda offered another. 'Yes please,' he said, 'I'm starved.' He ate two thick slices of bread covered with Yugoslav plum jam, gulped down the milk and asked for more.

It was getting on for one o'clock and Moda was increasingly anxious over an increasing number of things. They had a long drive ahead of them, and reason to fear that much of the route they had to travel would be over winding, narrow roads. Their timetable left little room for unexpected delays. She was worried that when the time came that Abdullah would ask her about her charge she was completely at a loss what she should say. His continued, quiet, behaviour, saying practically nothing and then only in monosyllables, left all the important questions unanswered, and raised a whole host of new ones. She pondered again on the unexpected, and disturbing, phenomenon that while Reuben showed no fear of her at all, she was feeling just a little afraid of him.

'You're very quiet. You didn't used to be so quiet,' she ventured, trying to draw him out.

He drained the last of the milk, and wiped a hand towel across his mouth.

'I was very hungry. I feel better now.'

'Good, I'm glad. We have rather a long journey ahead of us.'

'Where are you taking me?' he asked, still without emotion of any kind.

'We're taking . . . we're going to Libya.'

'Oh, I see.' He looked at her and for the first time they stared right into each other's eyes. They both had very similar eyes, dark brown, deep set, large eyes, sad eyes. For the first time both felt some unquestionable glimmer of sympathy in the other's eyes.

'Libya,' he continued in the same soft, velvety tone; 'why didn't you kill me at Zurndorf?'

'Karl, nobody wants to kill you!' she blurted the words out before taking a second to think. She never intended to talk like that to him; to use that personal, concerned tone of voice to him. It even sounded in her own ears as though she cared. Cared? No, she didn't care! When they were finished with him she didn't give a damn who killed him! Oh God, she thought, this isn't at all the way it is all supposed to be. She must control herself. She was engaged on a vital mission. A dangerous mission. She had called him 'Karl'. To hell with Karl! She concentrated her mind on Habash. On Haddad. On what her sister had told her. The whole process took thirty seconds, but she made it.

'Why are we going to Libya then?'

'So you can continue with your scientific work.'

He considered that a moment.

'Kaled told you about my work?'

'Yes, she did.'

'And that is why you . . . you, and your friends, kidnapped me?'

'Kidnapped is not a very nice word, Karl.'

'No, Moda, it is not.' He had used her name at last. Her fears about his memory receded. 'But it is the correct word, is it not?'

'Yes, I suppose it is.' Once again she found herself unable to resist the impulse to talk to him simply, frankly, like a friend. He's my enemy, never forget that! But my duty is to make him a friend. In no other way can our objective be achieved. The theory had all sounded so easy. Probably it was to Habash and Haddad. Moda was finding the application was in some danger of tearing her apart. But she believed she was getting the feel of it. She continued with a sufficient measure of calm this time, 'But we're at war, Karl. A lot of unpleasant things have happened.'

To her surprise he said something she would never have said; had never even thought of.

'That is true, Moda. Very unpleasant things. On both sides.' He looked very deliberately down at her hips where the bulge of her gun was just barely visible. 'You are PFLP too, aren't you?'

'I must serve my people,' she said firmly.

'Of course, I know that. That is what Kaled said when your people recruited her.'

'You knew Kaled had joined the PFLP?' she said horrified.

'Of course. We had no secrets from each other.'

Moda registered that here was one thing Kaled had *not* told her. The implications needed thinking about. Did Habash know this? There was no time to go into it now. They could both hear the three men in the hall, and knew that any moment there would be a knock on the door.

'We must go,' she said, 'wrap your toilet things in a towel and I'll put them in my rucksack.' She heard Abdullah's voice and called out, 'Just coming.' A very important hurdle had to be crossed. Right now. She turned and walked toward him, stopped only a pace in front of him, looked up into his face and came directly to the point, 'Karl, believe me, nobody wants to kill you. But, if you cause trouble . . . one of those men might decide he has to.'

He smiled at her, showing no sign of anxiety at all.

'I'm sure they would. And so would you, my dear.'

She very nearly spat in his face!

CHAPTER TWELVE

Despite the horrific implications of Jacob Kleinhart's discourse, and rather more stiff Scotches than he was accustomed to, Rupert had slept well. It was a habit, like many others, he had learned as a young soldier under the exhausting conditions of wartime, and he was careful never to lose it. As he showered and shaved his normal exuberance was struggling hard to reassert itself after the melodramatic series of unrequited batterings it had taken in the last forty-eight hours; but it was uphill work. There was no Sandra smiling across the breakfast table at him with those luscious big brown eyes of hers, and that ever so slightly sad smile that massaged a strong protective male hormone somewhere inside him; and Frau Kröner didn't come in until ten on Saturdays so he had to get his own breakfast. He read yesterday's London *Times* and found not a cheerful item in it. *Die Presse* carried a few lines in the stop press section about the death of a policeman and a car explosion at some obscure little town on the Hungarian border, no details had yet been issued. The United Nations World Intellectual Property Organisation were to have a meeting in Vienna. For heaven's sake, what do you suppose they do? He recalled once hearing an intellectual defined as a person who had been educated beyond the point of common sense. Experience had taught him it was true more often than not.

He walked downstairs into the gallery at nine o'clock as usual and said good morning to Heinz and the girls and then one flight back up to be assailed by the emptiness of his office. No Charlie. Neither on the right chair nor the wrong one. Then he remembered Jo Liebmann had promised the police would bring Charlie home sometime today. He suddenly remembered all the promises he had made in connection with getting Sandra home too. Frau Hauptmann was instructed to pack a suitcase of fresh clothes: 'You know, just the things she'll need, dress, stockings, shoes, I suppose, that's all.' Men never understand what is really important to a woman. Heinz rushed the case round to the hospital with a message that as soon as Sandra was ready to leave she was to phone and Rupert would come for her himself.

That out of the way he was ready to face his desk. Thank goodness there wasn't much on it. He looked at the letters for his attention still lying in a neat pile in the centre of the blotter where they should have been dealt with yesterday. There was a long, rambling letter from David Hughes, the irascible but brilliant young Welshman, whom Rupert had recently put in charge of the London gallery when he moved Nigel Coleman to Chicago. David's artistic knowledge was monumental for his age; his sense of values was profound, which in the art business means always remembering whether you are buying or selling; but like a number of the up and coming generation in the trade he was more interested in the artists than the customers, which really wasn't quite the right balance. He would dress like the artists too, which was not at all Rupert's style. Anyway, he had great affection for David; he tried to fathom what this long rigmarole was all about and made a note for Frau Hauptmann to make certain enquiries.

His heart wasn't in it. He knew there was no hope of getting to Semmering this week-end. He didn't like being restless. The usual sedative was music. Music? Mozart? Good Lord, Mozart! What on earth have I done with young Reuben's papers? In all the excitement he had completely forgotten that cheap little suitcase which he had purloined from the tower room. He thought for a moment, hurried upstairs to his apartment. There it was sitting in the cloakroom, right where he had left it. Picking it up with a sigh of relief he carried it into the drawing-room and sat down at the piano. Now he was very much in the mood for music. The first sheets he looked at were such a mass of scribbles and scratching out as to be unintelligible. Then he found some that looked more familiar. He hummed a few bars and then tried them out on the keyboard. That has the authentic ring of Mozart all right. He turned a few more leaves and came to a sheet on which someone had written 'revised score for the fifth variation on B flat'. It completely stumped him. It was unhummable and undoubtedly unplayable. If Mozart wrote that he must have been drunk. Or did Mozart write it? No of course he didn't, Reuben did. Maybe Reuben had not intended it to be played?

There was a gentle but firm tapping at the door, and Frau Hauptmann put her head around it. Please, could they finish his letters before lunch? Rupert returned to work full of apologies.

Where was I? The mail. Of course. He sat down, lit a pipe and turned a somewhat calmer mind to the letters in front of him. A French lady living in Switzerland, very rich, who bought pictures from him from time to time wrote a long, involved letter and enclosed a sheaf of photographs of chairs. Why all these chairs? The letter disclosed that she had recently bought a set of sixteen fine dining-room chairs at an auction in Lausanne for an inordinate amount of money; she had thought they were English Georgian, but there was no authentication, and did dear Monsieur Conway think she had been cheated? Since she knew he was too busy to come to Switzerland – too damn mean to pay my fare, the old bitch, was the somewhat uncharitable thought which flashed through Rupert's canny brain – she wondered if the dear Monsieur Conway could give an opinion from the photographs she had had specially taken, just for him.

Authenticate Georgian chairs from photographs? What does she think I am? Rupert looked at a selection of them on the desk and something in the design rang a faint bell somewhere in the back of his mind. He picked up a magnifying glass and studied them one after another meticulously. Then he wrote some notes across the back of the lady's letter for Frau Hauptmann to incorporate into a suitably flowery letter, 'the chairs are very handsome and at today's ridiculous prices' – Rupert didn't sell chairs – 'I should think you got value for money. So far as their origin is concerned I feel sure they are English, I suggest you turn them all upside down and carefully lift the seats out; I suspect that inside the frames of at least one or two of them you will find a little label that reads Maple & Co., Tottenham Court Road, London, and a date somewhere between 1920 and 1926.' He felt reasonably confident that great expert on English furniture, his old Gloucestershire friend Arthur Negus, would agree with him. He nearly added, 'send her a bill for a hundred Swiss francs', but thought better of it. She might want to buy another picture one day.

His elderly and saintly partner, Max Kallendorf, came tottering into the office; still hobbling on a cane from his most recent accident but smiling benevolence on the entire universe as always. Max looked round the office through his thick ungainly glasses and said, 'Where's Charlie this morning?' Rupert smiled, and without getting too involved in all the tangle of yesterday's adventures explained what had happened to Charlie.

They looked at each other in smiling silence for several seconds until Rupert said, 'Something I can do for you?'

Max pondered a moment, there must have been some trifle on his mind. 'Oh, yes. I quite forgot. That pretty little Dutch picture in the window . . .'

Rupert was well acquainted with Max's custom, perfectly sincere, of referring to any great work of art less than two thousand years old as a 'pretty little something or other', but this was a bit steep.

With mock severity he said, 'Are you referring to that superb painting by Nicolaes Van Verendael?'

Max's cherubic old face brightened, 'Yes. That's the fellow. Quite nice. Modern Dutch stuff.'

'Modern!' Rupert laughed. 'My dear Max, Van Verendael was born in 1640.'

Max looked positively impatient. 'Of course,' he said, 'I know that. And died in 1691.' The old boy taught fine art at Stanford University for five years during the Second World War and never let Rupert forget it. Having made his point he just sat there, smiling.

Rupert looked at him patiently for a moment, then he said, 'The Van Verendael, Max, what about it?'

'Ah,' Max animated himself again. 'There's a man in the gallery who wants to see the authentication.'

'Does he now? What sort of man, Max? Does he look as though he could afford one million schillings?'

'Definitely not,' Max shook his head. 'I know the type; he's probably some small town dealer fishing for information to impress somebody else with.'

'Tell him we keep such documents in the bank vault and he'll have to write for an appointment.'

'Quite right,' said Max and tottered happily out.

Just before eleven, and while Frau Kröner was in the act of carrying the coffee tray around to all the staff, the benign calm fitting to the headquarters of a famous international dealer in objects of fine art was shattered almost beyond repair. The coffee cups totally beyond repair. The door opened and a police-man released twenty pounds of yapping, shrieking, writhing, kinkly brown haired canine frenzy. Rupert rushed down into the gallery as fast as his very sore right leg would allow him and Charlie hit him at a full gallop which nearly knocked him down.

'All right, old chap, all right. God bless me, what a fuss! Yes, yes, it's good to have you back.' Rupert patted him from wriggling head down writhing back to the gyrating stub of a tail.

Charlie rushed from one person in the gallery to another like a wild thing, slipping and falling all over the highly polished floor, crashing into the debris of the coffee tray over which Frau Kröner was clucking like an angry hen and pushing broken china all over the room. In twenty-one years with the Herr Doktor Frau Kröner had never dropped the coffee tray before! It took Rupert longer to calm her down than to calm Charlie. Peace was eventually restored.

At eleven-thirty Rupert went for Sandra who returned home showing little outward trace of a very harrowing experience, and over a salad, cold meat and a glass of Chablis upstairs Rupert gave her a résumé of all that had happened since she disappeared Thursday night. So far today, there was no news of any kind, and no initiative he could think of to try. Crime detection can take a long time.

After lunch Sandra went to rest and Rupert continued his fitful attempts at normal work. Just after three Mini buzzed the phone on his desk and announced, 'Herr Hofrat Liebmann for you, Herr Doktor.' Rupert's heart jumped with elation, and he reckoned his adrenalin flow must be upsetting his blood count somewhere.

'Yes, Jo. What news?' he said eagerly. Jo must have news. He just has to have news. Or why would he be working Saturday afternoon?

'There is rather a lot, Rupert, and it's pretty complex. Werner is up to his eyes in this confounded Schleyer kidnapping, and has left this one to me. Freddy Kuso and I have just called a conference for four o'clock and we think you and your friend Dr Kleinhart will be able to help us. Can you make it?'

'Yes, of course I will,' his old enthusiasm for the hunt was fully in the ascendant again.

'Would you like me to send a car for you?' Jo said thoughtfully.

'That would be kind, Jo. To be quite frank I overdid the running around yesterday. My right leg's damn sore.'

'Ten to four,' Liebmann said and rang off.

They met in one of the conference rooms on the top floor of the Polizei Praesidium again. There were the same officers as at the meeting yesterday, plus Kuso himself with an aide, and two secretaries with a plethora of electronic equipment to ensure not a word or a thought missed the record. Liebmann took the chair, and with the help of the individual officers concerned with each stage of the saga proceeded to spell out the chapters of a very disjointed story.

'As of fourteen-forty-five today we have a number of reports, from several parts of the country, which may, or may not, bear some relation to each other. There has not yet been time to come to any firm conclusions. Perhaps this meeting will help. Since the pieces are a little confusing, and, I repeat, not necessarily related, I shall put them before you in strict time sequence.' He looked down to study his pages of notes, and checked a point with Kuso.

'Exhibit One. I think everyone round this table knows, we put out an emergency caution signal on a black Opel four door saloon car at eighteen-o-seven hours last night. Reports this morning show that one hundred and twenty-seven black four door Opel saloons were checked between then and o-eight-hundred. One hundred and twenty-five of them were readily identified as belonging to owners living in the vicinity of the observation, and whose movements were easily accounted for. The one hundred and twenty-sixth is a bit of a diversion, but, I expect you would like to hear it. It may well cause someone a hell of a lot of trouble, but, not us, I think. The vehicle in question belonged to a lady in Linz, and it was found parked in a country lane in the possession of her husband. According to the official report of the officer involved, a copy of which I have here, "at the moment I approached the car the male occupant was in the back seat having intimate contact with a female occupant who was not the owner." Not our business, I think.'

'There are two separate reports on the hundred and twenty-seventh which reached us from different sources some seventeen hours apart. The first one is that at nineteen-thirty last night the car was seen driving south from Wiener Neustadt on the main Graz road. A patrol car followed it, passed it, and made a careful observation. Since a male driver was the only occupant, and the car bore a diplomatic badge, the officer reported it and broke off contact. The licence number, by the way, we found shows that the car belongs to the Czech embassy. Point one that may, or may not, be significant.

'Sticking to time order, Exhibit Two, the next report that interests us comes from the border crossing into Hungary at Helligenkreuz, and reached us here at twenty-two hundred hours last night. The relevant facts appear to be these. Somewhere between twenty-one hundred and twenty-one fifteen

137

last night an unknown vehicle drove up to the frontier police-man's hut; the policeman was shot through the back, killed instantly. About the same time, presumably, a few minutes later, a vehicle blew up right on the actual border line some eight hundred metres from the police hut. The Burgenland forensic section have set up an emergency lab at the police station in Furstenfeld. The Minister has ordered two of our most experienced bomb experts to help them.' He looked at his watch. 'They should be there by now. Every man that can be mustered is on the job, but at present we have very little to go on. The last report we received states that no witnesses of any kind have been found; which is not surprising, it was a filthy night. The explosion caused such total disintegration of the vehicle that it will take hours to piece together the details. The officer in charge of the investigation will only say three things positively at present: one, the explosion was of such force that a bomb of some kind must have been planted in or under the vehicle; two, the total amount and general nature of the debris so far examined indicates that it was a large car, definitely not a truck or van, and that it was black; three, there are sufficient human remains to show that at least one, and possibly more, were in the car at the moment of explosion.

'We have two complications resulting from the actual site of the incident. It is possible, unlikely but possible, that some-how or other the cause was one of the landmines with which the Communists like to litter their frontiers. That would raise the awful problem of how the damned thing got on our side of the line. The other, of more immediate practical importance, is that the force of the explosion was such that a good deal of the wreckage was blown over to the Hungarian side, and as you would expect, they won't even allow our people to cross the border to look at it until everyone has gone through the proper channels and Budapest has sent its bloody permission, etc., etc., etc. Makes you sick! Can you imagine it? All these high priced bureaucrats sitting around in Belgrade arguing about "*détente*" and our friendly, peace loving neighbours will not even let a police officer six feet on their side of the border to investigate a

138

murder without applying to the Hungarian embassy for a visa! God alone knows what the Hungarians think happened there last night; they had armoured cars with machine-guns lumbering all over the place all night long.'

Jo took a drink from the water carafe in front of him, took out another, pre-loaded, pipe, and paused for breath.

'Now. So much for that little lot. Exhibit Three. A report received from Wiener Neustadt at thirteen-o-eight today. And I must admit I like this one. This is the second report on the black Opel. It seems that our colleagues at Wiener Neustadt have a thriving police cadet organisation. Yesterday afternoon from sixteen-thirty to seventeen-thirty a group of the boys were at police headquarters having a demonstration on road safety. Some time between seventeen-forty-five and eighteen hundred hours one of these bright lads was going home on his bicycle when a car just ahead of him suddenly turned into a driveway without giving any warning signal and he nearly ran into the back of it. Well, he didn't think he had power to arrest the driver, and he didn't get the licence number; but he did get a good look at the car and the occupants. Just before lunch this morning this lad went back to police headquarters to pick up a book he left behind last night, and being a keen type he stopped to look at the notice board on his way out. He read the notice with the red emergency sign over it about a black four door Opel saloon with a girl driving and two men passengers, so, he trotted along to the duty officer and says, "That must be the lot I nearly ran into last night." '

'Well done the cadets,' murmured Rupert.

'Well done indeed. I should darn well think so.' He turned to one of his assistants and said, 'Make a note; we must get that kid a citation of some kind. However, gentlemen, if Freddy and I are thinking clearly this afternoon, this is where a few threads look as though they're coming together. The duty officer tells a sergeant to hop in a squad car and the kid takes him right to the spot where the car turned in the gate. Sergeant notes the address and they return to station. Then they turn up two funny things. The lady who lives in that house came round to the station at five past nine this morning to report that during the night someone had stolen her son's car from her garage. A green Fiat station wagon; note that. Second funny thing, when the Security officer working on the black Opel case in that office saw the lady's name it sounded familiar to him. He spent some time going through his files and found out why. You all remember the OPEC ministers' kidnapping, at Christmas, nearly two years ago. Nobody in this building will ever forget it,' he said with heartfelt emphasis. 'Well now, this officer had been involved in the investigations to try to find where Carlos and his mob had been staying, and amongst a long list of possible suspects in those files he found this woman's name. Nothing had ever been proved against her, but she was a suspect, and it was known she was a person with a grudge against society. Our own government in particular, apparently. We're holding her for questioning, and of course we have full particulars on the green station wagon.

'So, the officer in charge of the investigations at Wiener Neustadt decided to play a hunch. He sought, and received, authority to put out an emergency caution signal on the green Fiat station wagon, same as we did on the Opel last night. And that leads us to Exhibit Four. Less than an hour later a squad car making a routine check on all gas stations that stay open late called at a station, way down in Styrmark some place,' he looked down at his notes and adjusted his glasses, 'just outside a town called Radkersburg. The man who owned the station sent for his son who was on duty last night, and bingo! A green Fiat station wagon with four men and a girl filled up there somewhere about twenty-three hundred hours. He says he remembered them particularly well because he was puzzled by something he heard them say. He says they spoke good German, but he was sure they were foreigners, and as they were dealing with the change he distinctly heard the driver say, "It will take us two days to reach the Yugoslavian frontier." He says he was about to tell them that the Yugoslavian frontier was only five kilometres up the road when they drove off.'

Liebmann sat back and rested his enormous arms on the sides

of his chair, 'And that, gentlemen, is the latest news hot off our wonderful computerised communications system. Anybody got any ideas?'

The discussion centred first on the Hungarian border incident. While they were talking a girl came in and handed a telex to one of Liebmann's assistants who read it and passed it straight over to his boss. Liebmann studied it and looked up saying, 'This may be helpful. The forensic lab at Furstenfeld have identified some piece of machinery that proves, to their satisfaction at any rate, that the blown up car was an Opel. They also now think that there was only one occupant, but it might be two.' He thought for a moment and said, 'So, instead of three or four people in the black Opel we now have one, or two. They kill a policeman, and head across for Hungary. Be interesting to see if the Czechs report the loss of one of their cars. We'd better be careful not to bring it to their attention. For a day or two at least.' He changed meerschaums again. Kuso picked up the train of thought, thinking out aloud: 'And the rest of the party were seen two hours later,' he consulted a map, 'nearly forty kilometres farther south, and five kilometres from the Yugoslavian border, where someone says it will take them two days to cross it.'

There was a long silence. Liebmann looked across at Kuso, 'These two incidents must be part of the same story, Freddy.'

He replied, 'Looks like it, Jo. Let's think about it along those lines for a bit.'

A lot of theories were put forward and tossed back and forth across the table. Then Liebmann said, 'If only one, or even two people were in the car that blew up while crossing into Hungary – leave aside why it may have blown up for the moment – and four, how many was it in the green Fiat?'

His assistant checked back through the telex sheets in front of him; 'Five, Herr Hofrat. Two men in front, a girl and two more men in the back.'

Liebmann thought a moment. 'Then at least it is clear that the car containing Reuben, I think we can safely assume they did kidnap Reuben, was the green Fiat. Freddy, no further report on it?'

'None, I'm afraid,' Kuso said, 'it has not been seen since the incident at the service station, twenty-three hundred hours last night. No record of it at any border crossing.'

Liebmann pondered again, 'So the kidnappers, with their prey, are, or were late last night, in a green Fiat station wagon, hiding somewhere in southern Austria. And, for some reason we don't know, they won't attempt to cross into Yugoslavia for two days. Hmm. Seems an odd thing to do, doesn't it?'

Kuso's aide interjected, 'All border crossings in Styrmark and Karntner have been sent a special, very detailed warning, both about the station wagon, and such descriptions as we have of its likely occupants. No report has come in from anywhere.'

Rupert said, 'Excuse me, Jo. But could you just repeat, what exactly was it that the garage attendant reported them as saying again?'

The telex was placed in front of Liebmann.

'It will take us two days to reach the Yugoslavian frontier,' he read out.

Rupert repeated very slowly, 'Two days to reach the Yugo-slavian frontier.'

Liebmann caught the inflection in Rupert's voice.

'Yes, Rupert. Go on.'

Rupert gazed at the ceiling for a moment, and then said, 'How many frontiers has Yugoslavia got? Six? Seven, isn't it?'

Liebmann seized the point at once.

'Italy, Austria, Hungary, Romania, Bulgaria . . .' He paused. Then half a dozen people sitting round the table exclaimed almost in unison, 'Greece,' long pause . . . 'and Albania!'

Haddad's carefully planned diversion had failed.

Liebmann looked around the room and said, 'Anybody here know the border between Styrmark and Yugoslavia well?'

It was Kuso's aide who spoke.

'Yes, Herr Hofrat. I come from there.'

'How easy is it to get across that border at night without being seen?'

'Not too difficult, Herr Hofrat. When I was a young constable down there we were always having trouble with smugglers. There are plenty of farms and woods that run right along it. The Jugs are not quite so relaxed as we are, but they don't patrol it regularly. Certainly not on a dirty wet night like last night.'

Liebmann summed up somewhat tentatively, 'Then, gentlemen, the picture would appear to be that our quarry are, very probably, now in Yugoslavia, and heading for a frontier which is two days' drive from Styrmark.' He considered for a moment. 'That really only leaves two possibilities. Hopefully, Greece. From our point of view, very unhopefully, Albania.'

Kleinhart stopped rubbing his glasses along the edge of his huge nose and asked anxiously, 'Just what is the state of police co-operation with each of these countries?'

'Starting from the top, and working rapidly down,' Liebmann said, 'with Greece it's good. They work well in the Interpol network; as long as their internal politics are stable we get good co-operation. Yugoslavia generally the same; on straight criminal matters good co-operation. On things like this though, where there are political overtones, it can be tricky. Right now, as you well know, Dr Kleinhart, President Tito is very close to Prime Minister Sadat, third world and all that. Egypt's relations with your country are all too clear, I'm afraid. Just what Mr Sadat tells Mr Tito about the Palestinians I couldn't guess. The British or the Americans probably could tell us, but our Foreign Ministry would want to be awfully careful how we went about it. If I told my counterpart in Belgrade that we were looking for an Israeli kidnapped by Palestinians and suspected of being in Yugoslavia, well, difficult to judge his reaction. On a purely personal basis I'm sure he'd try to be helpful, we're good friends; but, drag politics into it, I just don't know. Albania, dead loss, I'm afraid. Nice people, polite and all that, but they never answer a telegram under three weeks.'

'Assuming they can be intercepted in Yugoslavia,' Rupert asked, 'how serious a charge could you issue against them, with any hope of getting an extradition order?'

Liebmann passed that to Kuso.

'Even that is complicated, my dear Rupert. And takes a lot of time. We want the man who murdered the policeman. What Dr Kleinhart is after is Reuben. While we around this table all have strong reasons to believe these people killed our policeman and kidnapped Reuben, without finding the man himself we have no evidence that would stand up in court. Furthermore, there is the awkward fact to be got over that there is no legal proof Reuben ever entered Austria in the first place. The only person who saw him was old von Eck; he'd have to swear affidavits and that sort of thing. All takes time. I think the best we could do, through official channels, would be to request that they be held for questioning in relation to the murder of the policeman at Helligenkreuz. And,' he added ruefully, 'we have to admit to ourselves that at present we haven't a shred of real evidence to support such a charge.'

Liebmann said, 'I'm sure we could get them stopped at the Greek frontier, if that's where they're heading. But, Albania? They wouldn't even acknowledge a personal request from Chancellor Kreisky under a week: and they don't belong to Interpol.'

Rupert looked across at Kleinhart. 'At the moment, it looks as though this is another case for some intrepid Israeli private enterprise, Jacob.'

'I can't see even Dayan mounting a commando operation into Yugoslavia,' he said mournfully.

They had been at it for nearly two hours and everyone was beginning to feel jaded. Liebmann felt they couldn't get much farther sitting round that table.

'I'll do everything I can, Dr Kleinhart, and at once. We want the man who murdered that young policeman; we want to help you if we can. I'll get on the phone to my colleagues in Belgrade and Athens right away. We'll confirm all details to both of them by telex within the hour. If they will, which means if they can, co-operate, I'm sure they will do all they can to help us. The murder at the Hungarian border is public knowledge now. That will serve as a holding charge. There can't be many green Fiat station wagons driving round Yugoslavia with

Austrian licence plates. Assuming it still has Austrian licence plates. But, if they reach Albania . . .' He shrugged his huge shoulders and sighed.

He looked across at Kleinhart and said very seriously, 'If I were in your place, Dr Kleinhart, and speaking purely unofficially, off the record, you understand, I'd be inclined to explore Rupert's suggestion about, what did he call it, some intrepid private enterprise.' Then he smiled and added, 'In my personal opinion you could not find a more intrepid private enterpriser to help you than Rupert Conway.'

The meeting adjourned.

CHAPTER THIRTEEN

It was clear that a lot of people around Polizei Praesidium were not going to get much gardening done that week-end. One of Liebmann's officers escorted Rupert, Jacob Kleinhart and Yitzak Sokol down in the elevator. They all brooded in silence. In the main hall the sparkle of the lights coming on in the Schottenring was already dancing on the large bullet proof glass doors. They paused to consult.

Kleinhart said, 'Have you got your car, Rupert?'

'No, I haven't.'

'We have a chauffeur from the embassy, why not come with us, we've plenty to talk about.'

Sokol said, 'As Ambassador Doron is away, I suggest you come back to my apartment. We can talk there in peace.' He paused and looked at them with a touch of a smile. 'Oh yes, at diplomatic prices I can afford Johnny Walker Black Label? OK?'

Rupert grinned broadly and said, 'Very much OK. Lead on, MacDuff.' Sokol looked a bit baffled but Kleinhart knew his Shakespeare.

The car drove across town and pulled up before an apartment block just off Neulinggasse in the heart of the diplomatic enclave. It was, like most of its neighbours, one of those solid six storey square blocks with an ornamented stone façade built during the latter years of Franz Josef for a more spacious and elegant age; a pleasant district to live in, but a little long on dignity and grandeur and a little short on such mundane things as plumbing and central heating.

Rupert and Jacob were offered the Johnny Walker Black Label. 'Fit for the Gods,' was Rupert's comment. Their host drank orange juice; not from choice but because, like top security officers in many countries, he suffered from ulcers. They settled in the living room, comfortably cluttered with books. Serious, thought provoking books. There was silence for a few moments, broken by Rupert saying, 'They're halfway across Yugoslavia now. Got any maps?'

A security officer's apartment is always equipped for such discussions. Sokol went and got Kummery and Frey's map of Central Europe, folded it to show the area between Vienna and the Mediterranean and laid it on the coffee table between them. He moved a standard lamp to give a better light.

Rupert sucked his pipe and thought out loud.

'We assume they crossed the border about here.' He pointed to the area between Klagenfurt in Austria and Maribor in Yugoslavia. 'To get to Greece or Albania their direction has to be south-east. Now, let's see. There is no main road going across the country that fits. Anyway, that's all mountains in there. So, what do we deduce? If they were heading for Greece they would swing more to the east and go down through Belgrade. Right? That would give them an option of two routes, the Morava Valley, here; or the other side of that range of mountains there; giving them the choice of two crossing points into Greece. Let's see, what are they called?' He took out his jeweller's eye glass and studied the small print. 'Here, just south of Bitola; or there, at, what's it called, Gevgelija? Unpronounceable. Anyway, they are well over a hundred miles apart by road.

'Now, taking the worst case, if they're heading for nobody's chums in Albania; hmm . . . that's fairly simple, isn't it? These secondary roads cutting across the mountains would take 'em a week to navigate. So, they'd head over here, to Rijeka and drive down the Dalmatian Coast road which ends at,' he took up his glass again, 'yes, there it is, Titograd.'

Kleinhart had been following this carefully, it was obviously new territory to him; his owl-like expression and penetrating brown eyes evidenced total concentration.

'Yes, I expect that must be right. What's the distance? 600 kilometres. Winding roads, probably more. Unless they drove solidly for forty-eight hours, which seems unlikely, they could not reach any of those points before, well, to be safe, say late tomorrow afternoon.'

'So,' Rupert looked back at the map, 'at the moment they are somewhere in the neighbourhood of, hmm, either, Split if they're heading for Albania; or about a hundred kilometres south of Belgrade if it's to be Greece. I don't know what on earth we can do about it, but it's nice to know where our pals are.'

Kleinhart turned to their host.

'This is your line of country, not mine, Yitzak. What do you think?'

Choosing his words very carefully and deliberately, Sokol said, 'Yes, I think Herr Conway's analysis must be right. We're all working on supposition, of course. They may be stashed away in a barn down near Graz somewhere. Or even in the Tyrol. No, wait a minute, that's highly unlikely . . .'

'Why?' Kleinhart asked.

'Because the Austrians have a very efficient police service. Their road patrols at night are highly organised . . . as I know to my cost. After midnight wherever circumstances permit they note licence numbers of cars they don't immediately recognise, and they are all computer checked next morning. On a bad night such as it was all through southern Austria last night, traffic would have been light. That would much increase the chances that if the green station wagon went very far from the area where it was reported at eleven o'clock, its number would have turned up somewhere by now. That's only supposition too, of course . . .'

Rupert said, 'And even if it were wrong, if they still are somewhere in Austria, there is nothing we can do about that anyway. That possibility is in the hands of the police.'

There could be no supposition about that.

'And if they are in Yugoslavia?' Kleinhart addressed his colleague.

'If they are in Yugoslavia there's not much we can do about that either.'

Rupert interjected, 'And if they're in Albania there is damn all we can do about it! It's those three border crossings we've got to concentrate on.'

They kicked this around for nearly an hour until the pangs of hunger began to make themselves felt and Sokol phoned out to a Chinese restaurant to deliver some 'take-home' chop suey, crispy noodles and barbecued spare ribs. 'Don't forget the egg foo yung,' Rupert shouted out.

The pro and cons of innumerable possible courses of action went on all through the meal. Rupert and Jacob switched from Scotch to beer. Sokol stuck to orange juice. The guests thoroughly enjoyed the mixture of bamboo shoots and soya sauce with playing detectives, though their host, the professional, was also charged with making careful notes of the ideas that were flying across the table, and found the going a bit heavier.

When they finished eating, there was a pause for leg stretching and allied activities while Sokol went to the kitchen and made coffee. He made very good coffee; he hadn't learned that in a Kibbutz but during a tour at the Paris embassy. There are Israelis who regard Kibbutz coffee as a term of abuse. The phone rang. It was one of Liebmann's aides. His boss had asked him to let them know that the interrogation of the suspicious lady in Wiener Neustadt was going well; they had not yet found out exactly how she fitted into the overall picture, but their knowledge about her son's so-called stolen car had trapped her into saying that it was at this moment somewhere in Yugoslavia. She couldn't or wouldn't give any information about its final destination. If any more hard information came in he would keep them posted.

Kleinhart asked Sokol to summarise his notes and clarify their deductions.

'One. Interception in Yugoslavia. Israel has no resources to intervene. Dependent on what co-operation Liebmann can get from his police contacts. Possibilities, no better than fifty fifty. Greece. I can signal my colleague in Athens tonight; he can talk frankly to the Greek secret service people and enlist their help. As an added precaution he can send two, maybe three, men to each of the two crossing places to watch for the arrival of the green station wagon, and ensure whatever action is possible. Three, inside Albania no action possible. Mounting an Entebbe type raid is politically not on. That's where we got to.'

'Albania fascinates me,' Rupert said. 'If we find they do get there, or perhaps better to put it, if they don't turn up anywhere else, and we have to assume they have gone there, what would you people do?'

'Both Dayan and Eklund would have a fit, for a start, I should think,' Kleinhart said. 'But I don't know about these matters. What would we do?'

Top security men either never smile, or, like Sokol, they smile reassuringly.

'Quite a bit. The position would not be hopeless. The Albanians' relations with the Arab countries may be a little more cordial than with other countries, but not much. President Hoxha is the world's champion isolationist. It seems to me most unlikely they would stay in Albania; there is absolutely nothing there that ties up with the PFLP in any way. Indeed, this is the first time I have ever heard Albania mentioned in these matters, and I've been in this game for twenty years. No, I think what is happening is that they have to get Reuben to . . . somewhere . . . somewhere in the Middle East or North Africa, right? So how are they going to do it? I think they paid the Austrian police service the compliment of deciding they couldn't smuggle a live body out of this country in an airplane. I'm quite sure they were right. They might have tried getting him down the Danube to the Black Sea on a barge, but here again, too dangerous; the river community is a tight one, there would be too many people involved; too many borders to cross. Anyway, they came up with a solution through either Greece or Albania. We think.

'So, I think we can safely concentrate our attention on a nice little conundrum: having got a live body into Albania how do you get it out again? Only two possible ways. By air. That narrows the field considerably because Tiranë, the capital, is the only properly equipped airport in the country. It would also require the co-operation of the Albanian authorities. Possible, I suppose, but I've never known it happen. I think I'd better signal my headquarters in Jerusalem on that tonight. We monitor all airline traffic over the Mediterranean, Tiranë's traffic is small and the pattern routine. Any change from the normal pattern, even the entrance of one plane, would be immediately noticeable. Once we had picked up the call sign, frequency, and so on, not difficult to track. We'd know where he was landing before he touched the ground. After that, well, the next step would rest with people a lot senior to me; but, obviously young Mr Reuben is not going to come up with any miracle monstrosity next week.'

Kleinhart interrupted, 'Or next year.'

'Or next year, so, we would have time, and we would know where to start looking.'

Rupert looked unhappy and pulled his lower lip. He said, 'If they did get him out, and set him up, somewhere in the Middle East, North Africa, and if somehow they forced him, persuaded him, to go on with this appalling work . . . you'd have to kill him, wouldn't you?'

Kleinhart looked across at the security expert who nodded and said, 'Fortunately, he'd have plenty of time to think. But, I expect you are probably right.' Rupert asked: 'Do you think it likely they will try to fly him out?'

'I simply don't know. I'm a policeman, not a fortune teller. We must consider the alternative of course. If they are planning to take him out by boat, we might, it's just possible, we might be able to do something rather more effective.' He glanced over at a desk calendar and said, 'Just possible. There is a boat awaiting orders in Messina right now. She's just a hundred and twenty ton coastal freight carrier; but if anyone tried to chase her they'd get quite a surprise at the speed she could put up. And the armament she carries. Provided head office didn't veto my suggestions I think she could be somewhere off the north end of Corfu by noon tomorrow.'

They all looked back at the map and what they saw was encouraging. 'Durrës is the only seaport of any size in Albania. They probably wouldn't need a very large ship for an operation like this, but the whole coast is very rocky, they haven't let Lloyds people, or even the United Nations, in to up-date charts of this coast for years. The Straits of Otranto are only fifty miles wide at that point; our . . . ah . . . boat could sit out there somewhere and monitor everything that passed.'

'Could she really?' Kleinhart said impressed.

'Within reason, yes. Her radar range is well beyond that, but what's more important it is fully computerised and she has twelve channels you can lock on to a target and give you a continuous print out of that ship's course as long as you can keep within about a hundred miles of her.'

Rupert asked, 'Traffic is pretty heavy through there, surely?'

'That would add to their problems, certainly, but most of that traffic is well known, and the number of ships that call at Albanian ports is minimal. I'm not guaranteeing anything, but I do say we'd have a pretty good chance.'

Kleinhart looked at his watch.

'Gentlemen, do you realise it's nearly midnight? I think we have done all we can tonight. Can you send off your signals from here, or do you have to go back to the embassy?'

'I have a direct line to the embassy. And my coding key here.'

'Rupert, I'll give you a lift home. You must be exhausted.'

CHAPTER FOURTEEN

Rupert was indeed tired, and he went straight upstairs to bed. He found a nice little good-night note from Sandra pinned on his door; she had had a snack supper and gone to bed early as planned; she felt much better. He went through the usual routine of his toilet, got into bed and picked up his night-time book. It was Jack Higgins' latest, *Storm Warning*. Just his kind of book.

But even the excitement of Higgins at his best failed to hold Rupert's attention that night. He kept losing the thread of the story, and his mind kept wandering back to that forbidden, mysterious Albanian border; even amongst his wide circle of friends he had never met anyone who had been able to get into Albania since the British airborne commandos had left in 1945. He recalled that his old friend Julian Amery had written a book about it and made a note to look it up. A mountain fortress, a regular Tibet right here in Europe; impenetrable, inscrutable; it fascinated him. Somehow he was certain that was where this drama was going to move to next.

His Welsh grandmother would have told him it was his natural Celtic vision, something to do with little green men in the garden. He couldn't remember. He couldn't concentrate. He got up and went downstairs to a cupboard in the hall of his apartment where he kept maps, found the one he wanted and took it up to bed with him. For a few minutes he just sat and stared at it. Dubrovnik was about a hundred odd kilometres north of that fateful and tantalising border line but somehow his eye kept coming back to it. Dubrovnik. Why am I thinking about Dubrovnik? Of course! Thorney was going to Dubrovnik. What was the name of the hotel? All thought of sleep was forgotten.

Villa Dubrovnik, that was it. The Hotel Villa Dubrovnik. Without a moment's consideration of the time, or the probable response of the Yugoslav telephone service in the middle of the night he reached for the phone and dialled 'international'. He was pleasantly surprised to get a quick response from a young night operator who seemed delighted to find something a little novel with which to occupy himself. Rupert asked to place a personal call to a Mr Thornhill Biddle at the Hotel Villa Dubrovnik and the operator promised to call him back as soon as possible.

Ten minutes later he did, with the news that Mr Biddle had left the hotel but had given another number at which he could be found in some place called Ulcinj. Certainly, sir, be happy to try to raise Mr Biddle at Ulcinj. Call you back.

'Ulcinj,' Rupert muttered to himself. 'Trust Thorney to get himself into some place called Ulcinj.' Rupert made a note of it. 'Where the hell is Ulcinj?' His eyes went to the map where he soon discovered that Ulcinj was the southernmost town on the Yugoslavian coast. Only a few kilometres from the Albanian border. What sort of a dump would he stay in way down there? Must be one helluva lot of ducks around Ulcinj. He tried to turn back to *Storm Warning* while he waited, with some success this time.

It was nearly half an hour before the operator came through again.

'Sorry to keep you waiting, sir. Ulcinj is a bit off the beaten track, but the international exchange in Belgrade finally got through for me. I think your friend Mr Biddle was asleep but he's on the line now. I'll put you through.'

There was a short pause, two bleeps and innumerable squeaks then Rupert heard Thorney cursing at the top of his voice.

'Getting me out of bed at this hour in the night. Who the hell's idea of a joke is this?'

'Thorney. It's Rupert, and this is urgent.'

'Rupert! For God's sake, old man, what are you playing at? I was sound asleep. It's nearly two o'clock down here.'

'It's nearly two o'clock here too, Thorney, but I have to talk to you. Urgently.'

The note of excitement in his voice came across the wire clear enough to Thorney. He was ready to listen.

'All right, old boy. I'm listening.'

'Thorney, are you on speaking terms with the local gendarmerie?'

'Am I what? The police, you mean? They haven't locked me up yet if that's what you're worrying about. Why?'

'I can't go into the details on the phone, it's all very complicated, full of international politics, and all that. Briefly, a man has been kidnapped and we believe the gang that nabbed him are heading your way.'

'Pal of yours?'

'No, you ass! Anyway, that doesn't matter. The point is we want him back here; that is the police do. So do I.'

'So you want me to tell the local cops to grab him, is that it?'

'No, Thorney; please be patient. All the official stuff has been done. The Jugs have been asked to stop them, but it may not work. I must confess we're not certain, not quite certain, they are coming your way. But we think they are. We think they are heading for Albania, that's near where you are, isn't it?'

'Just the other side of the marsh. Some of the birds I shoot come down on their side of the river and I can't retrieve the brutes. They have nasty things like land-mines all over the beach.'

'Could you find anyone who can watch the road to the frontier for us? Spot a car so maybe we could alert somebody?'

'Chap to spot a car? I don't know about that. I've picked up five damn young Jug kids who are mighty good at spotting ducks; I suppose I could spare a couple of them to spot cars for you.'

Rupert gave him full details of the green Fiat, licence number, occupants and so on and Thorney promised to phone back as soon as there was anything to report.

Having achieved the satisfaction of actually doing something Rupert went happily to sleep.

At six o'clock he woke up with a start and asked himself, 'What the heck is the good of that if nobody is there to do anything about it?' He thought of getting Kleinhart out of bed then and there, but decided he had better think the next step out a bit before doing that.

Just after eight his patience gave out and he called. Kleinhart was already up and dressed; he got Sokol on another line and they agreed to reconvene their conference at nine-thirty. By nine-forty they were back in position around the coffee table, and there was a large pot of coffee with all accessories beside them. Rupert went straight to the map and passed his finger along the frontier area.

'My mind is stuck on this area right here,' and he pointed between Ulcinj and Titograd. 'There is a chance the Jugs may stop them. None of us rates it high. There must be some way we could, I'm not clear; that's why I wanted to talk again. Something might gel. I appreciate we have a few years in hand before young Reuben finds out how to give us all radiation disease and Gaddafi or Amin or some other raving lunatic takes it into his head to try . . . can't quite remember how I got involved in all this, but I've developed . . . ah . . . a kind of hankering to meet Mr Reuben. If you see what I mean?'

'No, I don't really. But I'm glad to hear it. What's buzzing in that fertile brain? What was it Liebmann called it? Intrepid?'

Rupert replied, 'My policy toward flattery has always been to accept it gracefully. Just don't inhale. No. Seriously, let's look at this again. If the Yugoslavs let us down there are only two options left, Greece and Albania. You've got Greece covered. Right?' Sokol nodded. 'Albania is wide open. If they go that way it must be better to try to stop this skylark on the Jug side of the Albanian border. Right?'

'Undoubtedly.'

'Right. That means we ought to raise the odds that the Jug frontier authorities don't let 'em out; someone or other must block the blighters long enough for Jo Liebmann and all the official channels to do their stuff. Now, how would a really intrepid man do that?'

Kleinhart was both amused and intrigued, and showed it.

'OK. Intrepid, how do we do it?'

Rupert mused, thinking out loud again. 'Well,' he said. 'It's difficult to plan anything definite in a vacuum. We don't know the set-up. The main crossing is just south of Titograd; seems unlikely, having got there, they would go all the way round to the other side of the country and cross over those mountains. Therefore, unless all of us have been putting together a farrago of nonsense, some time this afternoon, or evening, that green station wagon with all this gang on board is going to roll up to that Yugoslav frontier post . . . there . . . just south of Titograd. Now . . . my guess is that a fellow who was really intrepid would be there, with a reception committee to meet 'em. How's that?'

Kleinhart seemed to enjoy this droll idea. Sokol listened intently. He was back at the orange juice again. Kleinhart said, 'Great. Suppose we were there. What do we do? Have a running gun battle while the Yugoslav police act as referees?'

That was a very English kind of humour to which Rupert knew how to respond. 'Don't talk balls, old boy. That's not at all the way my mind works. No violence, I'm a man of peace. Think about it. If we were there first, not doing anything in particular, admiring the view, having a picnic, any confounded thing you like. We're just there; car parked as near the frontier post as possible. Right? Now, our Arab friends arrive; we can see them coming up the road. Surely with our imaginations we could contrive some kind of incident, we could protest, shout and yell, jump up and down, throw stones at their car; scream "Murderers! They murdered the Austrian policeman!" Got it? Anything to get the police boys all excited. Anything to delay them so Jo Liebmann and Co. can do their official stuff.'

'And the police might oblige us by arresting them?'

Rupert looked whimsical and said, 'Come to think of it, they'd almost certainly arrest us too. Naturally.'

'Oh, naturally,' Kleinhart was trying to see the funny side, and the wrinkles on his massive nose quivered right back to his ears.

'I'm told the Yugoslav jails are much improved these days,' Rupert observed cheerfully.

'Charming thought. Must remember to tell all my friends.'

Rupert thought a moment more and then said, 'But you know, that's right. That's exactly the ticket. If the whole gang of us are all in jail in some God-forsaken little backwater the Jugs have got a nasty international incident on their hands. Austrian police want the Arabs for questioning on a murder charge, that gets their embassy in the act. You get your embassy in. I can easily drag the British embassy in. I'd enjoy that. With luck we might even get some brilliant young "investigative" reporter to come down and hash the whole story up, we'll be headlines all over the world! There'd be a glorious old muck-up. In all this hullaballoo there's one thing certain: Reuben would be sprung! The moment the Jug police lock him in a separate cell he's as good as a free man.' He stopped to consider what he had just said. 'I know that sounds Irish, but you see what I mean.'

'Rupert,' said Kleinhart, 'you're brilliant. Would you believe it, I've never been in jail before in my life, it's taken a cockeyed genius like you to arrange it. On behalf of the government and people of Israel, I thank you.'

'There is still of course the little problem of getting there,' Rupert said almost sadly.

Kleinhart looked at Sokol. He in turn looked at the map.

'We could get there, certainly. Let's just look at the time factor.' He picked up a pencil, laid it along the kilometre scale and then traced a path down the map. 'Assuming we can land at Titograd – and that is by no means certain – but if we can, then, the distance is, let's see, about five hundred kilometres by air. There is a charter jet we use in emergencies – assuming we can get it at short notice on a Sunday – its cruising speed is four hundred kilometres per hour. Allowing for the usual hold-ups in take off and landing, call it the better part of two hours, switch on to switch off. They would have to clear a flight plan with the Yugoslavs' northern sector control, that's at Zagreb, that could easily take two hours, a lot will depend on what kind of a cock and bull story you intend to put up as the reason for this sudden, unscheduled flight; the Yugoslavs still have a few Communist hang-ups, you can't just drop in. With luck they might get us clearance to Titograd. If that's not open there is no landing field open at this time of the year nearer than Cilipi, south of Dubrovnik. What do we do when we land, get out and walk?'

'Surely there are plenty of taxis in Yugoslavia?' Kleinhart said.

'Oh sure. Plenty of them in Dubrovnik. I wouldn't know about Titograd. It's well off the tourist beat. Anyway, add it all up, *if* this and *if* that, and an hour to get out to Schwechat, and the time taken for the pilot to file a flight plan; let's see, it's nearly ten now; we'd be lucky to be off the ground by twelve, land Dubrovnik or Titograd somewhere around two.'

He looked at the others who were weighing up the host of imponderables in this unlikely package.

'Want to try?' he said.

Kleinhart nodded his head and said, 'Well, I can't think of anything better to suggest. I don't know what Doron will say when he comes back and finds a whopping great bill on his desk for a charter flight, but I suppose a little trip to the other end of Yugoslavia is as good a way as any of spending a quiet Sunday.'

At half past eleven they were sitting in a charter office at Schwechat airport filling in rafts of paper, and at a quarter to one they were actually airborne. Heading for Dubrovnik. At the last minute a signal had come through that landings at Titograd were not permitted without authority from Belgrade. Being

Sunday, the ministry was closed. There was a duty officer but he only spoke Serbo Croat. This was a considerable blow to their timing, but fortunately Cilipi airport was twenty kilometres south of Dubrovnik and near the highway; it was still worth trying, and the trip had acquired its own momentum. They were stalled over Dubrovnik for no apparent reason and put into a circuit at six thousand feet out over the Adriatic. If one had been in a mood for sight-seeing the huge craggy rocks and deep purple water streaked with bronze in the late autumn sun were a magnificent sight. It was ten past three when they finally completed the inquisition from an exceedingly polite, but rather puzzled immigration officer who spoke just enough English and German to complicate everything. Rupert tried to phone Thorney but found it nearly impossible to make himself understood, and failed to get through. Finding a taxi proved to be the least of their problems; they got in the first that offered and instructed the driver to take them to the Albanian border crossing south of Titograd as fast as possible. The driver looked perplexed by such a request, but believing they were either Englishmen or Americans he decided that they were probably crazy but would have plenty of money. In his best tourist guide English he smiled and said, 'Gents, cost of such trip is most definitely nine hundred dinars.' They soon discovered that 'most definitely' was his favourite, possibly his only, English expression.

Rupert always liked sitting up front next to the driver; talking to taxi drivers was a habit he always enjoyed, and from which he believed, or at least said he believed, he had over many years collected an encyclopedia of unusual, not entirely useless, information. He went straight to his desired seat, Kleinhart and Sokol got in the back. Once they cleared the airport complex and were out on to the coastal highway heading south, Rupert tried in his best pigeon English to elicit from the driver what time the frontier closed for the day. After a lot of explanation, counter-explanation, and re-explanation, he came up with the somewhat odd conclusion that the post on the Yugoslav side closed at six o'clock on a Sunday, but the one on the Albanian side closed at five. He decided it would be more trouble than it was worth to try to plumb the logic of this odd arrangement. Then he looked at his watch. It was now twenty-five past three and nearly a hundred kilometres to the frontier. Rupert noted a cross country road on the map that looked as though it might knock a few kilometres off the journey but the driver firmly announced, 'Not good, that road. Most definitely not good, gents.'

Fortunately, as many tourists know, the Dalmatian coast road is good, most of it is four lane now. After a few minutes they passed into the ancient state of Montenegro, one of the six more or less autonomous republics that make up 'The Union of the South Slavs', and into some of the grandest scenery on the whole Adriatic coast. It crossed the minds of all the passengers that it was a pity they had neither the time nor the inclination to enjoy properly the magnificent views of mountain on one side and ocean on the other as the road wound upward to the top of the great cliff that carried it south into the romantic old city of Hercegnovi, with its ancient walled town hanging over the very edge of the precipitous cliffs of the Gulf of Kotor. Probably the most spectacular view in the whole Adriatic. Grand Canyon flooded with deep purple water. The cheerful driver, good patriot that he was, tried to the limit of his inadequate vocabulary to cajole them from their purpose long enough to admire one superb scene after another; but to no avail. The thoughts uppermost in Rupert's mind were whether at any moment they might catch up to a green Fiat station wagon. Or how long ago had it passed down this same road? Or was it behind them? A car chase over this road he thought would meet the wildest requirements of Mr Brocolli who produces James Bond movies. They were just approaching a hairpin turn with a sheer drop to the jagged rocks a thousand metres below on which the waves dashed themselves with spectacular fervour. The driver had now obviously made up his mind that if he could not impress them with the glorious scenery of his beloved native land, then he damn well would impress them with his driving. He went round that bend at sixty kilometres an hour with all tyres screeching, and braked within a hair's breadth of the back end of an enormous truck which could not have been doing better than twenty. They were all nearly thrown out of their seats, and Rupert whispered to himself, 'My God, I'm not James Bond, he is!' Having completed this blood curdling feat the ever so anxious to please driver turned and gave them all the full benefit of his big, round smile. He was triumphantly satisfied that his driving had impressed them.

A few kilometres beyond Hercegnovi they had the dubious pleasure of looking across the gulf and down at the old Venetian walls of Kotor. It was only about seven kilometres away from them, as the crow flies. By road it was another agonising thirty. By the time they had completed the circuit and wound down the rocky side of the Ovcen mountain back to the coastal strip it was coming up to five o'clock and the border was still more than sixty kilometres away. The map showed them they were approaching a town called Petrovat where the road forked to travel either side of Lake Shkodres. The border ran right through the middle of the lake; the only crossing was some fifty kilometres inland. It would be closed for the day long before they could reach it. Thorney's duck hunting headquarters at Ulcinj lay straight ahead and a good deal closer. After some consultation in the calmer atmosphere of a reasonably straight and level road they decided the only thing to do was to go to Ulcinj and seek information, if any was to be had. The genial driver assured them there were 'most definitely good hotels in Ulcinj', which would be more comfortable than spending the anticipated night in Titograd jail.

Soon after making this fateful decision they hit the only section of the Dalmatian coast highway which has not been rebuilt; the asphalt was worn out and they found themselves bumping uncomfortably over pot holes and intermittent patches of gravel. It was dark when they finally drove into the picturesque *mélange* of seventeenth century Turkish, eighteenth century Venetian and modern concrete and glass structures which make up the extraordinary oriental flavoured little seaport-cum-holiday town of Ulcinj. During the last part of this epic, and now appearing somewhat hare-brained, journey Rupert had been wrestling with his realisation that he had the phone number of Thorney's hotel but not its name.

CHAPTER FIFTEEN

The drive south from Rijeka in the green station wagon had been entirely free of problems. Nobody said very much, though it was increasingly clear that the young Japanese was getting hourly more restless, and more dissatisfied with the half understood explanations for the continued absence of his *confrère* and senior partner, Okana. The language barrier proved a blessing to Abdullah and his team. Karl Reuben had responded to the fifty milligrams of promethazine administered in his milk; he managed to stay awake a good deal of the time but in a state of lassitude, lethargic both in body and mind. They spent Saturday night in a pleasant, small hotel in Split; the water-front lined by trees and flower beds was a welcome change from Rijeka. He and Moda shared a bedroom again without embarrassment or noticeable reaction of any kind. There being a small private bathroom *en suite* each of them, with a perfectly natural modesty, had gone into it to undress; she came back into the bedroom wearing a man's shirt that hung down to the middle of her thighs; Reuben kept his underpants on.

He saw her place her gun under the pillow but felt no inclination to do anything about it. The promethazine acting on that sensitive and tired, strained intelligence still produced a state of childlike docility.

Sunday morning she cut the dose to twenty-five milligrams; by tonight they would be safely over the border into Albania and on board the boat waiting to take them across the Mediterranean to Libya. She wanted him in a receptive enough state of mind for some serious discussion. There was a lot she had to try to get into his head, and the sooner she started the better her chances. The comparative calm and quiet of the drive down the Dalmatian coast had given her some time to think. Confidence in her ability to play out this strange role, which had been riding a roller-coaster since Friday afternoon, was on the rise again. If he didn't go berserk or get belligerent she felt she had her emotions under control now. There would be no more outbursts like the one just before they left Rijeka. She found herself thinking a lot about how charming and kind he had always been with Kaled, and she kept trying not to think it.

They left Split just after eight and went straight down the coastal road without incident of any kind. They filled the car with gas and had lunch at a roadside café like any other tourists. They found the unexpected beauties of the Gulf of Kotor concerned them far less than the very unwelcome delay caused by the winding and precipitous highway around it. As they drove along the north shore of Lake Shkodres and saw the Albanian mountains tantalisingly close on the other bank Moda felt her heart begin to pound with rising excitement: excitement at a dangerous and important mission now so nearly completed, and at the thoughts of what lay ahead of her in Libya. By this stage her thoughts about being a heroine of the PFLP, of how pleased Habash and Haddad would be with her, were hopelessly entangled with speculation about the future: her destined role of filling Kaled's shoes, of being Karl Reuben's mistress, seducing him into giving up the secrets lurking in his incredible brain to her, her friends, her cause. If Haddad had known how far she was back-sliding from all the dogma of pure hatred he had tried to instill in her he might well have shot her himself.

They all felt an inevitable sense of apprehension, an increase in tension, as the road left the lakeside and headed north again to make the long circuit around the marshlands, twelve kilometres up to Titograd, and as many down the other side again. When they passed through the last Yugoslav village, a tiny near-deserted place called Tuzi, they could at last see the frontier posts lying in the soft afternoon haze across more marsh only a few kilometres ahead; an untidy shambles of concrete huts, barbed wire and the inescapable array of arms and armour. First the Yugoslav post, a little farther on around the arm of the lake, the Albanian. Abdullah, Moda and Yali were well aware this was the critical moment of the journey; they were experiencing the alternate heights and depths of hope and fear, tensing themselves for the exultation of success, or could it still happen, some unforeseen disappointment, even disaster at this eleventh hour? There were now just two immovable, unmoving Yugoslav sentries between them and the first barrier. They came to a stop and were just beginning to wonder who took the first step in this simple but momentous little game, when an officer came out of one of the huts and walked unconcernedly over to them. He had an automatic, but it was securely anchored in its holster. He was polite. He even smiled. He spoke good German. He directed them into the main compound, the sentries raised the barrier, they drove ahead a few metres and stopped. They were asked to go inside another small building taking all their papers. The inside of the building was just more bare concrete, but the benches they were shown to were clean, the counter where two uniformed officials thumbed through their passports, sending for them one after another, showed no signs of menace; gave no indication the officials themselves were aware of the drama in which, for these vital minutes, they were playing the principal parts. The benevolent countenance of President Tito beamed his fatherly approval on all that happened here. Moda had to translate for the Japanese boy, but the officials accepted without demur the rather unusual story that his father was Austrian, he got his racial appearance only from his mother, and was indeed an Austrian citizen. Karl remained docile and Moda's story that he was her fiancé and an invalid was accepted without question. They were going to visit relatives. There are many Austrians and Yugoslavs who have relations in Albania; they are just about the only people who can secure entry to that romantic but forbidding country.

The formalities took twelve minutes; the Yugoslav officials seemed to enjoy having something to do; Yali had been born with the callousness that makes a good terrorist; Moda and old

Abdullah went through a lifetime of emotional stress, their spirits ebbing and surging as one of the officials alternately smiled or thought of yet another question to ask.

Quite suddenly, it was all over. Their passports were politely handed back to them, everything seemed to be in order. The officer gallantly opened the door for Moda who had her invalid 'fiancé' by the arm and gently but firmly steered him back to the car. The barrier at the other end of the compound was raised and they drove into no-man's-land. Within a few hundred metres they entered a sea of barbed wire and ditches; of glaring luminous signs proclaiming 'Drive with extreme caution', 'Do not leave the road', 'Do not stop or get out of the car', 'Danger – mine field ahead', in four languages. All these threatening portents were lost on Moda and her colleagues, disappeared in a beautiful mist of rising expectation, of longed for relief. From here on they would be safe, in a few hours they would be at sea, in two days in Libya.

This very special mission was approaching success. After the series of disasters which had nearly overwhelmed their cause in the last two years it was a heady sensation. They drove along the ill-kept gravel road almost to the shores of Lake Shkodres, then around the narrow arm of water through which the border line runs. At the head of the arm, the most northerly tip of the lake, the road made a slight dip; they passed the sign which read 'You are now leaving the Federal Republic of Yugoslavia', turned sharp south again and were face to face with that longed for message, 'You are now entering the People's Republic of Albania.'

For two kilometres the roadside showed no visible sign of human life; nothing but marsh, inhospitable scrub land stretching away to the shores of the lake in the south, to the very edges of the mountains in the north. To the three weary Palestinians it might have been paradise. They reached the Albanian frontier post with a feeling of eager expectation that was like the dawn of a new world after the last nine days. It looked almost exactly like the post they had passed five minutes ago; it would have taken close examination by an expert to tell exactly what were the differences in the drab khaki uniforms and various insignia worn by soldiers and officials whose jobs, and indeed very lives, were pretty well identical with those whom they had just left. The only immediately noticeable difference was the substitution for the Yugoslavian tricolour by the Albanian black double-headed eagle on its blood red background. The second difference was the unpleasant discovery of an almost insoluble language problem. No one here spoke good German, nor good English, just a few words of each, and a smattering of Italian. For them to understand Albanian in any of its various dialects was beyond the realm of possibility.

The sentries and officers were as correct and polite as their counterparts on the western side, but there was an atmosphere of suspicion, of wariness about all of them that put a small damper on the Arabs' spirits. They received the usual directions more by sign language and gesture than by word; they drove into the usual compound, got out of the car and took their precious passports into the usual sparse concrete hut and handed them over for inspection. As they awaited the routine questions that accompany all border crossings outside the countries of the European Common Market, where have you been, where are you going, how long will you be in Slobodia, they were apprehensive of nothing more than the difficulties of making themselves understood. Somehow or other, by means that did not concern them, they knew that the way was carefully prepared for PFLP operators by friendly Arab diplomats abroad as it so often was; the safe house, the stolen false passports and visas, the escape network; everything in their mission had gone like clockwork. Haddad was a meticulous planner and those who formed his overseas connections, be they Libyans, Iraqis, Algerians or stateless Arabs wearing many hats, had great experience in the subtle arts for which they were well paid.

After they had somehow or other managed to stumble through all the pitfalls of translation of the routine questions and answers, one of the officials politely indicated that they should return to the bare wooden seats provided and wait. He then picked up all their passports and went out. Their high spirits took another jolt, though on consideration there was nothing essentially foreboding in this. As the minutes dragged on and the sun began to sink behind the mountain range on the horizon somewhere over Italy they became first a little bored, and after fifteen minutes with no sign of action from anywhere, a little concerned. Then the official holding their passports came back accompanied by another, obviously more senior man; the glum looks on their swarthy faces could only be omens of trouble of some kind.

The senior officer's German, if hardly fluent, was at least more coherent and intelligible than his predecessor's. He asked them to come to the counter where he spread out their passports all opened at the page containing their Albanian visas. As these were stamped in a completely unknown language and alphabet they had had to assume, up till now correctly, that they were perfectly in order. To their intense relief the senior officer started by assuring them that they were. With one small exception. He drew their attention to the clearly understandable figure '17' which occurred in the same place in each document. He was very sorry to inconvenience them, but it was his duty to point out that there must have been a slight misunderstanding: if they had understood the words of the visas they would have seen that they all specified very clearly they were valid 'to enter the People's Republic of Albania on the 17th of October.' Today was the 16th.

No word that could be said in any language could shake him. He was very sorry. The regulations must be obeyed. If they would come back tomorrow when the frontier opened at nine o'clock he would welcome them most heartily to Albania. Before then it was impossible. Out of the question. No, he was very sorry there was no accommodation of any kind at the frontier post for civilians. No, they certainly could not spend the night in the car in the compound. It was his duty to order them to return to Yugoslavia at once. Any time after nine o'clock tomorrow morning they could enter the People's Republic of Albania legally. Not before.

Bitterly disappointed they made their way back over the winding road through the marshland, consoling themselves in the thought that it was, after all, only a temporary set-back. The officer had assured them half a dozen times they could cross tomorrow morning when the frontier opened. They only had fifteen hours to wait. On their return to the Yugoslavian frontier they were met with the same politeness as before; the officials there understood; this kind of thing happened often. Why the Albanians only allowed entry on a day previously specified was a mystery to them; everyone knew the Albanians did not welcome tourists, but this particular rule seemed needlessly bureaucratic. They then proceeded, inevitably, to go through the whole process of recording the unwilling travellers' re-entry into Yugoslavia complete with stamping of passports, filling in of immigration forms, and cheerful assurances that if they drove back to Titograd they would easily find a hotel for the night. The formalities finally completed they exchanged good-night greetings and the assurance that they looked forward to seeing each other the following morning.

But what a let-down! They should have been on board ship in a few hours, to sail on the first tide tomorrow morning. For reasons which it was not their business to know, Habash had been particularly insistent that they sail on the seventeenth if humanly possible. They had no knowledge of the tides in the Adriatic but assumed they could still do it sometime tomorrow. Clearly at Habash's level there was some relationship between their movements and that of Akache and his team wandering round over Arabia and North Africa in their sky-jacked Lufthansa Boeing. For the last few hours they had been too preoccupied with their own problems, and the car radio could pick up no intelligible news programmes in daytime; they hadn't thought about the sky-jackers all afternoon. Surely the Boeing had landed somewhere by now, in some safe haven? Surely they would still sail some time tomorrow? The orders of the commander of the small ship were to wait for them.

To try to cheer them all up a bit Abdullah now switched on the car radio and darkness brought its usual plethora of sound waves from all over Europe. They drove north unwillingly through the deserted little village of Tuzi accompanied by a rendering of Bizet's overture to *Carmen* coming through loud and clear from the powerful transmitter of Deutsches Rundfunk at Munich. This was immediately followed by a series of excited, breathless commercials for a variety of products ranging from toothpaste through brassières and sexy garter belts to beer. Then followed the news. The first item was, as they expected, the story of latest developments in the saga of the Lufthansa Boeing 737. They thrilled to every word of it and were still able to convince themselves that the PFLP had pulled off another triumph that would shake the lazy, indifferent people of the western world to the terrible injustices inflicted on the suffering Palestinian people. It was hard to avoid, however reluctantly, the unwelcome fact that this was the third day Zohair, his team and their unwilling passengers had been wandering aimlessly round the airports of Asia Minor being refused permission to get off. Something clearly had gone wrong with the landing plans. Had the mercurial Gaddafi changed his mind and left them high and dry again? It would not be for the first time. This saga might be getting a little out of hand.

The German news reader surveyed the world from Washington talks on cruise missiles and the lack of something called an energy policy, through the Panama Canal, a quick dash to East Africa for a war between Ethiopia and Somalia that was fast becoming bloodier, a minor political scandal in Bonn. For a moment they thought he had finished. He hadn't, quite. The next words that fell like a time bomb on the five weary and hungry people in the green station wagon were:

'The Austrian government have informed the international police organisation and the governments of all neighbouring countries of an incident on the border between Austria and Hungary on Friday night in which an Austrian policeman was murdered. It is believed that the murderer was a member of some Middle Eastern terrorist organisation and is now in Yugoslavia.'

The first fifty-five of those words were pretty much as expected; in a way they were surprised it had not come out before. It was the fifty-sixth word that was the thunderbolt. Yugoslavia! The announcement should have said they were believed to be in Hungary. How had the Austrian police penetrated Haddad's brilliant plan? Had the alarm worked down the channels of the Yugoslav police yet? Did they have details of the party? There was no mention of Reuben. Nor of the green station wagon. How much did the Austrian police know? How much did the Yugoslav police know? Did they know anything?

Should they drive on? Should they stop? Was it better to brave it out, go into town, act on the assumption it was still too early for anyone to be looking for them down here? Or should they take to the woods and find a lonely barn in which to spend the night? Whichever way they moved they still had to face the frontier post tomorrow morning, come what may. Their brief trip through no-man's-land left no possible room for doubt that any attempt to cross that border by unauthorised routes would be certain death. The Japanese boy had hardly spoken all day. The three Arabs had been hurled from the heights of elation to the depths of despair so many times in the last few hours they felt punch drunk. Karl Reuben was absorbed with the extraordinary experience of beginning to realise that the effects of the drug Moda had been giving him had completely worn off. He felt sluggish and headachy, but his brain was now quite clear.

The taxi driver into whose hands fate had entrusted the lives of Conway and company drove triumphantly into Ulcinj; it may be off the beaten track but nobody would ever say it lacked either history or atmosphere. Starting life as a Greek colony some hundreds of years before the Christian era its stormy past has embraced every species of Balkan overlord, and the Turks, Moors, Venetians, Austrians, Hungarians and Italians. Its present law-abiding occupations, primarily fishing and tourists, probably represent its most peaceful epoch; Rupert's aesthetic eye was too often assaulted by the outcrop of concrete, glass and neon signs that are rapidly swallowing up the remnants of a romantic little town. Even if it did smell!

The first friendly passer-by to whom they could communicate their problem intelligibly directed them to the town office of tourist information. They found it after three tries. Not open on Sunday nights after the first of October. It took three more stops before they could find a telephone they could use to enquire the name of the hostelry they were seeking, and how to find it. It was called, with faultless logic, the Adriatic, and lay some four kilometres east of the town along the coast road; just at the beginning of the Velika Plaza, the Great Beach, a wide ribbon of fine, pale grey sand running right to the mouth of the Bojana river: the border. Tired, stiff and a little crestfallen after their hair-raising five hour drive, it was half past eight when Rupert, Kleinhart and Sokol finally reached the Adriatic; exactly the same moment as their elusive quarry was approaching the outskirts of Titograd some seventy kilometres to the north. The taxi drew up to an old-fashioned wooden veranda which did a good deal to break the unlovely outline of the concrete box of a building, and faced straight across the beach and out to sea. It was a superb cloudless night and the lights of Bari on the Italian coast opposite danced like diamonds on a black velvet curtain.

On the hotel veranda they could dimly discern two men sitting enjoying a quiet drink. The taxi drew to a blessed halt and its stiff, weary and bruised occupants tottered out, stretching, yawning and rubbing their backsides.

'Rupert! We've been phoning all over Austria looking for you!'

One of the figures on the veranda was Thorney, tottering on to his disjointed legs and dropping his cane. All Rupert could think of to say was, 'Lafayette, we have arrived.' Everyone talked at once; the grizzled giant sharing the slivovitz with J. Thornhill Biddle, Junior, was the owner of the Adriatic and obvious lord of all he surveyed, Draǧa Janszcowicz. He bellowed orders in all directions; three rooms would be available at once; two boys came running for the luggage. Rupert introduced his companions. The taxi driver made elaborate farewells a thousand dinars richer with repeated smiles and bows and assurances, 'Most definitely gents, it was an honour, a great honour, a most definite honour to drive the gents.'

A waiter appeared with three glasses and another bottle of Montenegran Slivovitz. Sokol asked for orange juice. Rupert, normally a careful and fastidious drinker, was in no state of mind for detailed examination. He picked up the first glass offered, put his head back and hurled the longed for liquid into it. Fire water! He choked, spluttered, coughed.

'What the hell was that?'

Draǧa roared with amusement.

Thorney handed him a glass of water and murmured, 'Pure kikipoo joy juice, old boy. Don't you remember prohibition?'

The water put the fire out and Draǧa good-humouredly sent for scotch. Everyone was still talking at once. Rupert hastily explained who his companions were and how they had got there. All they wanted to know was what happened to the green station wagon? Did you see them? Have they been stopped in Yugoslavia? Where are they?

'Patience, patience,' Thorney said. 'We haven't got them; but all is not lost. Just let me tell you. We went over to the border crossing first thing this morning. As you asked. It's eighty kilometres from here, you have to go right round the lake, up to Titograd and down again. I came back here about two o'clock; it was really hot out there today, we just couldn't put the ducks up. Lazy brutes. I'd just finished lunch when the boys phoned, the first time. Your pals in the green station wagon arrived there about four o'clock.'

'Did they get across?' Rupert and Kleinhart both said at once.

'Wait for it. No, they didn't. I tried to get through to you but it took half an hour. Your answering service had a message to try the Israeli embassy; they raised someone there who knew about you, and he found someone else who phoned back and said you'd gone to some charter office at Vienna airport. Then the local telephone lines went out of order . . . well, anyway you know we didn't find you. About five the boys called again. They'd hung around the frontier post while your Arabs were going through the formalities, one of the lads has a cousin in the police who was on duty, there were four men and a girl as you said. All Austrian passports and apparently all in order so they let them through.'

The audience of three felt sinking hearts.

'Be patient. Just after six the lads called again. The car had been refused entry to Albania and came back.'

That good news was pure joy.

'What happened,' Kleinhart said hopefully, 'their papers didn't suit the Albanians?'

'Well,' continued Thorney, thoroughly enjoying himself, 'we don't exactly know, but Draga got on to the kid's cousin and it seems they got into some kind of problem at the Albanian side. Draga tells me language is an awful problem, even the Albanian officers speak very little but their own lingo, and a bit of Serbo-Croat, but that apparently didn't help your chums very much. From what we can make of it their visas to enter Albania specifically stated valid to cross *on* the seventeenth; this being the sixteenth they told them to return tomorrow and sent them back.'

'So they're still in Yugoslavia?'

'Without a doubt.'

'Do you know where?'

'Sorry about that, they drove off down the road toward Titograd, but my boys aren't very experienced in this sleuthing business and it never crossed their minds to follow them. So, they phoned here again and reported the news.'

Rupert said, 'The key point clearly is that first thing to-morrow morning they'll try again, and the odds are that this time they'll make it.'

'I guess that's it.'

'Unless we can get there first and stop 'em.'

'Sounds like a great idea,' said Thorney, 'how do you plan to do it?'

Kleinhart and Sokol looked at Rupert to explain the plan. When he finished Thorney turned to Draǧa and enquired, 'Draǧa, my friend, what do you think of that?'

Draǧa's massive, heavily side-burned and mustachioed face looked puzzled. He and Mr Biddle were by now good friends, he spoke English well, but he still had no reason to understand just what this was all about. Being a good citizen and a stern upholder of Yugoslavian law and order he doubted he wanted to get involved in creating a border incident.

'Mr Thorney,' he said in his deep, throaty voice, 'I would like to help your friends, of course. But, I would like to know more about this plan. I think your friends here would understand, I'm part of what you call the establishment down here. I represent this area in the state parliament, our government are very sensitive about this border. Our relations with the Albanian government are very difficult, you know . . .'

Rupert understood the situation.

'Yes, of course, Mr . . . ah . . . Mr Jankowich. I hope I pronounce your name correctly?'

The big man smiled and the deep wrinkles fanning out from that huge nose played musical patterns around the edge of his fierce, bristling moustache.

'No you don't. In Montenegro many of our names are uspronounceable, even for us. Everyone calls me Draǧa.'

Rupert said, 'Thank you. I should like to. It is a long and complicated affair, Draǧa, but I'll try to give you the main points. Four of the people in the car are believed to be Palestinian terrorists.' He calculated, correctly, that a solid old disciple of President Tito would have no sympathy with terrorists, the Yugoslavs had had enough trouble with their own brand in recent years.

'The fifth is an Israeli scientist. They kidnapped him in Austria. They also murdered an Austrian policeman.' That got Draǧa's sympathy too. 'Somehow they managed to get right across your country without being stopped. It has all happened very quickly. The Austrian police contacted your people in Belgrade and asked that the car be stopped and the terrorists held to be questioned about the murder. But that was only last night, and today is Sunday. Clearly the message did not get through to your frontier post. All we are trying to do is delay their departure from Yugoslavia to give your own authorities time to take the necessary action.'

The explanation satisfied Draga. 'I think the best thing I could do, then, would be to get through to police headquarters in Titograd; it's our state capital, you know. If I could assure them that some such order was on its way?'

Rupert and the other two exchanged dubious glances; they hoped it was, but Liebmann's warning about delays due to 'political factors' left a large measure of doubt. Best to be absolutely frank with the old man.

Rupert said, 'I can only say I believe it is on its way. I hope very much it is on its way.'

Draga smiled encouragingly, 'Well, I'll try to get through to somebody.' Then he added ominously, 'The telephones have been out of order three times this week; I hope they are working now.' He went inside to his office to phone, and the rest of them sat anxiously awaiting the outcome.

After a few minutes Draga returned looking disconsolate. The telephones were not working. Rupert hoped there might be consolation that this admission of failure would encourage this proud man to feel some sense of obligation to his foreign visitors in distress. His hope was justified.

They sat in silence for a few moments, gazing out to sea, while Draga was deep in thought. Then he said, 'I think the only thing I can do, my friends, is to arrange an expedition to the frontier first thing tomorrow morning. Mr Thorney, I suggest we take the boys over with us in my mini-bus, it's a long ride for them on their motorcycles.' The words and the all-embracing import of them were enthusiastically welcomed by everyone. 'The bus won't hold all of us,' he continued, 'I take it one of you gentlemen can drive a car?' Rupert readily

volunteered: Kleinhart and Sokol were no gluttons for punish-
ment, they felt no need to challenge him.

Draġa stood up. 'My son, Branco, will show you to your
rooms. The frontier opens at nine so we'll leave here prompt
at seven. OK? Now, if you will excuse me, there is a lot to
arrange. I hope you sleep well, gentlemen.'

CHAPTER SIXTEEN

Yali drove the green station wagon slower and slower along the road back to Titograd as the three of them debated the best course to take. Finally just as they were entering the new city of concrete boxes, tree-lined boulevards and flag poles that have arisen on the ruins of the old one, reduced to rubble in the merciless struggle between Tito's Partisans and the German Army in 1944, Abdullah made his decision. They would split up. The map and the volume of trains and buses in the area both attested to the fact that Titograd was the main transportation centre of this part of the country; there would be plenty of transients about. He and the young Jap would find some place to hide the car and make their own way into town; it was a warm night, if necessary they could sleep in the park, or in the railway station. Yali would go with Moda and Reuben, she might need help. The thought jarred for a moment on Moda's pride, but the confidence she had felt three hours ago in her own ability to handle difficult situations had diminished appreciably in the meantime. She said nothing. Abdullah thought there would be no reason for anyone to question them; so long as they could keep their prisoner docile and under control they should be all right. He chose an easily identifiable spot along the highway for their rendezvous in the morning. At eight thirty sharp, there was no sense in exposing themselves one minute longer than necessary. The arsenal hidden in the car was undisturbed; if the frontier police had received orders to arrest them, well, they would have to try to shoot their way through. They knew when they had joined Habash that nearly every man's hand in the world was turned against them. Karl Reuben's reaction to that remark was not quite so fatalistic as the others; if there was to be a gun battle with him in the middle of it, the only unarmed person on either side, his chances of living through this minor Armageddon were pretty slim; the least he could do would be to try to ensure his captors got the worst cf it.

They switched on the car radio again and meandered around the suburban areas of the city awaiting another news broadcast from Munich. In due course it came. The sky-jacked Lufthansa plane had left Dubai and was now in Mogadishu. Akache's deadline to start shooting his hostages that afternoon if their demands were not met had come and gone. 'The leader of the gang, who says his name is Captain Walter Mahmoud, and members of the Baader-Meinhoff urban guerrillas still at large somewhere in Germany, have issued a further joint ultimatum demanding the release of nine of their number in jail in Germany and two in Turkey. They also demand a sum of fifteen million dollars and safe passage to Vietnam, Somalia or South Yemen. The terrorists now state that if their demands are not met by half past five tomorrow afternoon, local time, Herr Hans-Martin Schleyer, whom they kidnapped five weeks ago, and all the hostages on the plane will be shot. Chancellor Helmut Schmidt repeated this evening his firm refusal to yield to these demands.'

They both issued the same ultimatum at the same time: that's good, that means that Haddad's international network is still operating. But the German government won't budge. They're already in Somalia. South Yemen has said they won't have them. Syria and Iraq refused them. Something somewhere has gone badly wrong. Why haven't they gone to Libya? Abdullah muttered a private prayer to the revenging Allah of his own imagination. Yali was unmoved, indifferent to human suffering of any kind; even his own. A true bedouin. As Moda attempted to sort out and try to understand her spontaneous reactions her anxieties only increased. Three days ago she would have sworn and cursed and called these people pigs;

she would have carried on the way a true member of the **PFLP** should do, defying the corrupt bourgeois world in the face of death; it had sounded so heroic. A flash of Haddad's ringing phrases of hatred, of Habash's subtle reasonings to justify death and destruction to all their enemies, crossed her worried mind. But this time the flash didn't ignite very much. Only more doubts. The reality of practising terrorism was not living up to her expectations.

The news reader finished the bulletin without any mention of the murder on the Austro-Hungarian border. That non-news was the best they had heard or experienced for several hours.

None of them spent a particularly comfortable, nor congenial, night, but it was free from incident. Karl Reuben slept fitfully as Yali had hand-cuffed his ankles. They met at the rendezvous at eight-thirty as planned, unmolested. So far so good.

Rupert was dead tired and hoped, in vain, for a few hours' good sleep before an early call at six. The enthusiasts of the Swedish health club, he never found out exactly what that meant, seemed to be equally divided into two groups: those who sat up noisily chatting, drinking, rushing up and down stairs half the night, banging doors and shouting 'Good night' to each other; and those who, having managed by some miracle to sleep in peace, leaped from their beds at the crack of dawn, greeted all in sight with disgustingly hearty 'Good mornings', and charged noisily to the beach for their run and their first swim. How these two managed to get along together was another mystery Rupert never solved.

When the three members of what the Adriatic's harassed night clerk had entered in the register simply as 'The Vienna Party' tottered down to breakfast at half past six none of them was in the best of form either to appreciate the fiery, dramatic grandeur of the sunrise as it sprang up out of the Albanian mountains, or feel much enthusiasm for the unknown and unpredictable adventures ahead of them. At least the addition of old Draǧa to their company offered some assurance that they might not, after all, have to spend a night or two in the local jail.

At five minutes to seven the motley company was duly assembled on the hotel's front veranda. Rupert, Kleinhart and Sokol all looked far from debonair in their rumpled and totally out of place business suits, complete with collars and ties, which they happened to have been wearing when they decided to set out on this unpromising expedition from the capital city some six hundred kilometres farther north and a good twenty degrees colder. Thorney, fully dressed for duck hunting, would have brought joy to the hearts of Mr Abercrombie and Mr Fitch; his trousers, though mud stained, were pale grey cavalry twill and superbly tailored; he wore a bottle green viyella shirt and a yellow silk foulard, topping the whole outfit off with a hat, somewhere between a Sherlock Holmes deer stalker and an Ivy League freshman's pork pie, made of tweed. Draǧa was of a height, and with a chest and shoulders of such monumental proportions, that he looked impressive in anything, even the shapeless brown corduroy trousers and loose fitting dark blue blouse he was wearing this morning. The party was completed by his son Branco and four other boys in the fifteen to seventeen age bracket, all dressed in the inevitable scruffy blue jeans and tee shirts proclaiming, presumably, their allegiance to a number of local educational establishments. What lack of originality and character there was about their rig was more than made up for by their smiles and their enthusiasm. Mr Thorney's gang were a memorable crew, and why they were not fully engaged in more academic pursuits on a Monday morning at this time of the year was none of Rupert's business.

There were two venerable, but hopefully serviceable, vehicles: a red and white hotel mini-bus built by Simca of France many years ago, and an even older American Buick sedan. Both showed innumerable scars from long service on the atrocious local roads. Rupert suffered his first qualm that they might not make it in these chariots.

Neither Draǧa nor Thorney manifested any such faintheartedness. As they drove off in the antique Buick both Rupert and his companions agreed that perhaps they should have told the leaders of the home team a little bit more so they could more fully appreciate the seriousness of the situation and the grave international repercussions involved. They bounced and bumped and rattled through Ulcinj and turned north on the gravel road, with patches of asphalt. They would have to go all the way back along the coast road to Petrovac before they could join the main highway again, running north of the lake and up to Titograd.

Monday turned out to be market day in the little village of Krute which lay unavoidably in the middle of their path. Before they reached the edge of town they came up behind one, or it could have been two or three, or even more, farmers driving small herds of goats and sheep to the market. There weren't many of them, but the way they kept rushing madly back and forth across the narrow road, bolting into neighbouring fields and out again, with the farmers and their sons and daughters waving sticks and shouting and running in all directions trying to keep their flocks together, for all practical purposes they might have been an army, they presented an impassable barrier.

When they did get into the centre the situation was worse. Far worse. Every available square metre was a seething mass of people, goats, sheep, dogs, farm carts and horses, converging from all sides and directions. To add to such joyful, traditional confusion, modern industry has added motor cars, trucks and tractors far beyond the capacity of narrow old streets to handle. Immediately someone spotted their popular member of the state legislature driving the mini-bus and from then on a hail of friendly greetings further obstructed their progress. Draga tried in vain to get across to them that his party were in a hurry, but in Yugoslavia Communism wears a democratic face, these people had a vote, and he had to be affable to them.

Thirty vital minutes were lost before they reached the open road again. There was no point in getting angry. The crew of the mini-bus seemed to have enjoyed this unexpected encounter with so many friends and relatives, and the three trailing behind in the Buick had no one to express their frustration to except each other. From there on they made the best time they could but fate was against them: traffic in Petrovac was heavy; the causeway across the north end of the lake was single line operation while repairs were being carried out; in Titograd a slow freight train was taking its own sweet time lumbering over a level crossing. They hurtled down the road from the city toward the frontier post like tin cans full of stones rolling crazily down hill, and at a speed which taxed even Rupert's highly skilled driving, the Buick clanked as though it would lose a wheel or even the whole rear axle at any minute.

As they screeched to a dusty stop at the frontier barrier at ten minutes past nine they could see a green Fiat station wagon crossing the border line at the head of the lake. Draga went into the office and confirmed there was no doubt it contained the five people they were seeking. There was no telephone communication across the border. Nothing could be done.

They got out of the vehicles and stood helplessly watching the station wagon reappear over the tops of the reeds in the low ground and commence the slow climb up the undulating slope, now disappearing and reappearing from view, until it pulled up at the Albanian barrier. Through Thorney's binoculars, which were passed from hand to hand, they saw the four men and the girl emerge from the car. For twenty minutes their thoughts veered back and forth between hope and despair as they speculated on the chances that the fugitives might be turned back once again.

They weren't, and with heavy hearts they saw the green station wagon move off slowly into Albania. Yitzak Sokol with the help and influence of Draga, received permission to use the telephone in the passport office to try to get through to his embassy in Vienna. The station wagon disappeared once again over a small hill and was lost to view.

Draga told them that just beyond that hill was the beginning of the main road south to Tiranë, the capital; that was the only airport from which they could quit Albania; but, if they were going by boat, there were several small ports they could sail from.

The boys were chatting with the soldiers, Draga stood alone, visibly unhappy at having failed his new-found friends; Rupert and Jacob Kleinhart were deep in discussion about the possibilities of Israeli means of intercepting them. Thorney was scanning the opposite side of the lake through his binoculars. Suddenly he said, 'There they are again!'

Draga looked surprised, and sad, 'Where?'

Thorney handed him the glasses and he watched the movements of the distant car in silence for some seconds while the others stood, hoping, praying, he might say something encouraging, however improbable.

What he did say was, 'That's not the main road. What can they be doing down there?' He passed the glasses to Rupert, saying, 'Look. The main road runs straight south, over those hills, you can't see it from here. They're taking the old road along the shore of the lake.'

Rupert saw what he meant. The station wagon was jolting slowly along what appeared to be little more than a dirt track. 'Where does that lead to?'

Draga said, 'It runs right along the lake down to the coast. There is no road over the mountain on their left. Either they have made a mistake, or they are heading for the little port on the Albanian side of the Bojana river.' He thought a moment and then continued, 'Surely, it can't be a mistake. No one could mistake that track for the main highway.'

The curiosity of the boys having been aroused they had joined the group and were listening to the old man intently.

One of them said, 'There was a boat came in there a couple of days ago.'

'One of the local fishing boats, you mean?' Draga asked.

'No. Had a funny flag on it I've never seen before.'

All the men looked interested. Draga said, 'Hasn't been a foreign boat up the Bojana for years. How do you know this?'

'We were fishing off the point of Nikola island on Saturday night. We saw this boat just off the sand bar. Didn't know his

185

way in. We told him to wait till daylight, but I don't know whether he understood us or not.'

Another lad said, 'He went in Sunday morning; I saw him. He tied up at the old dock by the village.'

The little River Bojana linked the lake to the sea and the border line ran right down the middle of it; the area had been no-man's-land for thirty years but there were no land mines planted on the Yugoslav side; boys and a few adventurous fishermen knew their way around the marsh land in there. Those involved in smuggling knew it like the backs of their hands; Albanian tobacco and liquor, while abundant, were strong and harsh; American, English and French brands fetched a good premium. Rupert felt he began to see a ray of hope again. Was the mysterious foreign boat what the Palestinians were heading for?

'Well,' Draga said thoughtfully, 'if it's not they won't find anything else down there but fish. And if they stray off that road their chances of being blown up by a mine are too high for my liking.'

He looked through the glasses again. 'No. There's no doubt now, that's where they must be heading.'

Kleinhart asked, 'Is there any way we can get close to them, from this side of the border, I mean?'

Draga's granite face beamed, 'Not legally there isn't. But there are plenty of us know that marsh very well. Very well indeed. One night in 1943 a troop of those SS brutes followed us in there. We killed every damn one of them,' he said with relish.

'What do you suggest?' Rupert asked.

The memories of the murderous fighting during the years of occupation stimulated this old Partisan warrior. He considered for a moment, and then said, 'Mr Thorney, we won't be able to see any more of them from here, but if we go back to the Adriatic I think we could arrange something.' He turned to two of the boys. 'You two know your way through the mine field across the Bojana, I think?'

They did.

Rupert could not resist asking how?

'Mr Conway, there are two things you don't yet know about Ulcinj. More than half the population are Albanians; and all of us are descended from pirates,' he roared with laughter at the thought. Both statements were sober truth.

As Rupert soon learned, not only were more than half the population of Ulcinj Albanians, most of them had good reason to detest the government of President Enver Hoxha; in 1956 when strong repressive measures had been used to enforce the collectivisation of agriculture many of the dispossessed peasants had fled across the border to Yugoslavia. The whole of northern Albania was wild, rugged, thinly populated country and these men formed the core of a prosperous smuggling industry; they knew every hill and valley over there, many friends and relatives; it was very rare one of them ever got caught. The Yugoslavs did little to discourage them.

They were still waiting for Sokol who had just succeeded in getting through to Vienna. An officer came out of the post and said something to Draǧa. He listened, nodded, and turned to his companions. 'That's a pity, he tells me an order has just come through from Belgrade that that car was to be stopped. He told them it was too late.'

The news, though too late to be effective, added appreciably to Draǧa's commitment to be helpful. He felt that the honour of his own country was now at stake in this adventure.

Sokol came out bearing other helpful news. He had made a full report to his colleague in Vienna and in return received the welcome news that their boat, the fast one, had been awaiting orders in Messina, was now cruising north of Corfu, in the narrowest passage of the Straits of Otranto, available if needed.

The return trip to Ulcinj was a little faster than the one out, and they were back in the Adriatic hotel for lunch and a council of war by one o'clock. Thorney was a bit moody about having been done out of his duck shooting for the day, but his gang were enthusiastic for whatever escapade might lie ahead of them. The two Albanian boys were immediately despatched down to the Bojana to reconnoitre the far bank and report back.

After an hour of consultation and much studying of maps and charts of the local waters, Draǧa sent his son Branco off to see some of the leading fishermen in Ulcinj, while he himself went down the beach to talk to members of the Swedish health club. They were delighted with his idea that tonight he would like to arrange something special for their entertainment: a barbecue supper to be followed by a midnight swim; down at the far end of the beach facing the beautiful little uninhabited island of Nikola. Free transport would be provided.

While the hotel was temporarily quiet the Vienna Party caught some much needed sleep.

CHAPTER SEVENTEEN

The green station wagon made its way round the south-east end of Lake Shkodres in a long drawn out series of painful jolts and bumps; at best the old road down by the lake was a dirt track. When it approached the few sights of human habitation along the Albanian side of the border it was more clearly defined by the marks of tractors and farm carts; and for the same reason more full of pot holes. They drove through two small collective farms hugging the lake shore; they seemed to be neatly laid out and self-sufficient settlements; small clean looking houses and massive barns, garages and work shops each centred round a communal hall that served as meeting place, school house and offices. They reminded Karl Reuben of some of the smaller kibbutz in northern Galilee. It looked a peaceful, but frugal existence. From the equipment visible to a passer-by, and there could not have been many, one of them appeared to be engaged in fishing small shell fish of various kinds from the brackish tidal waters of the lake, and the other in cultivating sugar beet and tobacco in the rolling fields that stretched away toward the mountains in the south-east. A few people in each settlement looked at the car as it drove through; nobody showed any sign of interest. Once outside them they never saw a human soul. For most of the journey none of them spoke. On the rare occasions silence was broken it was usually Moda enquiring in gentle tones of Karl's health and comfort. She knew the drug had worn off. They exchanged cigarettes. She had obviously taken some trouble with her appearance. If she just let her hair grow she could look remarkably like Kaled, Reuben thought.

After nearly two hours of driving they left the lake and followed the track along the edge of the Bojana river through the marsh lands down, nearly, to the point where the river turned south and became the border. There was no problem about finding their way; the track they were on was the only one. Down here, toward the end of their journey, the marshes and scrub land were exactly like they had been at the other end of the lake between the two frontier posts; pretty much like marshes all over the world. The land was nowhere more than five or six metres above sea level, and occasionally so low that in rainy weather it must have become impassable. The reeds were as dense and stiff as bristles on a hog's back, with bald spots here and there created by a rare outcrop of rock, or glimmering pool of clear water. Once, the noisy arrival of the car frightened a young deer drinking who instantly disappeared into the tall rushes. Other than that this whole area which stretched a good twelve kilometres between the lake and the sea, and for as much again on either side of the border, was strictly for the birds. In a normal spring or autumn there were countless thousands of them as the local population of gulls, herons, sparrows and wild pigeon were joined by huge flocks of ducks and geese of many varieties making their yearly migrations between the Baltic countries and North Africa. There were so many of them that even Thorney Biddle was satisfied having only half the area to roam in.

As they got closer to the sea they could begin to hear its unmistakable voice across the marsh, that deep musical pounding as tons of relentless water casts itself with effortless abandon upon the rocks at regular, rhythmic intervals. On each occasion when the track came right along the river's edge its banks were noticeably farther apart, and the current of the water running faster as the ebb tide began to lower the level of the lake for the inscrutable purpose of replenishing the sea.

By one o'clock they were hungry and badly needing relief both to limbs and bladders. They had been travelling at no better than fifteen kilometres an hour and had seen no evidence of human life of any kind since they had left the shores of the lake, except the inexplicable, intermittent entanglements of barbed wire and the odd signpost which they couldn't read, but deduced, correctly, gave warning of mine fields somewhere in the vicinity. They stopped to eat at a spot where the track crossed an open space surrounding a large pool, but was completely enclosed by tall reeds. They sat or lounged against the car eating chunks of fresh bread and smoked ham which they washed down by passing round two bottles of the raw, red Montenegran peasant wine. The young Jap could no longer hide from himself that his colleague, Okana, had gone, somewhere, somehow; and Okana had never told him of any such intention. Although he was the most heavily armed of them all, he knew the three Arabs carried their hand guns at instant alert, and his limited vocabulary in any common language made him virtually their prisoner. Karl Reuben, having now gone for twenty-four hours without drugs of any kind was thinking quite clearly again. The frontier crossing had been a disappointment: Moda kept clutching on to him so closely that he could feel the hard bulge of her gun under her sweater. Yali's hawk eyes had never left him. His brain, unaccustomed to coping with this kind of problem, could see no moment when he had any hope of attempting escape without being killed instantly. He had spent the whole morning in the car sifting the facts and the probabilities first one way and then another, and was still no closer to any decision about his future. He was delighted to find that, like numerous highly strung, even neurotic people, the stimulus of real danger had a strange calming, concentrating effect on him. He might have made a good fighter pilot in the old days when men fought like gladiators and not as machine controlled robots.

Abdullah, Moda and Yali talked in Arabic; they must have known Karl spoke it as fluently as they did, and were careful to say nothing that might either aid or provoke him. It was clear they were highly pleased with the success of their own operation, but increasingly worried about their friends who had sky-jacked the Lufthansa Boeing and after five days were still, so far as they knew, sitting about some airport on the east coast of Africa. They had tried the car radio several times during the morning but it would pick up nothing down here in daylight hours except a couple of unintelligible local stations, and they were none the wiser. With the unexplained exception of that Munich broadcast mentioning the murder of the policeman on the Hungarian border, and an error of one day in their forged Albanian visas, Haddad's meticulous planning of their escape had been brilliantly successful. Up till now. Could anything still go wrong for them, as it clearly had for their comrades sitting at Mogadishu airport?

The early afternoon sun was pleasant and their map told them there were only a few kilometres more of this marsh land wilderness before their rendezvous. Having little idea of what privacy she would find thereafter Moda persuaded Abdullah to let her attempt a heart to heart with Reuben here and now. He had simply said, 'Ten minutes.' She walked casually over to where Karl was sitting in solitary silence by the edge of the pool, chucking pebbles into it and watching the ripples, like a small boy. He had taken his sweater off and the tight fitting tee shirt showed every muscle of his chest and shoulders; clearly his physique was stronger than his lean features and scholarly eyes suggested. She had given up trying to persuade herself he was not attractive. She concentrated her mind on trying to look like Kaled; to talk like Kaled. To be Kaled. During the long brooding hours of the morning she had admitted to herself the stimulus of danger and action in these last few days had had just the opposite effect to what she had anticipated. She could still hate the Israelis and the whole smug, bourgeois western world, but it took greater effort; the essential woman in her was struggling to reassert itself, the difference between fighting abstract ideas and real flesh and blood people turned out to be greater than she had thought. Millions of soldiers in many countries could have told her that. Her mind was haunted by the macabre image of sparks and smoke and sizzling flesh on the breast of that unconscious woman in the warehouse attic; she thought of her own mother and the association of ideas disgusted her. She had not yet brought herself to face why, but she tried hard to get it out of her head.

Karl didn't move as she came up and stood looking down at him. 'Mind if I join you?' she said with a smile.

'Please do,' he turned and smiled back.

She sat down, took a cigarette from her handbag and offered him one.

'Sorry I haven't got a light,' Karl said.

'That's all right. I should have bought you a lighter.'

She lit his, and they sat in silence for a moment watching two herons standing silently like statues across the pool.

Moda had determined to try to avoid abstract and political issues if she possibly could; to keep their conversation personal, even intimate if he would follow her. This strange setting, cut off from the world, surrounded only by the sights and sounds of nature, had a wild, almost gothic romance about it. Perhaps here a young man and a young woman might be just themselves. When he threw the next pebble in the water she threw another one near it and they watched the twin sets of ripples meld into one another and disappear. Just as she was about to open the conversation he spoke.

'Rather like us, don't you think?'

'What is?'

'The way those ripples come together. They didn't mean to. They didn't even exist a minute ago. Other people threw two stones; the ripples were born; natural forces, irresistible forces drew them together; they flowed into each other. And they're gone.'

'That's a very romantic thought for a scientist.'

'I'm a very romantic scientist.'

'I remember Kaled telling me that shortly after she met you.'

'Kaled was a romantic. Thank God. If she had not been she would never have gone back to her homeland to live.'

'And you would never have met.'

'No, we would never have met. We should have left Israel

and married. But, there were irresistible natural forces pulling each of us to our fate. We both knew it.'

'Why didn't you marry?'

'Surely she told you that? Under rabinical law it is difficult for a Jew to marry a non-Jew in Israel; we could have done, but it entailed sacrifices which were repugnant to both of us.'

'You really loved Kaled, didn't you?'

'My mother died when I was two. I never knew her. My father when I was six. I adored him. From that moment on until I met Kaled twenty years later there was no love of any kind in my life. Nothing but science. I think I had forgotten how to feel love for any human being. Sometimes, I think my love for her was so violent it frightened her. Do you believe she really loved me?'

'Of course she did. You knew that.'

'Most of the time I knew it. Sometimes I felt she could never quite forgive me for being a Jew.'

'Could you forgive her for being an Arab?'

For the first time he turned his head away from the water and they looked straight into each other's eyes. As he shifted to speak more directly at her their hands brushed against each other.

'You may find this difficult to believe . . . but it's true. I never gave it a moment's thought. To me, people are people. None of them can claim credit, or blame, for where they happened to be born.'

Moda considered all the fears and hatreds with which her own childhood had been afflicted, the horror she had felt when her much loved and admired elder sister had announced her intention to return to the land of their forefathers to live, and the gentle forgiveness of their parents; the exultation she felt when she later persuaded Kaled to work for the PFLP. The sequence of ideas made her shudder. For the first time the unthinkable intruded itself brutally into her mind: perhaps she was as much responsible as Karl Reuben for Kaled's death! Her lips trembled and she struggled to think of some way of changing the subject before tears forced themselves upon her when he saved her by speaking again.

'Perhaps it is something to do with my own birth. After all, my father was an Austrian. My mother was French, born in Algiers. I might have been born in one of a dozen countries. If the Gestapo had not smashed my father's fingers he might never have gone to Israel.'

Moda had never heard of the finger-smashing episode.

'The Gestapo smashed his fingers?' she said unbelievingly.

'Yes. Do you know why?'

'No. I can't imagine such a thing. What did he do?'

'He was one of the greatest cellists in Europe.' He paused and looked at her thoughtfully. Appreciatively. He began to feel he could talk to her in the same frank and open way he and Kaled had always talked.

'My generation of Israelis don't hate Arabs, you know.'

'I find that difficult to believe.'

'Yes, I understand that. We were born in your land, but that was not of our doing.'

'But your fathers took that land.'

'And the sins of the fathers must be visited on the sons. So it has been since the beginning of time, for all generations. What you say is true; in a way. But it's not the whole truth. Did you know that the early Zionists believed there were no Arabs in Palestine? When Herzl tried to buy the land from the Turks he thought it was only inhabited by a few wandering tribes. If the Turks knew better they never told him. It is a classic example of how humans hurt each other, and themselves, because they are too impatient, often just too lazy, to find out the whole truth. Then it all goes wrong; as Amos Elon wrote, the early Zionists were revolutionaries, and like the human will revolutions cannot be programmed. Since my generation were born there we have to live with the consequences. Or die.'

Moda considered that seriously for a moment, and then said, 'Who is Amos Elon?'

'He's a writer, an historian. Same generation as I am. He

wrote a great book about us. Amos, I think, speaks for our generation. We have much sadness in us. And determination. We will defend ourselves to the death. But, we don't hate.'

They sat in silence for a moment and she felt the time deserting her. She had to get some inkling of the future into his mind, and try to judge his reactions.

'Karl, will you come willingly with us? With me, I mean?'

Once again they were looking straight and deep into each other's eyes. Without any change of tone at all he said simply, 'Where do you want me to go?'

'To Libya.'

'They don't like Jews in Libya,' was all he replied.

'I promise you this will be different.'

'On whose authority, my dear Moda, do you make such a promise?'

There was no hedging possible; she had to face that one.

'We have it from Gaddafi personally.'

Gaddafi! That Jew hater? The very name made him flinch. Moda followed his thoughts. She was ready for this moment.

'You know well, in the whole Arab world there is not one scientist with your knowledge.'

'That is true. The same could be said of nearly all of us working at Technion. And at Rehovoth. What do you want me to do?'

That was the key sentence. 'What do you want me to do?' Habash's clear and definite instructions came flooding back into Moda's consciousness: 'keep your mind concentrated on what your sister told you.'

'Continue with your work. There is a fine, modern hospital where we're going. The latest equipment, from America, and from Germany. Gaddafi has promised you will have every facility you can wish for. If only you will pursue your work . . .'
What work? Did they really want him to assist in relieving the suffering and carnage of human cancer? Or, the other thing? Had Kaled told her sister about 'the other thing'? And what would they do to him when they found out he was determined never to delve into it any further? He was trying to

196

formulate the correct leading question when this private little world he and Moda had created in a few, fleeting minutes was shattered by the voice of old Abdullah: 'Moda. It's time we started to move.'

It was just after three when the track finally wound out of the marsh land and into a tiny, primitive collection of huts and dilapidated wooden docks that constituted this isolated fishing village at the mouth of the Bojana. The small boats nearest the shore were lying on the mud flats created by low tide. At the end of the largest pier where she was only just afloat was an eighteen metre motor launch flying the Turkish flag. The few fishing boats that still operated from the village – it had a name but they weren't there long enough to learn how to pronounce it – were at sea. There were only a couple of women to be seen going about their household chores, and an old man smoking his pipe and gazing idly across the water. No one paid any attention to two boys who beached a small row boat a short distance down stream and clambered ashore through the mud in their bare feet.

CHAPTER EIGHTEEN

The wheel marks of the track they were on, which was the closest thing to a road the village boasted, led straight to the head of the pier where the launch was moored. The area surrounding bespoke the entire industry of the inhabitants; fishing nets draped from crude wooden posts, a large concrete stand littered with barrels in which the catch was transported, two dilapidated trucks to carry it and which constituted the villagers' sole means of communication with the world which lay on the other side of this spur of mountains. A strange, lonely life, totally dependent on the forces of nature for livelihood and, in winter, for very survival.

The green station wagon halted by the pier and as they got out they saw their first signs of life aboard the launch. She did not appear to have a name, unless it was BJ 270, the only word on her hull being Larnaca across her stern, from which any seaman would conclude she was registered in Cyprus. Since she flew the Turkish flag there might, or there might not, be a connection. Her lines were those of a sleek luxury yacht, but closer inspection made it evident that no discriminating millionaire would charter her in her present condition. The foredeck had been stripped of all her fittings and now sported nothing but a sturdy, businesslike revolving jib crane. From the blocked out port holes along the whole length of her bow it was clear that what had been cabins for the owner and his guests were now used for cargo. What kind of cargo, Reuben wondered. Freight rates must be pretty fancy on a boat like that.

The rest of her was equally functional; her main cabin and bridge equipped with every navigational aid, radar and Sonar systems, but void of all frills. When one got close up to her it was obvious that her whole superstructure had undergone a good many changes in recent years and neither shipwrights nor electricians had ever been encouraged to waste time and money on finishing their work 'ship shape and Bristol fashion'. The watchword on BJ 270 was obviously 'get the bloody job done and get the hell off as fast as possible'.

The captain was an Australian. He had an engineer, Spanish; two deck hands, Greeks, and a cook, Chinese. Whether they had any language in common such passengers as she carried seldom found out; the captain was six foot two and had the chest and biceps of a prize fighter; he looked like an ex-naval chief petty officer turned pirate, which was just about what he was. The crew were obviously professionals and he had no need to communicate with them beyond a fierce bloody this and bloody that which was enough to send them all scurrying about their duties. He reminded Reuben at once of Anthony Quinn in *The Guns of Navarone*.

As they walked along the pier he came ashore to meet them. Formal introductions were not required by either side; he talked only to Abdullah, but his cold, predatory grey eyes were occupied in a detailed head to foot appraisal of Moda. It was so blatant she felt embarrassed, and just a little frightened. The upshot of the encounter was that they could come on board now and get themselves settled but must not get in the way of the bloody crew who were bloody busy. The tide would not be high enough to get them safely over the sand bar at the head of the river until a few minutes before midnight; even then it would be bloody risky, but he had rowed out in the dinghy himself and studied it carefully, and he didn't want to spend more time hanging around this bloody dump waiting for the next high around noon tomorrow. The cook would give them all a meal at six o'clock; they were free to come and go as they pleased in the meantime, but he would cast off at ten-thirty sharp and after that he was in command and would give all the orders. Is that bloody well understood? It was both understood, and unarguable.

The captain went back on board to go about his own business and the passengers returned to the car to collect their meagre personal belongings. Karl stood passively by gazing at the river, but he could not help being a little amused by overhearing their conference about what to do with the arsenal hidden in the station wagon. And what to do with the station wagon itself? They finally decided that in order not to arouse any suspicion either from the villagers or the crew, who could not help seeing them and watching them with curiosity, they would free all the guns and ammunition from their present hiding places, working inside the car with all doors shut, and repack them in the canvas gun cases and the duffle bag. Moda was to go and sit down on the ground somewhere to continue her absorbing task of trying to explore Karl Reuben's mind. The young Jap, armed only with his personal automatic, would stay outside the car as a kind of sentry; while Abdullah and Yali did the work inside. As an afterthought Abdullah told the Japanese boy to also make himself useful by removing the licence plates and any other obvious identifying marks from the vehicle as best he could, and throw them in the marsh. Might as well leave their trail as obscure as possible; it's a rule with terrorists.

There was a good set of tools under the floor at the back of the station wagon. They lifted the seats out and got to work on inside body panels, up under the dashboard, under the spare tyre, where Yali had carefully secreted them. At this point there was a warning cry from the Japanese youth indicating they were about to have visitors. Abdullah and Yali continued to work busily, but were careful to keep the guns out of sight. Perhaps the Albanian peasants could not have cared less. Perhaps they might get excited. There was no point in needlessly taking any risk to find out.

The old man with the pipe had gone to find a soul mate and the two of them were now sauntering toward the station wagon obviously brimming over with curiosity. A vehicle of that design was rare in these remote parts. They came slowly, smilingly up to the young Jap; Abdullah and Yali stopped working and poked their heads over the window ledges of the doors to appraise the situation. It was immediately clear that the language barrier was total and insurmountable. The old gentlemen smiled and made gestures, walked slowly round the car, prodding it and patting it. They stuck their heads through the windows and looked amazed at the two Arabs squatting on the floor. The young Jap was getting nervous; he looked appealingly to Abdullah and said in his faltering English, 'I chase, yeh?'

'No, no!' Abdullah said quickly. 'Just be patient; they'll go away.'

Before they did two boys whose bare feet were covered with thick mud arrived to join the party. Abdullah and Yali were temporarily stymied. Abdullah nodded his head in the direction of the boat and they both got out of the car. He said to the Jap boy in English, 'We can't work with this audience. You stay.' He went round turning the car windows up and locked all the doors. The old men meandered off, making no effort to hide that they regarded this unfriendly action as offensive. As he and Yali headed for the boat Abdullah said, 'Stay here and guard the car. We'll come back for the guns when those boys go.' It never crossed his mind that two bare foot teenage urchins in a remote Albanian village could understand English.

They didn't understand much, but the members of Mr Thorney's gang were a bright crowd; they had acquired a colourful and useful vocabulary of English words in the last week and 'guns' was one they understood particularly well. They moved away from the car a little and held a whispered conference. After the two men had gone aboard and disappeared below they walked along the pier after them; they had learned yesterday that the skipper of the boat talked English, who knows what other scraps of interest they might overhear?

They sat on the edge of the dock dangling their legs over the side and just, idly, listening. After about fifteen minutes the two came up on deck again just as the captain emerged from the engine hold aft.

'We still have some more luggage to deal with in the car,' Abdullah said, by way of making casual conversation. 'We won't be long.'

'Be as long as you bloody well like,' was the laconic reply. 'But supper's at six and we sail at ten-thirty.'

The boys sat quite still while the two men passed them and walked ashore to the car. They watched as the older one un-locked the doors and the two of them got inside again and closed all the doors after them. Their heads disappeared below the window ledges and the boys didn't need to guess any more what they were doing. Since the car was sitting right out in the open there was no possibility of getting up close to it unseen by the vigilant and nervous Jap. They ambled very slowly, casually, in his direction, hands in their pockets, as though they had not a serious care in the world. They hadn't in fact; this was just another exciting experience that had come into their lives with the advent of the remarkable Mr Thorney to Ulcinj, and for which their childhood training in hunting and smuggling had well prepared them.

They were close enough to hear the Jap call to his friends in the car, 'Kids come back!' and they had seen enough gun-play in movies and television to surmise that when the Jap put his right hand inside his shirt somewhere in the region of his left arm-pit he carried a hand gun there.

Abdullah put his head up from inside the car and said with annoyance, 'Be careful, you fool! No guns.' At the same mo-ment Yali climbed out of the car backside foremost carrying a heavy canvas bag. As he straightened up he hit his head with a wallop against the top of the car, dropped the bag and swore.

The boys chuckled and one of them, remembering one of Mr Thorney's favourite phrases which always made them laugh, said 'Clumsy bugger!'

Lightning struck the two men at the car instantly, and relayed itself to the boys. In the same second that Abdullah cried, 'Those kids speak English!' they turned and ran.

Abdullah shouted, 'Don't use a gun!' and the Jap and Yali chased after them. Within a few metres a path led into the marsh. The boys raced down it, the Jap on their heels, Yali, who had a slow start, some way behind him. The young Asian was fit and light on his feet; the ground was rough and stony; the boys had no shoes on. Suddenly they turned off the path and plunged into the tall reeds. The Jap went in after them. He lost sight of them for just a second, saw them again, and pushed his way into the reeds. The boys broke out of the reeds and splashed along the river's edge. The Jap was gaining on them. He reached the water only a short distance behind them and they cut back into the marsh. He went straight in after them, lost sight of them again, but could hear them crashing about only a few metres ahead of him completely hidden by the reeds. From the sounds he knew they had split up. He shouted to Yali who was now only reaching the water line, 'One that way. Behind.' Yali looked frantically into the reeds but could see nothing but reeds. Then there was an explosion and a piercing scream from the Jap, Yali stumbled into barbed wire. The reeds were full of it. He stepped back into the mud of the river, lost his footing, and slipped, crashing over backwards into the water. As he clambered to his feet rubbing the water and mud from his face he saw the two boys emerge from the reeds again fifty metres farther down the bank, regain their dinghy, and before he could get his automatic from its mud smeared holster they disappeared around a bend in the river.

He shook the water from himself as best he could and scrambled back to firmer ground. There was nothing more he could do. As he turned to find the path back to the village he muttered to himself, 'Well, Habash said the Japs were expendable.'

At the Adriatic hotel the custom of the siesta was generally practised and the whole place was quieter than at any time during the previous night. Rupert and his two companions awoke again about five o'clock, and came downstairs not only refreshed but more suitably attired for the festivities planned that evening. In Rupert's own case this consisted of slippers, swimming trunks, and a bathrobe; all borrowed and ill fitting but serviceable. He met Branco on the veranda and they walked off to the beach, where the boys had assembled all the complicated paraphernalia that brings joy to the heart of every enthusiastic scuba diver. Whenever warned, as he frequently was, that this was a hazardous sport for any man past fifty Rupert's customary rejoinder was along the lines, 'With a mashed up leg like mine what do you expect me to do, take up tennis?' In fact, from boyhood swimming and all its allied pastimes had been one of his greatest delights, and he was reasonably expert. They spent half an hour jamming him into a wet-suit, closely fitting goggles and flippers, and adjusting all the fine points of the harness, checking oxygen valves, weights and pressure gauges. When both Rupert and Branco were entirely satisfied that all was correct they waded into the water, checked underwater watches and flashlights, and then disappeared westward into the sea.

It was beginning to get dark by the time they returned and Rupert expressed himself delighted with the equipment. After that trial run he felt ready for anything the evening might bring. They loaded up both sets of equipment in the mini-bus, together with spare tanks, weights, and twelve metres of fishing net. As Branco drove off he called to Rupert, 'Pick you up at ten o'clock sharp.' Rupert grinned an acknowledgement and walked back to the hotel. As he went in Draga came out of his office to tell him that the two Albanian boys had returned from across the Bojana, to report that the boat would sail at ten-thirty and one of the terrorists had stepped on a mine and was almost certainly dead. They went over details of the full party, now four passengers, five crew, and a general description of the boat. The point that concerned Rupert most was that she had twin screws. He must remember to warn Branco on that point. Risky though it seemed, they now knew their hunch was right, the boat would leave on the night's tide. A boy in the village had told them about the captain's reconnaissance of the sand bar, and they all reckoned that there would be sufficient water to get her safely over it by about eleven-thirty. Only the north channel around Nicola island was navigable and lit with buoys so there could be no doubt exactly where they would have to pass. Draga knew the passage would not be at the exact spot the boys referred to, but there was no need to explain that to them.

As the goddess of luck was with them the sunset put on one of its most spectacular performances, the sky was clear as a bell, and the muted zephyr from the south might have been bearing rose petals. Everyone in the hotel was in high spirits; the Swedes congratulating Draga and themselves on what a perfect night had been chosen for their barbecue and mid-night swim; the Vienna party, Mr Thorney and his gang, and above all old Draga himself, all enjoying the eagerness of anticipation. Dinner was early, and though the wine flowed rather less than normally its absence was not noticeable from the exuberance of their behaviour. As they were sipping coffee on the veranda just after nine they watched a beautiful ballet of lights dancing across the water in front of them as the Ulcinj fishing fleet headed out for its night's work. The fact that the enterprise they were about to launch was hazardous in the extreme, that a running gun fight culminating in one or more people being killed was a very real possibility within a couple of hours, was something nobody wanted to mention.

Over on the southern shore of the Bojana conditions were rather different. The dinner served up by the BJ 270's cook was appetising, and the rough Cypriot wine passably refreshing. The four passengers dined with the captain but they were all in one way or another preoccupied with their own thoughts, and the skipper's taciturn manner did not encourage social chit chat. There was no doubt what happened to the young Japanese so there was no point mentioning him. For some unknown reason the natives had paid no attention, it was clearly none of their business. After the meal Moda and Reuben walked across the pier and sauntered along the river bank. Yali did not exactly intrude but he ostentatiously kept a watchful eye on them and they both knew his hand was never far from his gun.

Moda had hoped that as the hour of final liberation from European soil approached her own mood would rise to meet it. She was disturbed to find that, on the contrary, the thoughts racing round in her head kept constantly coming back to her conversation with Karl earlier that afternoon; what he had said about Kaled, and about himself. For his part, Karl had now accepted that there was no escape, alive, from the fate these extraordinary people had planned for him; while he no longer believed Moda would herself shoot him if he showed signs of making a dash for freedom either Abdullah or Yali were constantly on watch and they would not hesitate. Even if he did make a break, where did freedom lie in this desolate place? Surely, some time, an opportunity would show itself: certainly not here. When they found out he would not pursue the course they had set for him would they kill him then? He could easily stall that off for months, perhaps a year or more, but sooner or later they must either tumble to it, or lose patience. For the first time he remembered all those papers strewn with calculations which he had left behind in the tower room at Zurndorf. Who would find those? And what would they make of them? Old Jacob Kleinhart would soon figure them out. Wonder if he'll ever see them?

To take his mind off such speculation which was both point-less, and not a little frightening, he let it dwell on more congenial matters. He continued to be reassured by his own reactions to this strange and unsought for experience. After the first twenty-four hours he had been reasonably comfortable; the men were hardly cosy companions, but Moda was obviously trying hard to make him feel at ease and the total break from his work was almost a holiday. And she was damnably like her elder sister, wasn't she? He put his arm through hers and was pleasantly surprised that she offered no resistance. Have a love affair with Kaled's sister, a dedicated PFLP terrorist? What a ludicrous idea! On second thoughts, it was their idea, not mine.

They walked up and down the bank like this for nearly ten minutes in total silence. It was a gorgeously romantic night. Karl thought, if only that thug with his gun were not standing over there watching us the whole time what might develop? Moda broke the silence.

'If only . . .' Whatever had been in her mind to say, she thought better of it.

'If only, what?' he responded. 'Sounds like the title of a song.'

'I . . . I . . .' she hesitated, 'I don't know the words.'

'Let me try,' Karl said softly. 'If only there could be peace between our peoples. I often think like that.'

Moda had reached a stage where she could not bring herself to think about Haddad and his dogma of hate any more. The useless deaths of the two Japanese boys affected her deeply. They were not abstract symbols. She knew them.

'Someone, someday, may be big enough to try,' he continued. 'I always believed Nasser would have, if he had lived long enough. Sadat, maybe?'

'Maybe,' she whispered, with just a touch of longing.

'Your people would kill him for it though, wouldn't they?'

Moda knew only too well the PFLP would try. A peaceful settlement was the last thing they wanted. She said nothing.

They walked slowly along the pier and back on board. The engineer was already warming up the two twelve hundred horse power engines and checking gauges; the crew coiling ropes, screwing down hatches and generally making ready for sea. The uncommunicative captain was poring over his charts and the notes he had made exactly locating the sand bar, the buoy and the rocks; he would have to go a little more to the north than he would like to be absolutely certain of avoiding the bar, and there were sharp rocks on the north-west point of Nicola island to be watched with great care. At that point the limit of Albanian territorial waters was nothing more than a line drawn on the chart. Wind four knots, speed four knots, he must make some allowance for drift. The odds, he believed, were heavily against anybody noticing if he went over the line at that hour of the night, but the Yugoslavs did patrol their coast, and he was leaving nothing to chance; he had decided to move completely blacked out until he reached international waters. His last two runs with drugs out of Alexandroupolis had failed, he dare not put back into Larnaca for fear of arrest on smuggling charges, and the price he had been offered for this charter was the highest he had ever known. Half of it was in the boat's safe below deck and the other half to be paid on delivering his passengers safely at Benghazi. His mind was wonderfully concentrated. When he was completely ready he ordered the crew to remove the canvas top which covered the whole bridge and saloon area so that nothing would interfere with his vision over the critical period it would take to get out into open water.

He turned and surveyed his passengers, sitting, standing around the saloon and aft deck.

'It would be better if you went to bed, but if you want to stay and watch us sail, sit on that bench there, behind me. And I mean sit. No movement, no word, no smoking, don't move one bloody inch until I tell you to. Understand?'

He turned back to his charts and did not notice Yali place a canvas duffle bag under his seat.

Two hired buses from the town's transport system rolled up at the Adriatic just before nine o'clock. Draga shepherded the Swedes aboard in his heartiest genial host manner, assured them the hotel staff had everything ready for them down at the other end of the beach, and that he would join them later, after he had attended to some unfinished business. As soon as the fishing fleet had passed he got into the Buick and drove into town where he had a boat to catch himself. At ten Branco arrived with the truck for Rupert, while the rest of the party including the entire complement of Mr Thorney's gang all crowded into the mini-bus. They drove along the beach south-ward for a few hundred metres and then turned inland on to a track which wound down to the Bojana through the marsh, reaching it half a kilometre from its mouth. Above the reeds and half a kilometre to the west they could see the faint glow of the bonfire and hear snatches of laughter and singing; the Swedes' barbecue sounded like a big success. On their left, from the south-east they caught the first deep throbs of full-throated diesel engines being warmed up, and knew their timing was just right.

The 'shore party', Kleinhart and Sokol, Thorney and his gang, started to fan out along the bank westward, the boys moving like cats while Thorney hobbled along in his own peculiar gait and stationed himself in a clump of small pine trees where he could see the river mouth on one side and keep an eye on the vehicles on the other. Rupert and Branco stripped to swimming trunks, donned their driving gear, and slid noiselessly into the water.

For some twenty minutes, as the moon climbed higher into the clear night sky, slowly, imperceptibly increasing their range of visibility, the only noises to be heard above the silky rustle of the breeze through the rushes continued to be the occasional gusts of laughter and music from the beach, and the distant throb of those engines.

Suddenly the throb changed into a roar as, for just a moment, the captain of the motor launch tried his engines at full throttle. Then it stopped. Almost. The new sound was softer, steadier, slightly lower pitched. The launch had started to move downstream. Rupert and Branco moved a little deeper into the river, submerged, and swam toward the sea. The narrowest point in the river mouth, just over the sand bar, was almost exactly halfway between them and the open water that faced the revellers on the beach, bounded by marsh on the west and rocks jutting out from Nikola island on the east. They surfaced just over the bar and listened. The humming of those powerful engines was getting steadily closer. Branco surfaced where he was just hidden by the reeds; Rupert on the seaward side of the jagged rocks. He grasped on to them and looked cautiously around him. He was only a few metres from the buoy marking the Albanian boundary at this point. He was pleased to see it showed no light; somebody had carefully covered it with a thick tarpaulin. He positioned himself in the apex of the right angled bend in the river so he could get a good view in both directions.

The BJ 270 had cast off and was slowly, so cautiously, making her way downstream with not a light showing. The reeds on both sides of the river stood almost as high as her bridge, and the shadows they cast in the moonlight outlined his course for him as the river wound its tortuous way through the marshes toward the sea; only two kilometres as a bird flies, nearer four on the water. The crew crouched motionless at their stations awaiting any word of command. The passengers sat on the bench behind the captain each brooding over their own private excitements, fears and hopes, anxieties and thrills. At half past eleven the captain checked his watch and his position; he reckoned all his calculations were correct. The water had risen rather more than a metre, there would be ample coverage over the bar now. An experienced seaman and navigator, the feel of the hull under his feet told him the tide was fully in; he could sense rather than feel a slight movement in the current now once again flowing seaward; he reduced power a fraction to counteract the movement of the water and maintain speed exactly as he wanted it. At a quarter to twelve he could see the forbidding outline of the gnarled rocks atop the highest point of Nikola island looming over the reeds, and knew the final ninety degree turn west was just ahead of him. It had been a fine feat of seamanship to bring a boat this size through such a narrow, shallow channel in the dark and he felt justifiable pride in his achievement. Once round that bend, now so near ahead of him, over the sand bar, the position of which he had memorised in his mind as bearing one hundred and eighty two degrees magnetic from the Albanian marker buoy, and they would be in clear, deep water with no more obstacles between them and the open sea. From there he would make Benghazi in under thirty-six hours.

His passengers were no judges of marine navigation, but they too could observe how the rushes were thinning out, giving place to rocky banks that presaged the end of the river, the beginning of their emergence into the Adriatic. The triumphant end of their dangerous and nerve-straining mission. Moda, sitting packed tight between Yali and Reuben, felt her heart pounding with excitement that was almost uncontrollable. Without thinking she instinctively grasped Karl's hand and dug her fingers into his. She wanted to whisper something, anything to relieve the tension, but the commanding figure of the captain just a few paces in front of them ruled that out. Karl felt more calm and philosophic than ever before in his life; there was nothing he could do or say. He enjoyed the feel of Moda's hand in his.

Another three agonizing minutes went by. They seemed like an age to those sitting at the back of the bridge on BJ 270. They seemed like an age to those waiting along the river bank just around that turn, the hum of the engines getting every second closer, closer, drumming in their ears. The voyagers suddenly realised there were no reeds around them any more. Just rocks; and they were heading straight for the rugged north cliff of the island. The captain turned the wheel at exactly the right point and her bow started to come round to the north where the view of the sea was cut off by the island itself. They rounded the rocky point leading out to the sand bar.

The silence on board was broken by a whispered but vehement 'Damn!' from the captain. None of them knew why, but he had good reason. The lighted buoy was nowhere near where it should have been. He saw it all right but the light was many metres farther north. There was no time for checking charts or refiguring his calculations. He turned the wheel another seven degrees to the north to give himself comfortable clearance of the buoy. Out of the darkness suddenly there were lights; lights everywhere; a whole string of them, from one bank to the other, right across their path and less than a couple of hundred metres ahead!

The captain grasped the throttle and pulled it back to neutral, but their own momentum and the current carried them relentlessly forward. For a second he considered throwing her into reverse but decided against it for the moment. There was no room to manoeuvre on either side. He had no choice but to decide, somehow, as slowly as possible, to try to pick his way through.

'A bloody fishing fleet! Right in the bloody channel!' His passengers had no idea what would happen.

At the moment they had seen the black outline of the boat start to round the bend in the river Rupert and Branco had submerged and swum toward the centre of the channel. The dark shadow of her hull showed clearly above their heads against the silver screen made by the moon on the surface of the still water. She made an easy target and with their flippers they could swim faster than the two knots which was all she was now making. Suddenly the dark shadow above them became a luminous bullseye in the centre of a field of misty white light as the captain switched on all his navigation lights. The next instant there was a brilliant flash of white pointing straight ahead from her bows as the searchlight came on. Rupert and Branco moved silently in under her hull.

Now only a hundred metres ahead more than fifty men and boys in the fishing boats were on their feet shouting and yelling at the tops of their voices. Slowly, but with grim perseverance the yacht was closing the distance between them; heading straight for their nets! The fishermen were screaming 'stop, stop!' in a dozen different dialects of Serbo-Croat and Montenegran. The boat's captain had picked up his loud-hailer and was shouting at them to get out of his way. Neither understood a word the other was saying.

On the bank the Swedes had just taken off their clothes and started wading into the water; men, women and children all stark naked. All those beautiful lights. Now this lovely yacht. What a wonderful spectacle! And old Draǧa arranged all this just to entertain us! They hurled themselves into the water with screams of joy and started swimming out toward the boats.

Under the launch's hull Rupert and Branco had unwound twelve metres of strong fishing net and were cautiously closing in on her twin propellers.

On the bridge the captain decided the moment had come when he must reverse engines to reduce his forward movement; he pulled the throttle back into the reverse position and gave her a burst of power. At that very moment Rupert and Branco succeeded in getting the fishing net completely round both propellers. The instant their blades caught up in its strands the net whirled like a mad thing, entangling itself around them into tighter and tighter knots with every revolution. In a split second the gear boxes let out two ear splitting screeches and both engines stalled.

No one had to tell the captain what had happened. He looked back toward the stern in a fury, and saw nothing but darkness. Against that darkness he did see the silhouettes of his agitated passengers all standing up trying to get a better view of the bewildering scene going on all around them. He exploded, 'Sit down! Damn you! I ordered you not to bloody well move. Sit down!'

Then he saw Yali was wielding a submachine gun. He saw Yali start to move forward and it was clear beyond all doubt that he was about to start spraying the water ahead of them with bullets the moment that muzzle topped the glass windscreen of the bridge.

'Bloody homicidal maniac!' he screamed, and with one ferocious leap the captain was across the bridge and caught Yali with a haymaker to the jaw, a brutal kick on the shins and a karate chop to the left side of his neck. Yali stumbled under this rain of blows, but he didn't go down. He swung the gun round and tried to smash his assailant across the face with it. The captain stopped the gun on his left arm and grabbed on to it with both hands. Their bodies swayed back and forth for a few seconds, but Yali had been dazed by the stunning blows he had received and was no match for the captain in this condition. With one quick, vicious movement the captain brought his right knee up crashing into Yali's crotch, they staggered locked together by each other's grasp on the submachine gun to the side of the bridge, and before he could recover the captain caught him one tremendous kick right in the groin that knocked him reeling backward over the side and into the water. The submachine gun clattered to the deck.

It was all over within a few seconds. Moda and Reuben, being farthest away on the opposite side of the bridge, had cowered back in their seats staring unbelievingly at what was going on around them. Abdullah, without any clear idea of what action, if any, he should take, instinctively rose from the bench only to find himself grabbed from behind by one of the Greek sailors and dumped back on it again.

The captain leaned down, picked up the submachine gun and threw it as far as he could across the water on the other side of the boat. He turned, grabbed Abdullah by the throat and shouted down into his face, 'Have you bloody murderers got any more of those playthings aboard my ship?'

Abdullah could only gulp but the captain didn't wait for an answer. He released him and shouted at all of them 'Throw those goddamned guns overboard. We've no way of getting out of here. I'm not doing twenty years in any bloody jail for you lot. Throw them. Now! Or we'll throw you where he went!' They threw.

The captain stood helplessly by the wheel for a few seconds; with both propellers snagged there was no way he could control the boat's movement. The naked swimmers drew closer every second, and the fishermen, screaming louder than ever, did not seem to realise that his engines had stopped.

From the darkness immediately behind the fishing boats there was a shattering roar as twin powerful diesels started up and in the next instant the beam of a thousand watt searchlight lit up the bridge of the BJ 270 blinding them completely.

Across the water from behind that searchlight came a voice through a loud-hailer, speaking in English: 'You are in Yugoslav waters. This is Coast Guard cutter 135. We are fully armed and any resistance will be met with force. Stand by to be boarded.'

CHAPTER NINETEEN

The two bus loads of Swedes were the first to get back to the Adriatic. They were hilarious to the point of ecstasy, or drunk, as you cared to look at it. What a memorable night! What food, what weather, what liquor, what swimming, what fun, what excitement. What a cabaret! Draga was a great host. Yugoslavia was a great country. They couldn't wait to get home to tell all their friends. Everyone of them had a different version of what it had all been about. Smugglers was the most popular theory. Draga would know. Draga knew everything that went on around here. Draga was nowhere to be found.

Rupert and Branco had silently withdrawn under water when the Coast Guard came alongside the yacht, swam back to their starting point and clambered shivering, but happy, out of the water. They were met by Thorney and the boys all of whom had enjoyed every minute of it. They were standing round looking down at what turned out to be a body, half drowned but still breathing.

'Who's that?' Rupert said when he had got his breath back.

'Fella who got knocked overboard, off the yacht,' Thorney said happily. 'Didn't you see him?'

'Oh, that's what it was. We didn't see anything. The moment that net started into the propellers we got clear. Is he drowned?'

'Damn nearly. There must have been a fight on the yacht. Two of the boys saw him knocked overboard and lay in wait for him on the bank. When he crawled ashore they clonked him with a piece of driftwood.'

Rupert had got his air tank and harness off by this time and bent down to have a closer look.

'He's an Arab all right. Wonder if he's the fellow Jo Lieb-mann and Freddy Kuso are looking for?'

Thorney said, 'Branco can drive you back in the Buick. The rest of the boys and I will put this character in the truck and deliver him to the pokey. We can probably get to the harbour before Draǧa and the rest of them do.' The boys carried the still semi-conscious Yali into the first available cell and dumped him there. The officer knew they had all been out on some expedition with Draǧa, and Draǧa's authority was good enough for anybody in these parts.

Fifteen minutes later they could see the lights of the Coast Guard cutter approaching the harbour mole. She was towing the yacht. Draǧa was standing, arms akimbo, on the for'ard deck in earnest conversation with Kleinhart and Sokol. The cutter's searchlight was pointed directly astern lighting up the remarkable scene aboard the yacht. There were eight uniden-tifiable people sitting huddled on the bridge deck, one of them a girl; and there were four Coast Guard ratings, two in the bow and two in the stern, all standing with their rifles pointing at the group amidships. The car of the Chief of Police and two black marias were waiting on the dock to receive them. First off were the four crew members, silent and sullen. They were put straight into the first vehicle. Then Abdullah, quiet and calm, saying nothing. He was handcuffed and taken to the second. Moda and Karl were allowed to come off together. Karl was astounded on seeing Kleinhart standing waiting for him with a friendly smile. There was an emotional greeting; Karl was told he would go with them to the hotel; he tried to protest when they ordered Moda to be handcuffed and put in the black maria. Both of them knew his protest was useless. They had an emotional parting. Finally came the Australian captain complaining volubly about the rights of international maritime navigation. He was pacified only to the extent that they agreed he need not be handcuffed. Two particularly rugged looking policemen took up positions on the step of each black maria and they drove away. Draga and the rest of the party drove to the Adriatic.

It was nearly two o'clock by the time the whole of the party had returned to the hotel. The Swedes had all happily retired, but this night it was their turn to complain endlessly, and with total futility, about the noise. Once Draga and Kleinhart arrived with Karl Reuben, the living proof of the success of this most unusual evening's exercise, the entire dramatis personae were in a state of high excitement. Questions and answers flew in all directions. Nearly everyone had some part of the story known only to himself, and everybody wanted to know everything.

Draga was a naturally boisterous host and his joy that the honour of Yugoslavian hospitality had been so triumphantly vindicated overwhelmed himself and his guests.

'Wonderful, wonderful! So happy, so happy!' he exclaimed, and turning to his night duty waiter shouted, 'Slivovitz for everybody. On the house!'

'Draga,' said Rupert with solemnity, 'you are a great man, but if I have to drink any more of that fire water of yours there will be a break in diplomatic relations.'

'Relations?' the old man shouted. 'There will be a declaration of war! Find some Scotch for our barbarian friends.'

Rupert noticed that in the course of the next half hour Draga got through nearly half a bottle of White Horse himself. Yitzak Sokol forgot his ulcer. Jacob Kleinhart looked more like a pirate than a scientist.

Through the general clatter and excitement, and repeated toasts to the 'health of President Tito', 'the gallant Yugoslavian navy', 'Yugoslavian Israeli friendship', 'Yugoslavian American friendship', Rupert's toast to 'The Principality' was received with tremendous enthusiasm, but since he was the only Welshman present no one else had the slightest idea what he meant.

Karl Reuben was naturally the centre of everyone's interest.

'Who was the leader?'

'The older man you took away in handcuffs. His name is Abdullah.'

'They are PFLP, aren't they?'

'Oh yes. No question of that. They continually talked about Habash and Haddad. This operation was organised by them personally. With the help of some Japanese.'

'What happened to the Japanese?'

'One was in the car that Yali blew up on the Hungarian border; the other stepped on a mine and was killed this afternoon.'

'Wait a minute. Who's Yali?'

'The fellow who went overboard in the fight. What happened to him?'

'He's in the town jail now. Is he the one who shot the Austrian policeman?'

'No doubt about it, they talked openly in my presence.'

'Can you testify to that?'

'Certainly.'

'What was the point?'

'That was supposed to be part of Haddad's plan. It was meant to mislead the Austrian police into thinking we were going through Hungary. How did you spot it?'

'Old intrepid over there,' Kleinhart chuckled.

'Sir William Stephenson? I thought he was a Canadian?'

'You know that great man?' Rupert chipped in.

'No, but I've read the book.'

'Who hasn't? I'm Rupert Conway, from Vienna.'

'Rupert Conway? You're the man who found some of my father's papers?'

'Yes, but don't set your hopes too high. That was a ruse too, in order to find you.'

'Is there anything in them about my father?'

'Nothing personal. They're all music; I intend to give them to the Mozart Institute.' He paused a moment. 'Something has been puzzling me. Do you or don't you write music yourself?'

Young Karl suddenly looked very serious. He said, 'Not

like my father, I'm afraid. I use it as a code. Dr Kleinhart taught me.'

'Good Lord! So I did. I'd quite forgotten.'

Rupert made a mental note and said nothing.

Draĝa took up the cross-examination. 'What can you tell us about the boat?'

'Not much. The captain is an Australian. She was on charter to somebody. The PFLP, I suppose. He's a real tough nut, that captain. Probably a pirate; certainly a smuggler; but he prevented a massacre this evening.'

'Massacre!' There was immediate silence around the bar.

Draĝa said very seriously, 'Would you please explain that?'

'With pleasure. When we ran into the fishing fleet and all those people in the water, Yali pulled out a submachine gun. He was just about to start shooting everyone in sight when the captain knocked him overboard.'

This was a revelation to everybody.

Draĝa's massive eyebrows bristled. 'You mean that young Arab tried to shoot their way through?'

'No doubt about it. If the captain had not been as tough as he was, and as quick as he was, the water would have been full of corpses.'

'We found no guns on board.'

'You'll find plenty of them in the river. The captain made Abdullah throw them all overboard. What will you do with him?'

'Who? The captain, or the Arab?'

'Well, both of them.'

Draĝa thought deeply for a moment while they all stared at him intently.

'Technically, the captain's only offence was that he entered Yugoslavian waters without authority. And that, I think, could be looked upon as an accident.' He paused and looked across at his son. 'That buoy . . . we don't want another international incident with the Albanians . . ' Branco understood the message.

'And the Arabs?'

'The Austrian police can come and collect them as soon as they want. The sooner the better.'

'There won't be any slip-up over that, I hope,' Rupert said.

Draga smiled broadly all over his granite lined face, and Thorney said laughingly, 'I guess we forgot to tell you, Rupert. Draga's the magistrate here too.'

'And the girl, she goes to Austria too?' Karl asked.

'Certainly.'

Rupert said, 'Tell us about the girl. We know who she is, by the way. I take it she is PFLP too?'

Karl said nothing for a moment; only Rupert's acute eye noticed a definite trace of a blush, a softening of Karl Reuben's eyes.

'I think she was, at one time,' Karl replied hesitantly. 'I'd be prepared to testify that she is not now.'

Rupert and Kleinhart exchanged knowing glances.

The conversation subsided for a moment, and then they heard a door slam somewhere down the hall and the sound of running footsteps. The night manager came rushing into the bar shouting in great excitement at Draga. Draga leapt to his feet and shouted back at him. He seemed to be asking questions in a tone of total disbelief and the manager's insistent answers tumbled out of him; as they were shouting in Serbo-Croat with thick Montenegran accents none of the visitors had any idea what it was all about.

Then Draga turned to them with the look of a man who has world-shattering news to report, and said in English: 'He has been listening to the radio. The news has just been announced that German commandos have stormed the Lufthansa aircraft on the ground at Mogadishu. All the hostages have been freed. Three of the terrorists have been killed and the fourth badly wounded. What a triumph!'

For a moment everyone stood, stunned into silence by this astonishing news. Rupert, Jacob and Yitzak looked at each other and raised their glasses.

'Thank God! What a marvellous night it's been for the good guys!' Thorney said.

*

Tuesday morning Karl was allowed to pay a brief visit to Moda in her cell, but nobody knew what they said to each other. Being assured that Moda would be sent to Vienna within a day or two, he readily agreed to fly back with them. The local telephones being, fortunately, in action again Rupert phoned a full report to Jo Leibmann, and then got through to 5B Stephansplatz. Mini screamed with delight when she heard his voice on the line, 'Herr Doktor, Herr Doktor; we've not heard of you for two days! Are you all right? Mrs Fleming didn't sleep a wink last night! Even Hofrat Liebmann didn't know what had happened to you.' Sandra's voice was quaking with relief when he spoke to her, and he could hear she was choking back tears. She would take the car out to Schwechat to meet him however late he was arriving. Yes, she would bring Charlie.

It was just three o'clock when they all said goodbye, at the airport outside Titograd. Draga assured them the proceedings in court had gone exactly as he had promised they would. He had spoken to the Foreign Minister in Belgrade personally; the Palestinians would be sent to Vienna as soon as transport arrangements were made by the Austrian government. Thorney said, 'Great fun, Rupert, really great. You must come and shoot ducks with me in Wisconsin next year. There's nothing like it.'

It was a perfect day for flying, clear and bright with almost unlimited visibility. Nobody spoke until they were crossing the most easterly peaks of the Kamniske Alps which mark the border between Yugoslavia and Austria. Kleinhart was rummaging through the pockets of his suit and pulled out a crumpled piece of paper. He looked at it and leaned over to Rupert. 'Oh, yes. By the way, in all the excitement I quite forgot to tell you. That chap who was murdered at the opera two weeks ago, he was one of them. I had this note from Kuso on Sunday morning, just before we left.'

Rupert said, 'Oh yes?'

'Yes. You remember they took that woman in Wiener Neustadt into custody for questioning on Saturday afternoon.

Apparently first thing Sunday morning that security man down there, the one who dug out the information on her, he had another brain wave. They took her up to the hospital in Vienna and she identified the body right away. She's working hard to save her own skin. Kuso said there is no doubt he was killed by one of their own people for helping himself to the proceeds of the Italian bank raid.'

Rupert thought for a moment and then said, both to Kleinhart and Karl Reuben sitting quietly beside him: 'There is something I forgot to tell you too.'

'What's that?'

'When I was in the tower room at Zurndorf I packed up all the papers you had left there and put them in a suitcase. I have them in my safe at home.'

Kleinhart went slightly pale, and took a deep breath. He and Reuben looked at each other, both trying to search the other one's mind. Karl looked at the ceiling, then gripped the arms of his chair. The results of so many years of work. He leaned forward across Kleinhart and said to Rupert, 'Promise me something, will you?'

'Certainly.'

'The very first thing you do when you reach home – burn every single sheet, will you?'

'Mozart and all?'

'Mozart and all.'

Rupert did.